ANOTHER *Goal*

A WILDCATTERS HOCKEY BOOK

BOOK 4

ALEXA PADGETT

ISBN: 978-1-945090-45-5

Edited by Jessica Royer Oaken
Proofread by Charity Chimni
Cover design by Chris Philpot

For Lorissa.

*You have a truly unmatched generous spirit. I've enjoyed the kids'
play dates, the wine nights, and all the years in between. Thank you
for supporting my work (and me!).
You're a great friend.*

CHAPTER 1
Millie

A man—an *enormous*, strange man—settled into the chair across from me that Ida Jane had vacated at our table a few moments before.

I stared for a moment, and his smile widened. I didn't trust smiling, towering strangers.

Well, for the record, I didn't trust. My father had taught me that lesson, and refusing to believe in people—except my bestie, Ida Jane—made life a lot simpler and less painful.

My muscles tightened as my heartbeat slammed against my neck. I was stuck between my instinct to flee and the paralyzing fear that I wouldn't make it out of the restaurant alive. I took a deep breath, preparing to bolt while I screamed. Creating a scene was better than ending up dead.

"I'm Luka Stol," the blond stranger said with a quick flash of teeth. His smile was *mesmerizing*. "I'm your temporary date until your friend's finished dealing with her pest problem. He's a real douche canoe, huh?"

I blinked at him, my mouth hanging open and my tongue as heavy as a brick. I could not find the words to unstick my frozen vocal cords. The rest of me was equally as unmoving. This felt like some kind of prank.

He plowed on, seeming undeterred by my lack of response.

"My teammates call me Stolly. Speaking of, Maxim and Cruz will make sure your friend is safe. She was holding her own, but that pissant got mouthy when he fell in the puddle. Served him right—talking to a woman like that."

I melted a little with his words. I studied him, liking what I saw.

"Ah, dinner!" He smiled as the waiter arrived with plates. "Excellent. I'm starved."

He grabbed Ida Jane's cloth napkin, shook it out, and settled it over his legs. He picked up Ida Jane's fork, speared a shrimp dripping with bechamel, and brought it to his mouth with a smug expression. I watched as he savored her dinner, mouth gaping, unsure what to do or say.

Okay, maybe he was pretty on the eyes, but he shouldn't be eating Ida Jane's birthday meal. That was…Trent-like, and I didn't have anything to do with Trent-like men.

Never again.

"Ida—is that her name?—said you're shy, but don't tell me you're starstruck, please." He wiped his lips and peeked at me through his blond lashes even as he heaped up another bite. "I'm too hungry to deal with shrieking right now. It'll give me a migraine, and that'll kill my appetite. Creates a vicious cycle. You get it."

That caused me to blink, and a tiny smile flitted over my now-closed mouth. I had two choices: freak out or go with it. He made me want to go with him—er, it. "Good to know how to bring you to your knees, Stolly."

He smiled, lips closed until he finished the bite. Then he leaned closer, his light brown eyes warm with humor. I waited for the skyrocket of my pulse and the slickness of sweat to spread over my skin like a virus. I couldn't help my reaction to men, not since Trent had tried to force—

I buried that thought in my mind by going through the molecular structure of jet fuel. There could be anywhere from eight to sixteen carbon atoms, and I listed the isotopes of two before my pulse regulated and refocused on the beautiful male in front of me. *Affable* was the best way to describe him.

"You could just ask me," he said when he'd finished chewing. "I'd drop to my knees for a pretty girl like you."

I laughed, unable to help myself. I was in my nerd glasses that did nothing to showcase my green-gray eyes. My dress was a size too big intentionally. I never dressed to impress anymore. I didn't *want* male attention, but Luka Stol looked as if he saw me. Not the scared, scarred woman, but *me*: Millie Jones, the woman who craved adventure as much as she shied away from the terrible possibilities it would bring.

The sound of my amusement tinkled across the table, shivering over the silverware and warming my chest even more than Stolly's smile. He was beautiful, he was presumptuous, and… maybe he was just what I needed.

Luka Stol made me feel sexier and more alive than any other person on the planet that I could recall. Definitely more than anyone in years.

"Just so we're clear, I'm not shy," I said, emboldened by my burgeoning fascination.

There were four types of molecular attraction, none of which had anything to do with human attraction. Sexual attraction was based on a different type of chemistry—one I'd never studied. I'd taken some psychology classes to better understand my response to my father and to losing my mother when I was young, but I'd mostly been much more interested in chemical compounds than people's actions and reactions.

That was where I'd meet Ida Jane, though. In that regard, taking psychology courses was the best decision I'd ever made.

Stolly nodded. "Got it. Not shy. Just…quiet. Observant."

I nodded back. As long as I was in this city, near my father and Trent—his protégé-from-hell—I would remain so.

Stolly lifted Ida Jane's white wine. "To a lovely dinner companion and great food." He sipped right from where her lipstick sat. He set the glass back on the table.

"Should you be drinking that during the season?" I asked. "I'm assuming you have nutritionists and—"

"So you *do* know who I am." He preened. "We do, and I shouldn't, no. But it pairs well with my dinner." He winked. *Winked*. And I warmed further. "Eat up, pretty girl. We have a party to attend."

Nerves rushed back. "We…we do?" *No way*. I couldn't do that. I glanced around nervously. What if…

"Yep," Luka said. "Wildcatters after-party. You'll like it."

"I…" I squeezed my fork so hard the edges indented the fleshy part of my thumb. I didn't do parties. I didn't spend time with strange men—hence the no parties. Just as I didn't date. Or have fun. Or live an actual life.

Not anymore.

But he was tempting me with everything I wanted. Luka was

gorgeous, he was fun, and I desired him. I shouldn't. I definitely should not give in to the growing attraction I felt for him.

There would be consequences. There were *always* consequences.

Luka seemed to understand my warring, terrified mind better than I did because he smiled again, and this one was softly protective. "I'll be by your side as long as you need, Millie. Don't worry. We got this."

I shook my head.

"You don't want to go?"

Oh, I did. But I wasn't sure I could handle it. *Focus, Millie.* I sucked in a breath and began to list chemical compounds, my go-to stress-reliever.

Carbon-14 had eight neutrons but just six protons, making it a useful isotope for medical tech and nanobiology. I blew out a slow breath.

Luka waited, his thumb rubbing a gentle rhythm on the back of my hand. "What do you want?" he asked.

You. To be normal. So damn many things. I smiled. "Let's go to your party, hockey man."

I blinked away that memory of our first meeting as I met Dr. Perera's bored expression.

"Say that again," I said. Oh, I'd heard him. I just didn't want to believe him, to have the words be real.

Dr. Perera, the man who'd had the misfortune of being on shift in the hospital when I walked in, sat on his little rolling doctor chair. He waited as I gawped. No doubt I looked like a herring struggling to breathe, the opposite of sexy—not that I wanted to be sexy for Dr. Perera. Or anyone.

Just Luka.

He'd helped me move past one of the worst experiences of my life, and I'd always be grateful to him for that.

"You're pregnant," he repeated.

Cold reality slammed into me as I assimilated Dr. Perera's words. I was halfway around the world, working my dream job, just as I'd planned. I'd assumed that after I ghosted him, Luka must have moved on with many different female companions. I knew of his reputation *before* he sat down at my table. He made every woman he spent time with feel sexy and special. But I wasn't either of those. I couldn't be.

I'm Millicent Anne Jones. Seriously, even my *name* was boring.

We'd talked after our initial meeting at dinner, and I'd fallen further under his spell. Over that next week, I'd given Luka not just a little of my trust but a piece of my heart.

So stupid.

Still, I couldn't regret the night I'd shared with him. I'd known I was leaving the next day, so I took what I wanted: a hot, young professional hockey player with soulful brown eyes and a smile that incinerated my panties. The memory of it had burned deep into my mind.

And apparently my body.

The garish lights above me burned my eyes while the antiseptic smell of the room dug into my nostrils and drove a spike into my mind. I hated being sick, and I hated hospitals. But mostly, I detested that I couldn't stop thinking about Luka Stol.

I leaned over and puked in a plastic basin that smelled of bleach and looked like an anemic liver. The container was unpleasant but getting sick on myself, the bed, or the floor held even less appeal.

I knew this from experience. I'd spent the last thirty-six hours heaving my guts out pretty much nonstop. This wasn't the first time I'd vomited since I'd entered this hospital, but it was the first time I'd done so knowing the reason I couldn't keep anything down.

I wiped a shaky hand across my mouth and looked up at Dr. Perera. He never batted an eye. I decided it would take a nuclear attack to get this guy to show some emotion.

"You should let the father of the child know so you can make some decisions," he said calmly. "Is he here? I can call him in."

I shook my head. No, that was the last thing I wanted to do. *That's not true.* If I was being honest—and I really didn't want to be—I'd wanted Luka from the moment he'd smiled and those dimples flashed. "*I'm Luka Stol, and I'm your temporary date until your friend's finished dealing with her pest problem.*"

He'd winked—winking was usually creepy, something I ignored—but he'd been so disarming. He'd lifted Ida Jane's wine glass, sniffed, and taken a sip.

We'd talked as we ate… Well, mainly *he* ate, and I'd picked at the meal I'd been so excited to enjoy before Ida Jane dashed from her chair and outside to meet with her ex, Dillon. He was a terrible person on his best day—not that Ida Jane had realized that then. I'd had hope for her. I'd needed to have hope because I was leaving her on her own.

Luka Stol had peered at me, those damn adorable dimples flashing. "*Tell me your name and what you do. Why are two such pretty ladies dining here tonight?*"

Between bites of our shared meal—and the surreal experience of having a professional hockey player sit down at my table—I'd told him my name, occupation, that it was Ida Jane's birthday.

He'd eaten with precision, enjoying both Ida Jane's meal choice and her wine. Halfway through, when I fell silent and focused on my dinner, he'd leaned back in his chair.

"*Well, Millie, I know you're a good friend, smart, with a hard-ass-sounding job. Now, tell me the secret of how you get that definition in your arms. I think I need your exercise regimen,*" he'd joked.

I'd blinked at him, unsure what to say and still worrying over my decision to allow him to sit with me. Why had I believed him when he said Ida Jane was still outside? What if he planned to abduct us both? What if…

"*While you're at it, you can tell me about the nicks on your fingers. Did you teach your friend to pound face?*"

"*I…*"

He'd leaned forward, his warm palm enveloping my hand. "*Settle, sweet Millie. You did a good job. Your friend is beating the douche's ass, and Maxim is with her. You know Maxim Dolov?*"

I'd offered a quick nod. Luka's thumb had rubbed my sensitized skin, shooting electricity up my arm—and down to my core. I'd pressed my thighs together, trying to ease the building ache. He was attractive, attentive, sweet.

"Preg…pregnant?" I wheezed. I had missed my last period… and the one before that. I'd been so busy with my move—setting up my condo and office, learning the area, helping Maxim win over Ida Jane, and obsessing over Luka—that I hadn't realized the significance.

Fuck. Me.

Luka had. A little *too* well. I was eleven weeks pregnant. I shivered as I relived the feel of Luka's warm fingers trailing along my sides and the sensation of his lips as he'd worked his way from my jaw down my throat to my breasts. My belly warmed.

"That *is* what I said," Dr. Perera confirmed.

Splash of cold water on that brief fantasy. *Focus, Millie. Your world is spinning out of control.* "You're *sure?*" I asked.

Dr. Perera sighed, probably disappointed in the thickness of my skull, which wasn't usually so thick. Everyone in my department at work considered me a genius. But who cared about that right now? I knew *nothing* about babies.

Hell, I could barely care for myself.

"You're sure?" I asked again, voice rising, muscles tensing.

"Well, hCG levels don't lie. I'll get you something for the nausea, which seems extreme. And I'd suggest you get in touch with friends or your former lover—someone to support you. While pregnancy symptoms often calm after twelve weeks, your hyperemesis is severe and may require further intervention."

"What does that mean?" I crumpled the thin gown that covered my thighs. I tried to think, but I couldn't. I was pregnant. *Luka Stol got me pregnant.*

I mean, he was potent. Like...really.

Luka's eyes had made my heart pitter from that first moment, but by the time I saw him again at his friend's birthday party the next weekend, he'd made me *burn*. His smile when he saw me that night had made my tummy clench. His fingertips on my skin, when they'd skimmed down my jaw, throat, chest, caused me to cream my panties. But his kisses…

I was pretty sure the brush of lip, the swirl of tongue, his soft moan as he'd angled his head and deepened the connection between us had caused my ovaries to shove out eggs. He'd worshipped me—palming my breasts, his breath on my nipples making them harder than ever, the warmth of his tongue before they'd chilled from the cool air. He'd nuzzled against my skin, seeming to want to be closer.

And that first thick, deep slide inside my body… I swallowed hard, throat dry, holding back a moan at the memory of how good he'd felt in me, over me, staring into my eyes as if I was the only person to matter.

Yeah, no wonder I was pregnant. If I wasn't already, I would be now just from *thinking* about him.

I nibbled on my lip. But it wasn't just the passionate sex—where he'd shown his stamina as a professional athlete, I might add. And I'd gotten to cup that strong ass as he pumped into my body. *Is it hot in here?* No, I was hot because the *mere thought* of Luka Stol caused me to smolder.

Afterward, when we were both limp and sated, he'd cradled me. His big, hard body had surrounded me, his thick thigh across both of mine. I'd felt cherished. I hadn't wanted to leave. He'd whispered in my ear, asking me to stay.

Already, he'd made too much of an impression.

I'd told him I couldn't, that I was leaving on a business trip.

That was true, but I'd been vague, unwilling to tell him my "trip" would be for years. I hadn't wanted to let our connection go.

I'd met his gaze, searching for anything nefarious in his eyes. He'd let me look. He'd waited, patient, as he continued to caress my skin. I'd let myself fall into the feeling. With a deep, soft breath, I'd admitted Luka Stol infatuated me.

Shit. *Shit*! This was because I'd let myself feel something, want something. I'd wanted Luka with an all-consuming need, and now, two months later, I was having his baby. Luka Stol, the up-and-coming offensive star of the Houston Wildcatters. I was screwed. My throat clamped as emotions swirled through me. Fear drove the rest, as it often did.

Fear of the unknown, fear of being hurt, fear of being responsible for a tiny, defenseless baby. I'd moved to a foreign country. I was much too far from my friends. Ida Jane… What was Ida Jane going to say? I couldn't tell her. I had to tell her…

Once I told her, her husband, D-man Maxim Dolov, would know, and that meant I had to tell Luka before Maxim did.

I didn't want to tell Luka. I didn't want to be pregnant!

The chance to work in this paradise coincided with a need to show my bosses that I deserved not just this position, but a promotion. I clutched the gown tighter and groaned. This was a nightmare. I began to tick with molecular structure, needing the comfort of chemistry to calm myself.

Babies were made up mostly of carbon, but also oxygen, nitrogen, calcium, magnesium… I continued to list the basic building blocks that made up a human life.

I was growing a human inside me.

The very thing I'd fought so hard against when I was with Trent.

My hand slid to my flat stomach. I was having Luka Stol's baby. A kernel of excitement lit me up. I'd *never* planned to have a child. Now, now…oh, I wanted the baby.

I was having a baby!

This was my choice. *Mine.* Only mine.

I lifted my gaze to Dr. Perera's. "I can't function right now."

He nodded. "We may need to consider more drastic options than an antinausea medicine. And we might have to consider bed rest if you aren't feeling well enough to travel to and from work."

I shook my head, which made it seem like my neck was a string and my head a plummeting, snapping kite.

No bed rest. No. That—*no*, I'd lose my job, have to go back to Houston. Back to Luka. Yes, I wanted to see him, have him hold me, share this experience with me, but that also meant back to my father and Trent.

So, no. I wasn't going back.

I despised the anxiety that rooted through my body, its shoots flickering out into my petrified limbs and squeezing my quelled heart. I hated that I continued to give Trent the power to sear off my independence and well-built life and send me back to being a crumpled, shuddering form in the bed.

I gritted my teeth and forced away the memories. They lived in a small box with a blue lid. The blue was cesium, element 55 on the periodic table. They'd named it after the Latin word, caesius, which meant blue sky.

After a few more repetitions, I breathed normally. A child was simply a change of direction. I smiled at Dr. Perera, striving to be normal. Once he left, shutting the door with a soft, firm click, I rested against the bed. My eyes slid shut, and I moved through my breathing exercises.

Luka wasn't anything like Trent. And I wasn't the same naïve young woman who'd believed wholeheartedly in love and perfect marriages to a dream man. I was Millicent Anne Jones, and I was strong, forged into it by circumstances. I *was* in control of my destiny.

Behind my lids, more moments of my time with Luka bubbled forward. I'd handed him control of my body, but that had been only for one night. I'd made a calculated decision and reveled in every second. Adored it. I'd felt empowered by my decision, my choice, to be intimate with such a perfect man on my terms.

But even then, even *now*, I would never give Luka or any other man control over the rest of my life. Nonetheless, my future, the one I'd planned down to the freaking *hour* for the next three years, crumbled around me.

And I had only myself—and Luka Stol—to blame.

Luka

I woke up with Millie's name on my lips, my hips grinding into my tangled sheets. I collapsed on my back and stared up at the ceiling as I tried to regulate my breathing.

Shit. Fuck. *Damn*.

I looked over at the clock on my bedside table. Five forty-five. It was a cheap clock—and a cheap nightstand. Buying real furniture would happen once I was certain Houston wanted to keep me. I wanted a long-term contract like Cormac and Maxim had. Then, finally, I'd be able to move into my forever home. So I couldn't mess up this season by doing stupid shit.

My phone. Where was my phone?

I found it on the nightstand and called Cruz. He answered with a groggy curse, followed by, "Do I need to kill you or someone else?"

"Want to go for a run?" I asked.

"Hell, man, I was *sleeping*."

"And now you're awake. Run?"

"You're getting really annoying, you know that?"

I waited. He liked it when I spent time on conditioning—it was one of management's issues with me. The top brass seemed to think I didn't give weight training and diet the full respect they deserved. I liked to party. What twenty-three-year-old man didn't? Weirdos and nerds, that was who.

When I first sat down at that table the night we met, I would have classified Millie as a straight-up nerd. She'd worn *pearls* and a dress that buttoned to her neck. But when those pretty eyes met mine, not even her thick frames could hide the gorgeousness in those peepers.

After all the texts and a flurry of phone calls, after meeting up with her again, I was entranced by her brilliance. And she'd worn contacts to Naese's party the next week, so I'd had a clear view of her beautiful eyes and the sweet, soft curve of her cheek. I'd been half in love with her *before* we had sex.

And then the sex blew my mind. So much so that I'd passed on the chance to fuck a lot of women since. I hadn't been interested, because I was sure Millie had felt the connection, too. We could be so good together. We'd proven it—not just in bed, but with the thousands of texts that came before.

But she'd ghosted me.

I pounded my fist against the mattress and clutched my phone tighter. I had to stop thinking about her. She didn't want me.

That hurt like a motherfucker, but it was true. I had to stop hoping for more than she was willing to give. I wouldn't beg for crumbs of affection. Been there, done that, hated myself for it.

"Are you running with me or not?" I snapped.

Cruz sighed. "Give me twenty."

That's why Cruz was the best. I tossed my phone back on my nightstand and rubbed my hands across my face.

I *had* to stop thinking about Millie. Had to.

I didn't. I texted her instead: *Thinking about you. Missing you.*

Same refrain, different day.

Miraculously, though, this time those three little bubbles appeared. I held my breath. They disappeared, and my chest seemed to cave.

They reappeared again.

Hope fluttered.

You are the most amazing man I've ever met.

Score! She's talking to me!

But I'm in Sri Lanka for the next few years. I won't be coming back to the States. I'm sure you'll find someone in Houston you want to be with.

Why would she say that?

It's best that we don't talk any more. Nothing can come of it.

I slammed my fists into my mattress again and again. That wasn't what I wanted. I wanted to…

What?

I wanted to be with her even though she was halfway around the world? How would that work? Millie was being logical. Smart.

What was this about—*shit*! Emotions. I'd never caught feelings for a woman before, and then she'd moved away before I had the chance to explore what it could be like.

I rested my arm over my eyes and heaved a breath. Being with Millie had been exhilarating. She was smart, funny, and truly interested in *me*. Me, Luka Stol, the dumb kid who'd barely finished high school and still struggled to finish a novel.

She'd mesmerized me, and then she was gone. I *hated* her leaving even as I pined for her. And now knowing she was literally gone from this city—this country—somehow made it worse.

I hated her.

Focus on that emotion. Harness it.

It was time to get off my ass and focus on what I could control: my conditioning. Next year was a contract year for me. I needed to show my coach, Silas Whittaker, and Gunnar Evaldson, owner of the Wildcatters, that I was the best player in my position.

Plus, maybe the run would clear my head of Millie fucking Jones.

It did, and it didn't—story of my life. Cruz had set a punishing pace to torture me for waking him up. But I appreciated it, because I was worn out—sweat drenching my torso and sucking in great gulps of air—by the time we finished.

Today was a practice day. By the time we got to the arena, I'd tried to call Millie again. And she'd ignored me. *Again.* Which pissed me off. No doubt that was why I went in for the hard hit on Naese, shoving him into the boards. He pushed me off with a roar, dropping his gloves and pummeling my chest.

Coach blew his whistle, but it was Cruz and Maxim who plucked us apart—as if we were dolls in their big-ass world.

"Stop being a dick," Maxim growled.

"Tell Naese to stop being so quick to react," I snapped.

"Pot meet kettle," Cruz muttered. He shoved Naese into the boards, causing him to grunt and curse.

"Both of you need to get your heads out of your asses and back in the game where they belong. Hear me?" Cruz glowered, looking like an angry bear with all that bristling facial hair.

I hung my head. "Yes, Father."

He shoved my shoulder on the way past, but I caught a hint of a smile tugging at his lips—or it was a nervous tic? Probably a lip quirk because Cruz didn't do nerves. Lucky bastard.

"Stol, Naese, I want fifty laps. Then meet me in my office," Coach Whittaker yelled. He wrinkled his nose. "After you shower—you both smell terrible. Shit. I can't stand this BS."

Cormac Bouchard skated over, concern on his handsome face. It sucked having a team captain that looked like freaking Prince Charming and acted…well, like a charming fucker.

I couldn't live up to that standard.

I scowled as I dropped my chin to my chest, moving toward the exit. Maxim settled in for the skate next to me, matching my stride as I sped around the ice.

"Gonna do a cute little jump and spin?" he asked as I turned backward.

I rolled my eyes. The guys were *so funny*. "No, but I was thinking about shoving you under the zamboni."

Maxim pushed ahead of me. "You can try."

He didn't even say it with any heat. I wanted a fight, a release of tension. But no. Maxim, who was now with Ida Jane, Millie's best friend, couldn't even give me that. Just a matter-of-fact reminder that he was bigger, stronger, and more experienced than me.

I gritted my teeth and skated on. Cormac was still talking to Naese, who appeared agitated. At least I'd gotten under someone's skin.

"You gonna admit you're acting out about the nerd girl you hooked up with at his party?" Maxim tipped his head toward Naese.

"Her name is Millie, and no," I said. My legs felt like deadweight; I could barely lift my skates.

This conditioning had better help in our game this weekend. I needed a win—both in my stats and for the team if I wanted to stick around with Houston next year.

"Nothing wrong with a little vulnerability," Maxim offered.

"Have you traded personalities with Cruz? And yes, there *is*. You get hurt."

I clenched my fists inside my gloves, pissed I'd admitted Millie's refusal to talk to me hurt my feelings. I was Luka Stol, a hot-shot hockey star with the money and looks to bag any woman in hockey nation…except the one I wanted.

"What *would* be good is to channel that aggression into a W on Friday." Maxim smacked my shoulder hard enough for me to wince. "You have ten more to go."

He headed toward the exit while I considered what he'd told me, and what he *hadn't* said.

Gunnar Evaldson also slapped my shoulder as he exited Coach Whittaker's office when I trudged down the hall after my shower. I didn't have time to wonder why he was there, because Coach laid into me the moment I crossed the door's threshold.

"You either get your head together or be prepared to be benched."

I stared at him, halfway into the seat, my hand on the back of the chair. Instead of settling down, I popped up. "Sure, Coach. Whatever you say."

He thumped his butt into his chair as I turned toward the door, jaw tight with my effort not to spew the additional shit my ego demanded. That would definitely get me benched.

"Sit your ass down, Luka. *Now.*"

I returned to the chair and sat with my fists tight against my thighs.

"You're wound tighter than Mac was before we signed him," Coach said, leaning forward. The gray at his temples seemed more pronounced. He was still young, but he'd been through a lot of life changes since coming to Houston. I hadn't been here for his wedding or his adoption of his niece, but I knew about it. We all did because Coach had all the guys at his place a few times each season.

I liked both his wife, Paloma, and his daughter, Trix. Not that

I spent a lot of time with women or girls.

The closest thing I had to a mother, Alyssa, said that was because I didn't know how to interact with women, especially those who had potential to be in my life long term. I had to admit, she seemed to be on to something with that theory.

I preferred to keep my relationships with women superficial—some flirting, getting off, and getting out. Until Millie.

"I'm sorry," Coach said, scrubbing his hands over his face, which caused his glasses to push up on his forehead.

He'd gotten the readers this year, and I thought they made him look like a TV dad. Coach didn't seem used to them or comfortable with them yet, which made it funny as hell to watch him forget where he put them.

"You have so much promise, Luka. Such talent. It's hard to remember you're just a kid."

I stiffened, but kept my mouth shut. Barely.

"I know you're going through some stuff—who isn't? But I need you to keep your off-ice romances *off* the damn ice. You hear me?" He sighed. "You and Naese… I can't have my starting line this twisted up over women, especially when I know you boys were the ones who created the drama in the first place."

I didn't create shit with Millie. Well, I had, but I'd planned on it being more than a wham-bam-drop-the-man scenario. Silas Whittaker wasn't interested in my hurt pride, though. I wrenched my lips open enough to offer, "Yes, Coach."

He leaned forward, his expression implacable. "You're up for a new contract next season. Right now, you're looking like a good trade option."

I bit my tongue and met his gaze, though I wanted to drop my head. I'd focused on playing for Houston from the get-go. I'd followed hockey for as long as I could remember, and I'd liked what the Wildcatters owner, Gunnar Evaldson, was doing with this program. This was where I wanted to retire. Not only was Silas Whittaker a fantastic former player and brilliant coach, but he'd also managed the impossible and already led this new franchise to two Stanley Cup runs in five years.

Most teams never got that far.

I inhaled through my nose. "I understand."

"Do you, Luka?" Coach snapped. "You have the build, the speed, the stick work to be one of the greats. You *also* have a chip on your shoulder and an impulsive streak that screws up all that talent. I'm not sure I can coach you—not if you're not willing to trust me."

I inhaled again. "I hear you, Coach."

He waited, but I remained silent. "Get your act together, Luka. I've given you all the chances I can."

CHAPTER 2
Millie

Single parenting wasn't for the weak, not even when the baby was still inside me. Wiping my mouth with the back of my shaking hand, I flushed the toilet. I couldn't remember a time I hadn't been ill.

I rose, my legs unsteady, and rested my hands on the cool porcelain of the sink. Dark bags sat thick and menacing under my eyes. My skin was sallow, patched with dryness, and my hair was lank. But it was my eyes that caught my attention. I squinted, then shook my head.

They were bright, filled with some internal glow the rest of me was not feeling. My eyes told the rest of the story—the one I'd hidden for the last few weeks.

"You're okay, Mil-bil," I murmured. Using Ida Jane's nickname for me raised a longing in my chest. I missed her. I curled my fingers tighter against the sink. With a heavy sigh, I picked up my toothbrush and cleaned my mouth.

Then, before I could change my mind, I padded out of the bathroom and through the living room, ignoring my high-rise view, and to the bar in the kitchen where I'd left my laptop. I settled into the chair and opened the chat app. I picked up my now-cool tea, wrapping my fingers around the ceramic mug as if it were a talisman that would save me from the censure I would receive.

The digital chimes continued for a few moments until Ida Jane's pretty face filled my screen. Her tousled hair, droopy eyelids, and flushed cheeks told me I'd caught her at a bad time. Didn't matter. I couldn't hide from her any longer.

"It wasn't Dengue fever. I'm pregnant," I blurted, needing my friend's comfort.

Ida Jane's eyes widened, her lips forming a perfect O of surprise. "Okay. Well, that's not what I expected you to lead with. I'm happy if you're happy, which I'm assuming you are since you're telling me about the baby. Who's the father?" she asked.

Ida Jane and I had been fast friends since our college days at University of Houston, and she now practiced as an art therapist near the Galleria.

I relaxed enough to set the mug on the counter. Ida Jane wasn't judging me.

"Luka. Who else?"

Ida Jane gave a curt nod, her gaze flicking upward, no doubt to Maxim. I still couldn't believe she'd married the Wildcatters' D-man in a private civil ceremony nearly two months ago—not long after they'd met the night we'd gone to dinner. But she looked well-loved and happy with her decision, so I was happy for her.

"You're the first person I've told," I said, teary. "I'm not sure what to do."

"Be honest with Stol," Ida Jane said.

I twisted my hands together, nervous energy running through me. But I was too tired to get up and run or do kata. "Do you think he'll care? I mean, he must have moved on with, like, a million other women by now."

"He hasn't, and he's a better guy than you've given him credit for," Ida Jane snapped. "Look, he comes over every week. He's a good man. Thoughtful and responsible. He has a past. *So do you.*"

Damn her for bringing up my attempts at romance and love. Those had all happened before my father basically assigned Trent to be my husband, and before I knew my father had evidence of my failed relationships he could use against me.

"Don't hold that against him," Ida Jane continued. "Just like you wouldn't want him to see you only as a survivor."

"But…" I didn't even know what I was trying to say, just that fighting was easier than what Ida Jane was asking of me.

"Tell Luka about the baby," she said. Her voice was kind, her eyes filled with understanding even as she gave me her stern face.

I swallowed. "I know. I'm…I'm so scared."

Her expression softened. If I'd been in the room, she would have hugged me. I could have used one of her soft-but-fierce hugs. In fact, I craved them. I was desperate for any kind of touch. My night with Luka had rekindled my need for connection.

I'd been so closed off since finding out Trent's plans for me: get her pregnant, get the heir, cinch ties to the Jones' fortune.

Trent had hurt me, but now I was hurting myself—and I couldn't seem to stop. I wanted to connect, to be open and find love, but I was scared I'd end up a means to an end, an unwanted possession.

Like Trent had tried to make me.

"I understand, Mil-bil. You have every right to be afraid." She didn't add "*that's normal,*" and I loved her for it. Ida Jane always allowed me to set the pace of recovery.

"But Luka needs to know he's going to be a dad. And he deserves the chance to prove his interest in his child—however the two of you work out the details."

I sniffled. "I love the baby already, and I can't imagine not being there for…for everything."

"I'm sure you do." Ida Jane smiled. "You're going to be a great mama, Millie. Fierce, protective, but oh so loving."

I snorted. Leave it to Ida Jane to slam into the heart of the situation—of my fear. "I didn't have the best role model…"

Ida Jane sneered. "Your father is the poster man for what *not* to do as a parent. You're a smart one, Millie. You've already synthesized what didn't work from him and determined a different, better path."

I swallowed, trying to ease the ache in my throat. "What if I mess up?"

Ida Jane waved her hand. "Everyone makes mistakes every day."

"And you see the kids who result from those mistakes," I replied.

"No. I see the kids impacted by neglect, abuse, fear, and trauma. But a mistake? Rarely, if ever, have I met with a child who knew they were loved yet wanted to come into my office."

"Y-you're sure? I can't mess up that badly?" I shivered. My toes were chilled, and goose bumps exploded over my arms and legs.

"I suppose it's possible, but so unlikely," Ida Jane said.

That would have to do. "Okay."

"Love you."

"Love you, Idge."

Her expression morphed back into sternness. "Tell him, Millie. The longer you wait, the harder it is to spit out the truth."

I closed my laptop and stared out at the skyline.

In the days that followed, I ignored her advice—even as I continued to think about, even dream about, Luka Stol.

And like Ida Jane said, with each passing day, I found contacting Luka harder to think about.

Luka

Maxim stared at me *again*. His icy blue eyes tracked my every movement, much like a leopard just before it pounced.

We had one game left of the three in our away series. I'd implemented Coach's strategy to a T throughout the trip. No way I was getting bounced from Houston. This was my best chance for title contention.

But Maxim's continued observation was getting on my nerves. Big time. I refused to admit that *everything* got on my nerves right now. So instead, I focused on the game.

In the second period, I had a great skate down the ice with control of the puck, flipping it back to Naese, who passed it back to me. I slapped the shot over the goalie, where it hit the top of the post...and slid in.

I raised my hands in triumph. "Hell, yeah!"

That goal tied the game, and I was pumped. The next time my line was called, midway through the third period, I hustled down the ice, beating my opponent to the puck and passing to Naese just before the D-man slammed me into the boards. My helmet absorbed most of the blow, but as I shoved him off with some well-placed elbows, I felt a little woozy.

No time to worry about that, though, because Naese was coming back around the net. I tied up the defense with my back, skating the guy into the boards.

Naese zipped around and flicked his wrist, causing the puck to wobble over the ice and clink off the goalie's foot into the net.

I skated over to hug Naese, slapping him on the back. "Good goal!"

I side-eyed Coach, who was watching the two of us, a slight frown marring his forehead. What was that about? We'd played well. Coach had to realize Naese and I had won him the game.

After the final horn sounded, I skated toward the other team to shake hands. Maxim loomed over me, his gaze steady. When I glanced up at him, his expression was tight, almost as if he expected me to explode.

"What is wrong with you?" I snapped, shoving my shoulder into his side—the dude was a *giant*. The only one bigger was Cruz, and that fellow *had* to have been fed steroids as a baby. No person should be as tall and wide as a door. It was unnatural.

"Don't be a dick," Maxim said. His English was pretty much flawless, but dude still gave off harsh Russian vibes when he wanted to, which was pretty much always.

I bit back my response, because I didn't feel like fighting with him. I was tired, stiff, sore, and wanted to ask if his wife had talked to my woman.

Shit. I had to stop thinking of Millie as *mine*. She wasn't because *she didn't want to be.*

"You talked to Millie?" Maxim asked once we'd finished the

obligatory end-of-game salutations.

My head whipped up. "No. Why? What's wrong?"

He shrugged, but I caught the tightening of the skin around his lips and eyes. "She said she was going to talk to you."

"When?" I demanded.

"Few days ago," Maxim gritted out. The words were menacing, and a fire burned deep in his icy gaze. "I'll make sure she does."

I reached the exit and stepped up onto the rubber mat, grabbing my blade guards from the kid holding them out to me. "Nah, man, I don't want her pressured," I told Maxim. *Pressure her!* my mind raged. *Make her call me back and tell me what I can do to make something real between us.*

I swallowed the bitterness that came with those thoughts. I was Luka Stol, and I was a professional hockey player. I shouldn't be begging for a woman's attention. The ladies came to *me*—found *me*. And I hadn't been interested enough to even look at them since Millie.

I shoved my hands through my hair and clomped off toward the locker room.

I showered and found a seat on the bus that would take us back to the hotel so we could get home for a couple of days before we'd get on another plane, another bus, and do all this again, in another city. That was the season—constant grind. I shot Millie a text. *Maxim said you wanted to talk to me. So call. I'm around.*

Nothing.

Right. It was night in Sri Lanka. Probably late at night. I wasn't sure of the time difference because we were on the East

Coast, and the time-change math became fuzzy. I never remembered if I need to add or subtract hours to her time.

Well, I couldn't be too mad if she was sleeping. Except I was. I wanted her to think about me as much as I thought about her.

More.

I wanted her to cry into her pillow every night with how much she missed my awesomeness. I fantasized about the exact opposite of what she'd dished out.

I sighed, the sound so heavy it was more of a groan. I was so glad we'd finished this road trip. I wanted to hop in my Corvette, my pride and joy, and drive fast and free. I'd head home and play some video games. We had the day off tomorrow, and I didn't need to be at Cormac's until five to watch the footage for our next matchup. I glanced over at the phone again. Nothing.

Millie. That was Millie's picture requesting a video chat. I stared at my phone screen for a long moment the next morning. I'd just awakened and come out to the kitchen to grab a glass of orange juice in the T-shirt and athletic shorts I'd slept in. I hadn't combed my hair or anything remotely related to making myself presentable. But that didn't matter as I settled on the edge of my large, leather sectional.

Hell to the yes, I accepted.

I smiled, anticipation zinging through me. "Hi, beaut—have you been crying?"

She had. Her eyes were bloodshot and red-rimmed. The tip of her adorable nose was also red. She looked pale and tired.

"What's wrong?" I demanded. If some fuck-face had bothered

her, I'd… Shit. I was twenty-two hours away. What would I do?

"I'm pregnant."

"What?" I asked. My mouth fell open. My eyes widened so much, I was pretty sure they'd be dry for days.

"Luka, I'm pregnant," she said again. Her voice was soft. Resigned.

This was the first time I'd spoken to her in months, and all she said to me was, "I don't expect anything from you, but I needed to tell you I'm pregnant."

Before I could respond, she hung up.

I stared at my phone, my arms and legs noodly, my chest tight. Rage, elation, worry, and possessiveness crashed into each other, trying to cave in my chest.

"What the fuck just happened?" I gasped. My eyes refused to blink. They were dry, burning. I forced the lids together. Sweet relief—for my fucking eyes. But my heart…

Millie was pregnant.

I called her back. She ignored me.

I called her back again.

She declined the call.

"Oh, no you don't."

Millie Jones, the sweet, soft woman who'd snuck into my heart the moment I'd sat down at her table at the team's favorite restaurant, was having my baby. *My* baby. And she expected *nothing* from me.

That had been just a courtesy call—a heads-up.

I rose, driven by resentment and, yeah, anger. "*I don't expect anything from you…*"

She damn well *should* expect a lot from me, like being a father. I tried her again.

Nothing.

My legs gave out, and my ass landed hard on the edge of the sofa before sliding off. I ended up sprawled in front of my leather sectional, a hand-me-down from Maxim, my vision tunneling and anger pumping into my temples.

This was my kid, too. I would be part of his life.

Oh, hell! What if I had a girl?

My eyes widened, and I barked out a laugh as I leaned my head back against the cushion. That would be the universe's best joke, one I'd deserve.

I called her again.

Declined.

"Why the fuck are you on the floor?" Cruz rasped as he came to stand over me some time later.

Shit. I was supposed to be ready to go to Cormac's. I'd lost track of time, thanks to Millie's life bomb.

Cruz had taken me under his wing last season and acted like a big brother. Without him, I'd forget to go—or not want to deal with extra game-footage-and-strategy meetings. That didn't fly on a professional team, so Cruz, who lived in the same condo building as me, had become my nanny.

I hated that I needed him. But I did.

At twenty-three, some of this adulting shit was more than I could handle.

I typed out a message to Millie: *We need to talk.*

It showed read.

We're going to talk about this, Millie. And you damn well better expect something from me. That's my kid, too.

She read that message as well. I waited. No dots. Nothing.

Damn her smart, stubborn little head.

"Get your ass up. We're going to be late, and you know I can't stand being late." Cruz grumbled as he stalked off to my bedroom, cursing when he realized my bag with my notebook and playbook wasn't packed. "On your feet, Stolly. Let's go."

I rose, first to a knee with my hand on the couch. Then I wobbled to my feet.

"No shoes?" Cruz threw up his hands and headed back into my bedroom. He stormed out, face like thunder. Well, that's always how he looked. Something in my expression must have signaled how close I was to breaking.

"You okay?" he asked gently. "You on something?"

Cruz was a huge grizzly of a man with a thick, wild beard and a cutting stare. But he was also sensitive. He cried at commercials, but none of us teased him because he was all business on the ice, protecting our asses from the opposing defensive players, who wanted to pound us into the boards.

He, Cormac, and Maxim made up our most potent defense, the one that had led us to the championship in my first year with the team. We were well in the mix for another shot at the Cup. And I refused to do anything to jeopardize that.

"I don't do drugs," I said, offended. Then I blew out an unsteady breath. Swallowed. What to say? "The first woman I really, really liked—the one who hooked up with me at Naese's party months ago, who I couldn't stop thinking about—left," I told him. "That was it because she wasn't willing to try for more." I grimaced, hating how much that still stung.

"Now, she's back," I continued after a moment. "But only to tell me she's pregnant with my kid." I dropped my head into my hands, fingers tunneling into my hair. "That sounds…sordid. *Less* than what I wanted with Millie from the get-go."

I swallowed again, slipping my feet into the sneakers Cruz had dropped in front of me. He remained silent, letting me talk. He was a good listener.

"I think… I think I'm not okay."

Cruz laid his huge palms on my shoulders and stared into my face. "That's a shit story," he murmured. "A shit-ton to process all at once. Don't try. Just take the first step."

Cruz always knew what to say, the bastard. I loved him for it. He waited for my nod. "I made you one of those smoothies you like," he continued. "You can drink that on the way to Cormac's and try to get your head right."

He carried my gear even as he grabbed his from just inside my door. He shoved the drink he'd made into my chest and motioned me out. Once he locked up my place, I fell into position behind him and followed him all the way to his truck.

Cruz liked trucks. The bigger, the growlier the better. Same with dogs. Dude was always rescuing dogs, preferably former military ones, but he'd foster police K-9s as well. He never kept them, though I'd seen how attached he became to each one. Instead, he vetted the potential owners. Cruz let the dogs out of his care only when he was certain the person would make the dog's life better.

I put on my seatbelt and took a long swig of the smoothie. Sweet and creamy, the flavors of strawberry and banana burst on my tongue. I was hungry. I took another long pull, enjoying the taste and the slow filling of my belly.

"What do you know about kids?" I asked.

Cruz shot me an unfathomable look. "What age?"

"Um, tiny."

"Infants, toddlers, or preschoolers? Early-elementary age? What are you asking about?"

"Just-born kids."

Cruz pulled out of the space with a long-suffering sigh. "So, you mean what's it going to be like when your kid's born?"

"Yeah. That. I've never been around a baby."

He shook his head and launched into an explanation of infancy up to early-childhood education that would have made Keelie, Cormac's fiancée, proud. And I hung on his every fucking word.

Millie

I stared at the phone in horror as I pressed a hand to my still-flat stomach. *Why had I hung up? Why hadn't I let Luka speak? Why couldn't I respond to his messages?*

Anxiety pumped through me, along with fear and doubt and anger at myself. Sure, I'd been afraid, but I hadn't been mature. I'd run away from Luka, from my feelings, again.

Swallowing the hard, ragged lump of emotion in my throat, I switched over to my laptop and opened a video chat with Ida Jane.

"There's something wrong with me," I rasped out instead of a greeting.

"Besides the fact that you're growing a life inside you, and said life is sabotaging your ability to eat and drink like a normal person?" Ida Jane wrinkled her nose. "You're not selling the whole pregnancy thing."

"This is the most intense weight-loss journey I've ever been on, and it sucks," I said. "But besides that, which *still* sucks…" I laid my forehead in my upturned palms. "…I called Luka and told him about the baby."

"About damn time," I heard Maxim growl from the background.

"Shouldn't he be watching film?" I asked.

"He just got home," Ida Jane said. She smiled at what I assumed was Maxim off screen before she returned her attention to me. "Stol—"

"Luka," I snapped.

"*Luka* came by and mentioned it," Ida Jane said.

Maxim didn't bother to show his face—he was angry with me for not telling Luka sooner. I deserved that. I lifted my face and let Ida Jane see my wet cheeks, my red-rimmed eyes, my contorted mouth. I was an ugly crier, always had been.

"So how's our little Gordie?" Ida Jane asked, no doubt trying to distract me from my concerns.

I wrinkled my nose. "Gordie?"

Ida Jane shrugged. "Famous hockey player. Maxim likes him. Said he's Luka's favorite. I was just testing out names."

"Well, it sure as hell will not be *Gordie*."

She propped her chin on her fists. "Yeah, I wasn't feeling it once I said it either. That name doesn't suit your kid."

"How would you know—" I shook my head. "You got me off topic. So, I told Luka about the baby, who is *not* named Gordie." I paused, my throat thick. "And then... Then I hung up. Just *click*! I didn't let him say anything." I gasped, shocked at my poor behavior but also by the fear coursing through me. That combination caused me to sob.

"Oh, Mil-bil. You don't need to be so frightened. Women have babies all the time."

"Not that. Not *only* that." I looked around for tissues, a napkin... Nothing. So I used the sleeve of my cardigan and grimaced. Oh, that was going in the wash as soon as I ended this call. I didn't like bodily fluids—another reason I was freaking out about parenting. From what I'd seen and heard, babies eliminated from every hole possible, and often. The idea made me gag.

"What if..." I licked my lips. "What if Luka's like..." I didn't want to say his name. I shuddered. "What if he uses the baby to control me?" I whispered. *Like my father did.*

Maxim appeared behind Ida Jane, his bulk blocking most of the light. He peered in closer, his face softening as he took in my forlorn expression.

"Ah. Because someone has hurt you. Your father that you mentioned." He gave a sharp nod. "It is as I told Ida Jane. Stolly is one of the best guys I know."

"Luka," I said. "His name is *Luka*. And the baby is a *she*. I'm having *a girl*, not an it, and her name will definitely not be Gordie."

"We already ruled that out. You should have led with the baby's gender! You had the sonogram?" Ida Jane asked. "Is it the three-D kind where you can see her little face? Show me, show me, show me! I want to see her sweet nose and chin. I hope she has your chin, but maybe Stol—er Luka's cheekbones. That man's cheekbones are *to die* for."

Ida Jane leaned in so close, her nose had to be touching her laptop's screen.

I shook my head. "I have to wait almost six more weeks for the sonogram because the doctor said that's the best time to find out the baby's gender."

Wow. Eighteen weeks was…a good way through the pregnancy. Almost five full months.

"And you're right," I continued. "She really needs to inherit his cheeks." I groaned. "Dammit, now I'll be sad if she doesn't."

"No, you won't. She'll be precious no matter whose cheeks she gets."

"And you're going to be her godmother." I was on a roll now.

"Of course I am." Ida Jane smiled happily. "I'll spoil her properly."

"But not too much," I said, wagging a finger.

"You really think you're having a girl?" Ida Jane asked.

"I really do. It's a…feeling, I guess. But it's more than that. And I'm going to name her Bree, because I love that name and I love her, so she gets the best of everything."

Ida Jane's expression turned dreamy, a smile curing her lips. "She will, Millie. I know she will, because you're going to be an amazing mom."

I snuffled a bit, surprised at my show of emotion but, at the same time, pleased with it. I hadn't been sure I'd be able to love anyone after Trent. My hand crept down to my belly.

Ida Jane tracked the move, and she must have understood some of my thought process because her expression soured and worry glinted from her eyes. "Does your father know about the baby?" she asked.

"Not from me. I never plan to tell him."

And just like that, my burgeoning power drained out of me. My lower lip quivered. These hormones were *insane*.

I never cried. Not even when Trent had refused to use a condom that night. He'd told me he was getting me pregnant whether I wanted to be or not—which I had not—so I'd had to run away from the man my father had chosen for me. I hadn't cried when my father had stormed into my workplace, steam curling out of his mouth and raising his eyebrows as he shoved his face close to mine and told me I was marrying Trent *immediately*. And I hadn't cried when I'd begged Ida Jane to move into my new condo with me and started searching for out-of-country jobs.

I hadn't even cried when my father had taunted me with all that money, telling me I only got to have it if I was a good girl and did the right thing by Trent—that he and Trent deserved their next big merger, and I would not mess up a multibil-lion-dollar deal with accusations that should have stayed quiet between a man and his fiancée.

That's when I'd blended up my engagement ring, nicking the platinum before mailing it back and cutting all ties.

That was a lesson I would never forget. My father cared more about his precious empire than his only child. He'd been more upset on Trent's behalf than mine. I would never, ever put my baby Bree in a position where she had to deal with my father.

It was more important than ever that I stay tucked away, a long distance from my father's wealth and power.

"I don't blame you there," Ida Jane murmured. "Look, your dad's a piece of work, bless his heart, but St—er, Luka's not like him. Maxim just told you, Luka's great. And he really is, Mil-bil. He's around all the time for dinner, and I really like him." She gave me her most winning smile. "Don't go lumping him in with your father just yet. You need to give him a chance."

"You're right," I said on a sigh. "That means I need to call him back."

"You already did the hard part of telling him about the baby…"

"Bree," I reminded her. I'd better have a girl, because otherwise I was going to end up with a kid named Gordie. I shook my head. "I'll call him."

"Now."

I blew out a breath. "Now."

"As soon as you hang up," Ida Jane said, her expression stern.

"Talk soon," I said.

"Love you, Mil-bil!"

Sure, she did. She wasn't the one having to make this call.

I sucked in my breath and dialed Luka's number.

"Is now a bad time?" I asked when he answered.

"No! Don't hang up." He glanced away from the screen. "We're just hanging out. Cormac, I'm hitting your office."

I closed my eyes as Luka carried his phone to a different location, away from the tumult of voices.

"Okay. It's quiet here." He took a slow breath. "Thank you for calling me back."

He was angry. I could see the tension around his eyes and in the set of his mouth. I deserved that anger, but it made me feel small, mean—and I hated that. "I don't know how to do this."

"Do what?"

I glanced away as I swallowed. "I've been in one serious relationship." I shook my head. "It ended terribly." Understatement of understatements, but I wasn't getting into that mess right now.

"So you steered clear of men."

I met Luka's gaze, which had softened. "I did. I also was determined to see your entire gender as…" I pressed my lips together. Luka didn't need to know about Trent and his predatory behavior. "Then you sat down that night, and I…" I smiled, and it felt wistful. "You swept me off my feet, Luka. That sounds so ridiculous—"

"It was the same for me." He cleared his throat, his gaze direct. "I want to be involved. With the baby."

"Okay." I nodded, then nodded again, unsure what else to do.

"I'm serious, Millie. I don't know yet what that means, because we're basically a day's travel apart, but I want to be involved in my kid's life."

I nibbled my lip. "I have a sonogram. In six weeks. To find out what we're having."

"When?" Luka asked.

"You'll have a game—"

"When, Millie?"

I stuttered out the date and time.

"I'll see what I can do," he said. "But I want to be there."

"You're in the middle of a playoff run," I reminded him.

"So? I'm only going to go to… How many sonograms do you have?"

"Well, since I'm healthy, not that many."

Luka narrowed his eyes thoughtfully. "Right. So this is important. We get to find out what we're having." He squirmed. "I'd like that to be together." His supplication melted my heart.

"I'd like that, too." I bit my lip. "But I think she's a girl."

"Well, we'll find out for sure together." His smile beamed so brightly, I couldn't help but be dazzled once again by Luka Stol.

CHAPTER 3
Luka

Cruz tapped his fingers on the steering wheel as we headed home from Cormac's house. We'd stayed longer than he probably wanted, but I liked hanging out with the guys, especially this time of year.

"Something's up with management," he said into the silence.

I sighed, still focused on my conversation with Millie and how I was going to manage to be in the fucking room when we found out our baby's sex. I shifted in my seat. I wasn't completely reassured by Millie's comments that she was well and the baby was, too.

There were few things I'd wanted in life, and fewer still that I'd grabbed hold of with both hands. Hockey was one. The Wildcatters had been my dream team. But Coach's frustration with my performance could have me well on my way to fucking up that dream.

"I saw Gunnar heading out of Coach's office when I was up there. Figured there's a trade in the works," I said. *I won't let that happen. I can't.* I knew how to work hard. So I damn well better buckle down—with a brief break to go to Sri Lanka and see Millie in person.

Coach would never go for that.

Cruz grunted. "I know I'm supposed to stay open-minded about trades, but I like our team, our chemistry. Our playoff chances."

"Me, too." But it didn't change the fact that my name was out there as a trade option. "What are you doing after the season?" I asked, suddenly desperate for something, *anything*, that wasn't related to my new reality.

While we were at Cormac's, Keelie's cat, Slippers, had used my lap as her resting place, and I now swiped at the fur coating my pants.

My mind continued to whirl. I'd wanted more time with Millie, but I hadn't expected our hookup to come with a lifetime connection. Millie thought we were having a baby girl. A *girl*. I was having a daughter. Of course I was. And I was *excited*. Thrilled about meeting my daughter.

Last laugh on me there. I'd been more than happy to love and leave my share of women. But that had changed when I met Millie. She meant something to me. Somehow, during those days I'd spent getting to know her, she'd wormed her way inside.

I didn't know if what I felt for Millie was love—anger, rejection, and frustration overpowered the sweeter emotion. But what I felt for my baby was pure adoration. I loved my baby.

Now and always. Even if I hadn't already decided to be better about casual sex, the idea of my kid one day asking about my romantic life made me want to be a man she could respect, trust— and know I respected and trusted her.

Jesus. Less than a day into parenthood, and I wanted to become a monk.

"Gonna reunite more veterans with their dogs," Cruz said, pulling my mind out of my strange musings and back into the truck with him. "Maybe I'll bring one home with me this time.

Get a house and a yard. Do the whole responsible-adult thing."

I shook my hand, trying to get the fur I'd extracted from my pants to detach. The bundle got near the air-conditioning vent and shot up my nose.

"Fuck!" I batted at my face, coughing. I sneezed once, twice, three times.

Cruz stuck his finger in his ear and twisted it. "You're loud."

"Sorry." I used the hem of my T-shirt to wipe my face. Note to self: no pets.

"I'm hungry," Cruz grumbled. "Want some tacos?"

"Good idea. I'm buying."

He turned into a parking lot that housed a few food trucks, and we walked up to the window. Cruz ordered for us both in Spanish, then shot the shit with the wizened man while I paid.

"Stolly?"

I turned at my name, then winced.

Brenda…Bridget…Brittany? stood a couple of feet away, eyes wide, a panther's grin on her lips. She was tall, lithe, and bottle-blond with a banging body.

"Hey," I said weakly.

"You never got my number. Back when we were together."

That had been at the start of the season, about a month before I sat down at the table with Millie.

"Yeah, well, we had fun…"

She edged in closer, so that her cute, strappy sandals were on the toes of my sneakers. "I rocked your world—and you rocked mine." She bit her lip.

"It was fun," I said, stepping backward and bumping into

Cruz, who made a sound like a startled bear. "But, ah, I met someone."

Brittany? blinked. "You met someone. That's why you didn't call me?"

"Well, I didn't have your number, but yeah." *Focus, dumbass.* "We're, ah, together—exclusive."

She tipped her head forward so all that long, blond hair streamed over her perky tits. "You're telling me you're in a relationship?" She giggled. "Please."

I straightened. "Why is that funny?"

"Because your eyes were roving even while your hands were on me."

I wasn't that bad, was I?

"Food's done," Cruz said. "Let's go."

"Good luck with your life," I said with a halfhearted wave.

"Good luck having an actual relationship," she shot back.

I heaved a sigh as I climbed back into the truck. "Don't start," I snapped at Cruz. I grabbed my drink, shoved the straw in, and took a long pull. I shuddered. Unsweetened iced tea. Damn Cruz and his religious zeal for nutrition.

"I didn't say anything," he said as he started the engine. "She's pretty."

"She wanted to fuck a hockey player. I obliged."

Cruz said nothing.

"And I regret it," I said into the deepening silence.

He looked over. "I know."

Much as I wanted to yell at him, I couldn't. Cruz hadn't gone through the puck-bunny stage. Cruz had been a responsible adult from the time he was in diapers; I was sure of that. The man seemed to ooze dependability. He'd told me his dad had died when he was really young; he'd been a truck driver and didn't make it home from a haul. Cruz's older brother, Raymond, had been a K-9 handler for the Army. When Raymond died, Cruz's family spent years trying to get his dog, Zeus, home with them.

Cruz didn't talk about Raymond much, but we all knew he'd managed to track Zeus down, get him discharged, and bring him home. The two of them had been inseparable until Zeus died, right around the time Cruz started playing in the NHL.

I wasn't supposed to know that Cruz had bought his mother's house outright and gotten her and his sisters new cars, paid for their college. Cruz didn't like to make a big deal about supporting the women in his family, but they were damn lucky to have him.

Hell, I'd become like his little brother, using Cruz's sense of duty to get me through my workouts and the season.

I am a dad. That was so much more responsibility than dealing with adults. I needed to buck up, get my shit together. Be more Cruz than Cruz.

"I'm thinking it's time to buy a house near the rest of the guys," Cruz said. "I want a dog or three." He shrugged his heavy shoulders. "Plan to reunite more."

"Need any help?" I asked.

"You're going to be busy with a kid," he reminded me.

I sighed. "Not if I can't talk Millie into sharing custody."

"Then you better come up with a plan to do that."

I spread my hands on my knees, fingers as wide as they could go. "I'm not sure I want to."

Cruz glared at me so hard I was sure my skull cracked. "You don't want to be part of the kid's life?"

When a car horn blared, he turned back to the road, just missing a couple of parked vehicles.

"Oh, I'm definitely going to be part of my kid's life." I cleared my throat. "Millie thinks the baby's a girl."

Cruz chuckled. "That would be something—you with a sweet little baby girl."

I shot him a look. "My daughter's going to know I love her and want her and all that shit. I'm just not sure we should split custody. I mean, that messes kids up, moving back and forth between houses and friends and all that weirdness. I'd rather be an everyday part of my girl's life."

Cruz grunted. "That might be harder, especially if your baby's mom is on the other side of the world."

"Believe me, I know."

I might not even get to my kid's sonogram, and that bothered me. I needed to show Millie, our baby, myself, that I was all in. *Why* did she move so damn far away?

"Any ideas about what you'll do?" Cruz asked.

Well, the thought of having a girl was growing on me, for one. But that wasn't what he was asking.

I tried to ground myself as worries spun through my mind. I knew what I wanted—Millie in my life and my bed, our baby in her room down the hall. But Millie didn't seem amenable to that, and I didn't know how to talk her into it. It wasn't like I planned to give up my job; I loved hockey, and I made great money, thanks to the lucrative contract my agent had put together when

I was drafted.

I had to assume Millie didn't want to give up her job or her career. And it was in Sri Lanka—not a great way for us to share dinner at the table whenever I was in town.

"None."

"Talk to Coach," Cruz suggested. "He might help out."

I crossed my arms over my chest and grunted, hating the idea of getting Coach involved in my personal life. Not after our last "talk."

"Seriously, Coach knows stuff," Cruz said.

"Yeah, he's great at reaming asses."

"Well, you have been playing like shit for weeks now," Cruz said.

I winced. He wasn't wrong. "Maybe I need some positive reinforcement. Ever thought of that?"

"Nah, man." Cruz shook his head. "We've coddled you long enough. You need a fire lit under your ass. Maybe the kid thing is it for you."

Cruz pulled into our parking garage, and I jumped out of the truck, not interested in a lecture on my shortcomings. "See you tomorrow," I called over my shoulder as I slammed the door. If Cruz responded, I didn't hear him.

By the time I made it up to my place, I'd worked myself into a lather about the whole situation. It was only then that I realized I'd left my tacos in the truck. My stomach rumbled, but I had more pressing matters.

I knew *nothing* about kids, especially girls. I'd never planned to have a child of my own. Didn't *want* one. Not after my childhood. My parents weren't abusive or evil; they were eccentric. Or that's what Alyssa called them, but I'd never understood them at all. They rolled along together simply because it caused less friction, but they never married and never seemed particularly interested in each other's lives, let alone mine. They rarely attended my hockey games, nor did they make my high school graduation, my draft day, or any day of importance in *my* life. It hadn't mattered to them because, as they'd told me for as long as I could remember, "*We're people, too, Luka. And we have our own lives.*"

And their own lives rarely meshed with mine. We never sat down to family dinner at my house. I could probably count the number of times on one hand. My mom got me into hockey because the kids on the street played, and it meant she only had to drive the carpool once a week.

If I wanted a home-cooked meal and a caring hug, I headed down the street to Mike's house and hoped his loud, swearing mom didn't mind adding another place at the table. She hadn't, and over time I became one of Alyssa Romeo's favorite kids. She'd collected all of us from the neighborhood who hadn't had enough supervision.

I loved her more than I ever could my mother, which is why I dug my phone from my pocket as I collapsed onto my long, plush sofa and called her.

"Ma, I got a problem," I announced when she answered.

"You and seven other kids. Nice to hear from you, Luka. You played like shit last week. Is that what this is about? We talked about this. Cut faster—"

I stared up at the ceiling. "I played great this entire series."

"Better, yeah."

I hesitated. "I'm going to be a father."

For the first time I could recall, Alyssa Romeo was speechless. I didn't need to see her to know that in the silence, she inhaled from the cigarette that clung stubbornly to her lip and blew out a long exhale of smoke. Alyssa always had a cigarette, but rarely inhaled. It was an extension of her, like her cursing.

"You like this girl?" she asked. "I mean, really like her more than to—"

"Ma!"

"You screwed her, Luka. You should be able to talk about that. If not, maybe you aren't as ready for the screwing as you'd like to think."

I swallowed. Ma had a way of cutting through the bullshit. "I... Yeah, I like her. More than like her, really."

"What's her name?"

"Millie."

"That's a nice name. Old-fashioned and sweet. *Is* she a sweet girl? I wanna meet her. See if she's good enough for you."

I grimaced as a new emotion emerged. Longing. I hadn't felt that in...forever. I'd learned early that my parents didn't give a shit, and I made sure I didn't care enough about anything or anyone to be hurt by missing out.

"I'd like you to, but that's part of the problem," I said.

"She's a hooker?" Alyssa grunted. "Well, you're not the first—"

"No! Ma, she's a chemical engineer."

Alyssa hummed. I could see her in my mind's eye: lips pursed, eyes narrowed, dark, graying hair teased up in that weird puff look many older women seemed to like. She was wearing a pair of skinny jeans that sagged off her slight frame and one of my sweaters or Mikey's baseball jersey.

Her son, Mike, and I had gone on to two different big leagues. Alyssa wanted everyone to know how proud she was, so she always wore one of our jerseys. Old-fashioned sneakers with those tiny white socks with a ball on the back likely completed her outfit.

"Well, now, that job sounds fancy," she said. "Tell me more about Millie, the sweet chemical engineer."

So I did. I relaxed on the couch as I talked. "She's so smart, Ma. And when she talks, her whole face lights up. Her eyes—she has these thick glasses she wears sometimes, and I couldn't see them the first night. But when she wears her contacts, her eyes are like *jade*, Ma. They're pretty."

Alyssa chuckled. "Smart and pretty. Got it. How did you meet?"

I described how Millie and I met, then flirted via texts and phone calls for a couple of weeks before we spent the night to-gether…and how she left without saying goodbye.

"Ah," Alyssa said.

"What does that mean?"

She let out a dry rumble that turned into a long, vicious bout of coughing. I'd begged her to quit smoking, but she refused. I'd begged her to go to the doctor, but she asked why—she knew she had lung cancer, and there wasn't anything they could do to stop it.

"Mike and I have the money to get you treatment—"

"S-st-stop."

I shut my mouth because this, too, was an old argument. Instead, I waited for Alyssa to get her breathing back under control.

"It…means…Millie…treated you…like you…treat *them*."

Confusion settled over me, and my brows tugged low. "Them? Who?"

"The women you screw, Luka. Keep up!"

My ears and cheeks burned, and my mouth dropped open. I wasn't *that* bad. I gave the women I slept with a delightful night. We had fun. We both orgasmed—multiple times for her, though I'd never turned down a thank-you blowie—and then I ghosted. I never gave those women my number. I never looked them up again.

"Shit, Ma! Shit! What if there are other little Lukas running around and I—"

"Calm your titties. There aren't."

"How do you know—"

"I know stuff, and I especially wanted to know about pregnancies that could be used against you."

Of course she did. Ma was as no-nonsense as they came. She wouldn't allow a puck bunny to derail my career.

"Now, focus on Millie. She dumped you, moved to Sri Lanka for work, and called to let you know she's pregnant but expects nothing from you."

"That pisses me off," I admitted.

"Which bit?"

"The dumping, moving, and expecting nothing from me," I mumbled.

"Why?" Alyssa asked. "Based on your past behavior—which I'm betting she knows about since it's in all the tabloids—I would think you'd be happy not to have to deal with a child. The responsibility is awesome."

I rubbed my hand up and down my neck. Jitters had replaced the earlier noodliness in my body. I needed to run or skate until I collapsed. I hopped off my couch and paced; my sneakers made a soft squeak on the hardwood. "I *know* that."

"And you know that she knows about your reputation because *everyone* knows about it, Luka. You weren't discreet."

"I'm twenty-three!"

"And it's already biting you in the ass, hard, which should tell you about all that partying." She harrumphed.

"I…" What to say. How to explain. "Sex is simple for a professional athlete."

"I know," she groused.

"But it's also meaningless." I rubbed my chest as that horrible longing ripped through it again.

"Why's that?" Alyssa asked.

"Because…" How to explain something I didn't understand myself? "I want what you and Bob had, Ma."

"Aaaaaaaaah." She drew out the word. "I wondered."

I frowned. "About what?"

"You were always so eager for hugs, for praise. It made you an incredible athlete, but you've been using those women to give you connection—a sense of belonging with and to someone else. Like I had with my Bob."

"I… Yeah."

"It's okay to be affectionate, Luka. It's okay to want a deep, lasting relationship—to know that other person's gonna love you, be there for you, no matter what."

I shook my head because I didn't know how to get those things, but based on how achy my chest was and the sting in my eyes and nose, that was *exactly* what I wanted. I quit walking so fast, I tripped over my own feet. "With Millie, there was connection. We...clicked," I choked out. "But I don't know what to do."

Damn, these emotions were big. Fucking scary—like my mind was battering my body from the inside, and I didn't know what to do with these strange and terrible feelings.

"What *do* you know, kiddo?"

"That I like her."

"Yeah."

"That this is *my* kid."

"Yeah."

"Jeez, Ma, *fine*! I want to be involved. With the pregnancy and the parenting. I want this baby."

"And Millie?"

I chewed my lower lip, considering. Alyssa waited, her wheezing less pronounced, which helped me calm down enough to think.

"Yeah, and Millie. I want them both in my life, in my house."

"Well, now, that's something!" Alyssa's cackling turned back into that deep, hacking cough. "All right, bucko, let's come up with a plan."

"I can't do anything—"

"Until the end of the season. I know. But you can put pieces in place now. First thing we need to do is understand where she's coming from."

CHAPTER 4
Luka

It took me nearly six weeks, but I was finally able to put the first step of my plan in place.

"I can't believe you flew all this way for an appointment," Millie said, awestruck. I wasn't sure she'd blinked since she met me at the doors to the terminal.

I shook my head, trying to clear the fogginess of traveling for more than twenty-four hours. "I told you, this is important. Coach agreed."

"You're missing the game against the Avalanche tonight—"

"Just one game, which Coach approved because, depending how deep we go in the playoffs, I might not pull this off again for months." I shot her a hopeful look. "Unless you want to come to Houston."

Millie shook her head once, hard. "No."

I sighed, but I tried not to get discouraged. I was much, much further along than a few weeks ago when Millie wouldn't even take my calls. Today, this trip, was about building the foundation for more. We wobble and fall before we skate the full rink.

We talked every day now about the baby, her job, my job, and Colombo, which we were driving through at the moment. Sri Lanka's capital was larger than I'd expected. It was just as muggy as Houston, and it smelled both exotic and familiar—of exhaust and local spices and sweat. The high rises clustered all the way to the water's edge, reminding me a bit of Miami, but the roads, crowded with cars and mopeds and bicycles, were distinctly overcrowded and un-American in their traffic patterns. And then there was the way the pedestrians dressed and the signs over the shops and for the streets. I was in a strange new world, in so many ways.

The driver braked hard at the last moment, bringing us within millimeters of the bumper in front of us, much like a cabbie in Manhattan.

"You're taking a flight out again this evening?" Millie asked.

"Well, like you said, I'm already missing a game…"

Coach had seemed pleased to shift my place with the second-line left winger, Reece Hopper. That guy had been itching to show what he could do. I might well lose my starting spot after this, something Coach and I had talked through after my call with Millie in Cormac's office.

Coach had congratulated me on my impending fatherhood and helped me find flights. As I'd walked out, Gunnar Evaldson, the owner, had walked in—the second time we'd traded places in Coach's office that way. There was something afoot with management, and it made me nervous. Something was going on in the organization, and I had enough ego to wonder if it had to do with me. No doubt it had been Coach's plan to light a fire under my ass when he'd mentioned trades.

My agent claimed I was safe until the end of the season because the trade deadline had passed and I wouldn't be allowed to suit up for another team's playoff run, just as the new Wildcatter's player taking my place wouldn't be able to play.

But that was a worry for another day. Right now, I wanted to enjoy my sixteen hours with Millie before I headed back to Houston.

"So, I thought you'd like to take a shower and change before we walk over to my appointment," Millie said, tucking her hair behind her ear.

I smiled at her thoughtfulness. "Sounds great."

The driver opened the car door, and I helped her out, noting the slight curve to her belly. If I hadn't known she was four-and-a-half months pregnant, I never would have guessed. I kept my hand clasped around her smaller one as I grabbed my backpack.

"Lead the way," I said, still holding her hand.

She brought me in through an opulent lobby, dripping with chandeliers and polished marble floors. We took the elevator up to a seventh-floor condominium, which had a view of the ocean three blocks away. The water was a rich blue farther from the shoreline and a soft turquoise where it kissed the beige sand.

Her place was tidy. The darker wood floors popped against the white walls. The furniture was all new and had that soulless corporate ambiance that told me it had come standard with the place. Millie had added a couple of framed photos, one of her and Ida Jane and—I smiled, pleasure rippling through me—a candid shot of her and me together from the night we'd met. Well, that was a very good sign. Millie was infatuated with me, just as I was with her. She also had a large print of the periodic table above her couch…and that was the extent of her personalization.

Even my place, with its standard male furnishings, looked

more lived in.

"You'll have to use my bathroom," she told me. "The powder room doesn't have a shower."

I nodded. "Think I can get some coffee?"

"I asked the concierge to send up a full breakfast," Millie said.

Once I was showered and caffeinated, Millie and I walked to her doctor's office. Again I was assaulted by a jumble of sounds and smells that my mind struggled to assimilate. Columbo was fascinating—so different from any place I'd been before. When a man on a motorbike sped too close to her, I tucked Millie against my side, moving her over next to the buildings. Horns honked and the ocean breeze drifted through the acres of concrete, easing the worst of the mugginess. She glanced up at me as I looked down at her, the sunlight peeking through the tall buildings and limning her silhouette, making her appear Madonna-like. I squeezed her fingers, and she leaned into me.

"Had any food cravings?" I asked.

She laughed, and then I listened to her talk about her current fascination with fish sauce as I took in the bursts of color and harsh blares of horns and the soft sea breeze tinted with decaying seaweed and fish.

It was different from the oppressiveness of a Houston spring day, yet not. I wondered if Millie had chosen the location because of its similar climate. Something told me she had, though she'd shown no interest in returning to her hometown. As close as she and Ida Jane seemed to be, I couldn't understand Millie's desire to be so far away.

We entered the cool of the building, and once Millie gave her name, they ushered us into an exam room.

"They seem very efficient," I offered.

"They are. Much more on top of their schedule than my gynecologist back in Houston ever was."

I wanted to ask her again about returning, but I'd sensed her hesitation before naming the city and felt the slight tremor in her hand when she did. I remembered, clearly, Ida Jane's comment about Millie being hurt.

A knock sounded, and the doctor poked her graying head into the room. She smiled at the both of us and began the exam. Millie beckoned me over right before the doctor set a device to her belly.

A strange, fast *whop-whop-whop* filled the air.

"That's her heartbeat," Millie whispered.

My gaze sought hers and held.

"Sounds great," the doctor said.

Two important truths hit me then: there was an actual baby inside of Millie, and Millie expected that tiny life to be a *girl*.

I blinked back tears. I wanted to blame it on travel exhaustion, but I knew my reaction stemmed from my stunted childhood. I *never* wanted our baby to go days, let alone weeks, without seeing my face, feeling my hugs, and hearing me tell her I loved her.

I had no clue how I was going to swing day-to-day involvement if Millie insisted on living in Colombo, but I'd have to figure something out.

Soon.

Maybe I didn't need to play hockey.

The idea choked me, and fear settled in my guts.

What else would I do?

What else *could* I do?

There wasn't a professional hockey league in Sri Lanka. And it wasn't like I could just go down to the local ice rink and get a job as the ice manager. I didn't even know what that job entailed. I just knew how to skate and score goals.

That was a very limited skill set. One that made me millions of dollars, but still, that was only into my thirties if I was lucky.

"So today's the big day," the doctor said with a smile. "I'm assuming Dad's here to find out your baby's gender."

"Yes," I crowed. "I'm excited."

"He traveled from Houston to be here for this," Millie added. She smiled up at me from the exam table.

The doctor whistled. "That's a long flight. Well, let's find out so you can celebrate."

And start planning. I kept that thought to myself.

The doctor scooted back, and a lab technician rolled in a sonogram machine. She took about a million measurements, all of which told her whether our baby was growing well. Then, she said the four words that caused my emotions to squeeze my throat closed, even though I'd expected them: "Congratulations! It's a girl!"

Millie met my gaze, her eyes shining with emotion. Before I could think better of it or stop myself, I kissed her. She made a startled sound even as her lips clung to mine.

"Thank you," I murmured. "I can't wait to introduce our daughter to the guys. They'll love her."

Millie disengaged from me, turning her back to hop off the

exam table. "I need to get dressed."

She was doing it again; she pulled away whenever I mentioned my teammates, or Houston.

"I'll be in the waiting room," I said, shoving down my hurt.

When Millie appeared a few minutes later, I was pretty sure she'd been crying. But the duck of her head and the speed with which she scampered past me made it clear she didn't want me to mention it—nor did she want to talk to me.

"When do you need to get to the airport?" she asked as she stood next to me in the lobby, waiting for a car.

"I have a few hours," I said. "We can get lunch—"

"I should go to the office. I've already been away longer than I planned."

I gritted my teeth. "I'd really like to spend the few hours I have with you. You could show me your favorite spot in the city, or we could hit that market I saw on the drive to your place."

"I…I should really get to work." She fidgeted, unable to meet my eyes. "Just so you know, I'm having Bree here, in Sri Lanka. We're living here. But you're welcome to visit."

A sleek car pulled up outside the building, and a driver came around to open the door. Millie hurried outside. I followed more slowly so I had a moment to push down my frustration. Everything had been going so well. At least, I'd thought it was. But Millie was fixated on a path I couldn't join, and that hurt.

"My season runs nine months out of the year, sometimes longer with exhibition games and the playoffs," I said as I moved into the car next to her. "But I want to be involved." I hesitated. "I wasn't close to my parents, and I don't want my—our child to have experience. You know, to wonder if she's loved."

I reached for Millie's hand, only to realize she'd squished herself tightly against the other door—to make herself less of a target? Did she think I'd hurt her?

My frustration morphed into horror. The driver entered the car and looked back at us questioningly. As I debated what to do—try to push Millie into lunch or at least into going back to her apartment where we could talk—she told the driver to head to the airport.

Well, that told me where I stood. In Millie's eyes, I was just the sperm donor, just an irritant she'd have to put up with from time to time.

"I have to keep Bree here, Luka. I know you don't understand, but there's no way she can go to Houston. Ever."

"Why?"

She looked down at her clasped hands, and I noted how tightly she squeezed them. Even hurt and angry with her, I wanted to soothe her, to unclasp her hands and hold one while I helped her work through her fear.

Instead, I sat next to her, taut with nerves, as she stared down at her lap. She didn't say another word until we pulled up at the terminal.

Then she looked up at me, her eyes filled with remorse and yearning. She reached out, her fingers trembling as she touched my jaw.

"Goodbye, Luka."

I was so mixed up on days and nights, I had no clue what time it was when I got into Cruz's truck at the airport to go straight to practice. I'd slept maybe a couple of hours on the plane, my mind spinning on Millie's adamant refusal to return to Houston.

I didn't have a lot of options, not if I wanted to be part of my daughter's life. No doubt sensing my mood, Cruz drove in silence, but his eyes were suspicious, like he sensed I was on the verge of shattering.

"Millie said she can't move back to the States. She can't bring the baby here."

"She tell you why?" he asked.

I shook my head. "No, and that's bugging me."

I recognized her behavior, because I did the same thing when people tried to get me to talk about my parents, yet I was *still* smarting over it. I'd spent the entire layover in Doha walking around the terminal, replaying our conversation—or lack there-of—in my mind.

"Would bug me, too." Cruz made a deep sound in his chest. "Hopper fucked the line."

"Well, there's that, at least. Surely that means Coach will put me back in my spot."

"I hope so. You're better at reading the defense than he is. No one will say it, but his sloppy play cost us the game."

That made me feel good, but probably meant little. "Well, let's show Jacksonville what a real offense can produce," I said.

Cruz grunted, which I took as a yes. I managed an hour-long nap at the arena before I laced up for the pre-skate and warmups. With effort, I shoved my concerns about Millie and my daughter from my mind and focused on the practice. I scored a goal and offered Naese an assist during our scrimmage.

Our team won by two, and the guys were in a festive mood.

"You coming?" Naese asked me after.

"Nah, man, but have fun."

He shrugged, and I realized that he looked miserable. I wondered if, like me, Naese wasn't interested in the dating scene anymore. I was a family man now, whether or not Millie was ready to believe it.

"What's wrong?" Cormac asked, concern etched into his expression.

"Nothing. I'm just tired from forty-plus hours of travel."

"Right. How's your woman?" he asked.

"Good." She was healthy at least. Our relationship was not good, but I was too tired to go there right now. I just needed to fix it. I'd decided to call her at least once every day. I had to show Millie I was invested in her, in our daughter—in *us* as a family, if she'd believe that.

"And the baby?" Cormac asked.

I smiled. "I got pictures."

Naese stepped back, possibly weirded out by the black and white sonogram shots, but Cormac, Cruz, and even Maxim oo-hed over my girl's tiny features.

"Ida Jane said she hopes the baby has your cheekbones because they're, and I quote—'too gorgeous not to pass down.'" Maxim raised an eyebrow, amusement dancing in his eyes while Naese made gagging sounds.

"My kid will be adorable with whatever cheekbones she has," I said with all the authority I could muster.

"You're having a girl?" Cormac thumped my shoulder. "Aw, a little girlie Stolly skating around."

I grinned, prouder in that moment than of any of my hockey accomplishments—even holding the Cup. "Yeah. I'm a girl dad. She's perfect."

I touched the image, already missing Millie, frustrated to be so far away and not get to see her belly round with our daughter. I hated missing the first kicks or getting to talk to our baby in Millie's belly, which was why Alyssa and I would continue developing our plan for me to be as involved as I could be. Video technology would help.

Melancholy settled in, but I forced it down. I knew how to work hard—harder than most other people. I'd win Millie over. I had to. My future with my daughter was at stake.

I grabbed my bag and headed toward the door, catching Coach's eye on the way out. He gave me a small nod and a "proud of you" as I passed. Something else was in his gaze—something I wasn't able to place.

A rideshare dropped me at my building, and I headed upstairs, already dialing Millie's number. I desperately wanted her to answer; I needed to know that her dropping me directly at the airport hadn't been a more extended goodbye.

She answered the video call with a tired smile. I glanced at the clock: just after eleven here, which meant it was 9:30 on Saturday morning there. The ten-hour-and-thirty-minute time change would take me a while to get right.

"How are you?" I asked.

"Fine. Tired. Pregnancy's been hitting me hard."

"I'm impressed that you're awake so bright and early this morning," I teased, hoping to lighten the heaviness between us the way I had that first night we met.

She blushed. "Yeah, I just got up. You'd think I was the one who'd traveled a full day."

"I'd think you're the one growing our daughter," I replied. "Thank you for doing such a good job with her, Millie."

Her breath caught, and her eyes went soft. She was so much more open now that I was on the other side of the world. Best I could work out, the distance between us made Millie feel safe. There was no hint now of the closed-off, abrupt dismissal she'd dished after he doctor's appointment. Based on what Ida Jane had said, I was pretty sure someone close to Millie had hurt her. I didn't want to be right, but that would explain why Millie was so determined to remain far, far from home.

Ida Jane had also told me Millie was a black belt in jiu jitsu. That dedication to martial arts and my growing hypothesis would explain the starburst patterns on her knuckles, which I'd also seen on a lot of boxers and MMA fighters who hit punching bags repeatedly.

"I was thinking about names," she said, pulling me from my reverie.

This woman had so many layers. Peeling each one aside to get to her heart might prove more daunting than any task I'd ever completed—including getting the call to professional hockey.

"Great! I want to hear them. Is there one you love?" *Please don't pick one I hate.* I wanted to give Millie everything I could, but I drew the line at a terrible name.

She licked her lips. "Bree, short for Briana. I want to call her Bree."

"Bree…" I rolled it over my tongue a few times, then my mind. "That's pretty."

Her shoulders dropped and her smile grew. "Great! Now, tell me about your day. When did you get back? Did you make it for practice?"

~

I tossed the eighth grapefruit into the bowl on my counter after giving it a good huff. It smelled like Millie…sort of. I'd dreamed, again, about the night we'd spent together.

"*It drives me wild*," I'd groaned into her neck, nuzzling against her to release more of the fragrance. Just like I had that night.

I'd relived it in my dreams so often that I could recite every detail.

"*My shampoo?*" she'd asked, sounding shocked.

"*Yeah. I love it.*"

"*Um…grapefruit.*"

"*Mmm…*"

I'd dropped tiny kisses along her hairline and down her cheek until I'd hovered over her mouth. Her pupils were blown wide with desire, and she'd clutched at my biceps, shifting against my hardening cock. How many times had we gone at it? I didn't know—didn't care because it wasn't enough. I'd had a sinking feeling I'd never get enough of Millie Jones.

"*That's not it, though. There's a flower…*"

"*M-m-my lotion,*" she'd moaned into my mouth.

I'd kissed her with a languidness that spoke of the initial hunger quenched, but continued need. This had been unexpected. Beautiful. Just like the woman who'd kissed me back with abandon.

"What is it, pretty girl? What's the smell I want to bury myself in?"

"L-lilac?"

"Fuck, it's delicious. Like you."

I sighed, the memory fizzling as someone—probably Cruz—knocked on my door. The dude had been checking up on me even more now that he knew about Millie and the baby.

That could also be because I'd poured my heart out a couple of nights ago, admitting how much I cared about Millie, how deeply I wanted to be an integral part of my kid's life, how much I knew that mattered because my parents hadn't provided it for me.

I opened the door to find Naese, my friend and nuisance, on the other side. He looked...unkempt, and unhappier than usual.

"What's up?" I asked.

"Why do you have a shrub on your table?" he asked, ignoring my question as he pushed past me into my space. He bristled with testosterone. "Shouldn't that be in dirt?"

"It is in dirt, dipshit. And I've got a big pot for it outside on the terrace. I just haven't planted it yet. Oh, hey! I got a new picture of my kid. Look." I pulled the 3-D sonogram from my wallet and showed him Bree's cute little face. "Millie sent them to me last night."

I'd asked her to do this special procedure so I had something tangible of my daughter. Millie agreed to most of my requests, as long as they didn't include her returning to Houston or me bringing our daughter to the city.

"She's tiny. Cute," Naese said, handing the photo back.

Fine, he wasn't into the bonding-over-kids thing. Where was Cormac or even Maxim when I needed them? At their houses with their women.

Envy welled because I wanted that—what they had.

"Want to see the photo Millie sent me this morning of her bump?" I asked.

"No, man. Looking at your woman's belly is weird." He pierced me with his narrowed gaze. "Is *she* why you have a plant on your table? Are you practicing keeping something alive? Gotta say, I think the practice-with-a-cat thing makes more sense. Cuz it's like *alive* alive."

"Shut up, dickhead. I didn't buy a plant to practice on." I'd bought a baby doll, which was currently on the pillows of my bed, the closest thing I had to a full-time connection with my child. I scuffed my toe on the hardwood, refusing to meet Naese's gaze in case he figured that out and busted my balls. "Lilac reminds me of Millie. And since we need to complete the season..." I shrugged. "Made me feel closer to her."

Naese's ass thudded with an unrecognizable heaviness onto one of my barstools.

"Careful, man," I said. "I like those."

"And the grapefruit? Do you even like grapefruit?" Naese reached over and snagged the lilac, burying his face into the blooms.

"I love how they smell on Millie. But they're bitter and taste like a year-old orange."

He burbled out a halfhearted laugh. "Give 'em to Mac. He likes the juice."

CHAPTER 5
Millie

I lingered in my kitchen, feeling restless and listless after I finished my tea and hoping Luka would call. I hadn't seen him in nine weeks, and I missed him more with each passing day. Much as I hated to admit it, I cared about him. A lot. And talking to him was the highlight of my day.

I wondered how he was feeling. He'd seemed a bit down since they lost their championship run a couple weeks ago. The Wildcatters had been close to a title, making it all the way to the conference finals. I'd hated how defeated Luka had looked as he did a final lap around the ice after that last game.

When it didn't seem I was going to hear from him this morning, I went out onto my balcony and looked down at the city and the sea beyond. I loved the view but felt unsettled—no, worse than that. Luka never missed a day of talking to me, to find out about Bree. Yet he hadn't called yesterday. And he hadn't let me know he'd planned to skip today. Maybe he hadn't planned on it and something terrible happened.

Ida Jane would have told me, wouldn't she?

Or what if nothing was wrong, but he'd decided I was too much work with my cold shoulder and unwillingness to discuss my reasons for not returning to Houston. Maybe he was out right now and had met a new, beautiful woman.

Maybe he'd decided I wasn't worth the effort.

I couldn't blame him. I'd been shoving him away since we'd spent the night together. Melancholy clutched at my chest, and I blinked back tears.

If Luka had given up on me, I had no one to blame but myself. I couldn't be mad at him, and that brought my mood even lower. As I looked out toward the sea, I admitted that I missed Ida Jane fiercely. I even missed the smog and noise and humidity of Houston. But mostly, I missed Luka.

He'd been so kind, even when I'd kicked him out of the car and sent him directly back to Houston after Bree's sonogram.

He hadn't needed to be; I hadn't expected his kindness after that. But Luka, I'd realized, was inherently good, just as Maxim had said. He deserved better than me, better than the position I'd forced him into. But I was afraid—so damn afraid to go back to Houston, to let my father know I had a baby, to tell Luka the sordid details of my past.

The door's chime took me by surprise, causing me to spin around too fast. I grasped the balcony railing for support, waiting for the dizziness to pass. Then I headed toward the door, praying, as I always did, that my father wasn't on the other side.

My palms were sweaty as I eased closer and peeked out the glass side panel. I had to grab the door handle for support so I didn't collapse to my knees—or worse, fall flat on my face.

"I see you, Millie."

I gasped and backed away. Luka was here. In Colombo. *Again.*

I hadn't known he was coming. I'd talked to him a few days ago, right before Cormac and Keelie's wedding, but he hadn't called yesterday, and now I knew why. He'd been on a plane for…I tried to remember.

"Let me in. Please," he said. "I've been traveling for almost forty hours, and I left right after Cormac's wedding."

Luka's voice was deep and resonated in my chest, along with a warmth I hadn't felt since I'd last seen him. That settled in my middle but radiated outward. I was shocked by how much I enjoyed the sensation.

I'd already flicked the lock and turned the handle before I realized I was following his order. "Y-you're…"

"Here. Yes. To see you and Bree."

His hair was longer, his eyes intense even with the shadows under them. He was so beautiful. He wore a cotton T-shirt and cargo shorts. Those would also be made from cotton, which was ninety-nine percent cellulose. Cellulose was a long chain of glucose molecules where the carbon connected to oxygen… My mini science lesson didn't stop the vise that gripped my chest. Luka was here. I wasn't ready to see him. I was a mess of longing and anxiety.

When he leaned in closer, my fingers fluttered, desperate to touch his stubbled cheek. "But…" I settled my hands on my bump under my cotton tank top, needing to ground myself. My belly, warm and rigid, encased our sleeping baby.

"The season is over, as you know. I was in Hawaii for Cormac and Keelie's wedding, and I had to decide—go back to my lonely condo in Houston or come see you." His eyes filled with yearning, his gaze lingering on my pregnant belly, which seemed to grow each day. He shut his eyes, anguish in his expression. "I've hated missing so much of your pregnancy. Now, will you please let me inside so we can, you know, talk?"

I licked my lips. "I…" I was stuck on the fact that he'd traveled nearly two full days to get here. He must have spoken to me right before he caught the flight.

We'd been on good terms these past couple months, but I'd made it clear I wasn't coming back to Houston. I'd thought that was the end of his attempts to connect in person. I should have known NHL players were tenacious.

"It's okay, Millie," he said. "I just want to talk to you. You can do this."

He said what my mind told me, but what my body and heart feared were lies. Still, I shuffled back enough for him to step inside, which he did once he grabbed his duffle from the floor next to his feet.

He shut the door behind him, dropping his bag and doing the locks. He turned back in time to find me swaying, still blinking with shock.

Seeing Luka Stol, my baby daddy, in person, after all this time, made me break-out-in-hives, barf-up-my-guts apprehensive. And I'd done neither of those since I'd hit fourteen weeks of pregnancy—before he'd come out for Bree's sonogram. I wanted to keep it that way.

This second trimester had been much, much better on my hormones than the first. I refused to consider what could happen as I moved more deeply into the third trimester—or the fact that I was there now.

"You didn't mention you were coming," I said. "When we last talked."

We'd spoken regularly, so Luka was up to date on Bree, but we hadn't discussed *us* outside of the fact that he wanted to be present for the baby's birth and planned to take some time off during the preseason to help me with the early months after Bree's arrival.

"I couldn't stay away," he said.

My pulse fluttered in my neck, and I felt as I did each time Luka tried to bring up where Bree would be born, where we'd live. My mind spun with the unknown, further increasing my fretting.

He peered down at me, his attention focused, as if he were serious about me.

Me.

Tch. As if.

Yes, I'd heard what Ida Jane said all those months ago, and yes, I'd checked the gossip sites to see if Luka was with anyone else, and he wasn't. But that didn't mean I trusted him to want me.

I was so different now than when we'd first met. More had changed than just my growing belly and larger breasts. I was... Well, as Ida Jane had put it the other day, I was a hot mess. I'd thrown myself into my work so I wouldn't have to focus on my reasons for leaving Houston.

That hadn't worked the way I'd thought it would. In fact, I'd concluded that I'd made a mistake. A big one. I hadn't faced the trauma caused by Trent's actions, nor had I spoken to my father since I accepted the transfer to Sri Lanka.

That, too, had been foolhardy because I'd let Trent's actions—and my father's complicity—create a narrative around me: that I was a victim.

But I wasn't.

I was not. Nor would I ever be.

And now I was a mother. I had more to protect. More to fight for…more to lose.

I opened my mouth, closed it. What was I supposed to say to Luka? I'd told him I was sorry—that I hadn't intended to get pregnant, that he didn't need to do anything. He'd called me back the next day and insisted on a video chat. When his face appeared—so beautiful, his jaw tense, eyes broken but filled with hope—he'd told me he was Bree's father, and he would be involved in her life. *"Starting now, Millie. I know I can't be there every day, and that's bothering the hell out of me, but I want to know about all your appointments, her growth, your blood pressure and glucose levels, and all that shit."*

At least he hadn't asked to hear about my weight gain. That would have been awful. I'd started the pregnancy fit and strong, but my body didn't feel entirely my own these days. I still had an ass that rivaled Kim Kardashian's in size, if not roundness, with the thighs to support it.

"I should have given you a heads-up about me coming—" he began.

"Yeah, that would have been helpful…" Except, would it? From the get-go, Luka had tied me in knots, and I'd acted the fool. I would have tried to disappear if he'd told me about his visit—something he seemed to have surmised. No, if I were in his shoes, I would have surprised me, too.

"Um, do you want to sit down?" I asked, finally finding some equilibrium.

"Sure."

I led Luka into the living room and turned to face him. I didn't know where to put my hands, and I ended up settling them on my hips, which pushed my bump farther forward. Luka's gaze drifted to my belly.

"You're bigger that I expected," he blurted.

I drew myself up, mouth compressed in an angry line, but Luka didn't notice. He was focused on the baby snuggled in my midsection.

Dropping to his knees, he laid his hands on either side of my belly, shocking me with the vulnerability on his face. Luka seemed choked by the same emotions rocketing through me.

"Hi there, Bree," he said.

He hadn't fought with me about the name. In fact, he'd told me it was beautiful—as beautiful as our baby would be. So I'd sent him the image of her 3-D sonogram a couple months ago. He'd gotten to see her sweet, tiny little face. I'd fallen even more in love with him as he'd stroked the image, tears in his eyes as he thanked me for her and the picture.

"Hi. I'm your daddy," he murmured against my belly. He swallowed, a thick sound that told me his emotions were just below the surface. After a moment, he continued, "I've missed you—don't think otherwise. I got here as soon as I could. And I want you to know, you mean everything to me."

The man I couldn't stop dreaming about was on his knees with his face pressed against my belly, as if that was the most natural scenario in the world. If he only knew how right—and wrong—it was that he was my baby's father.

Luka

I glanced up at Millie, then wished I hadn't. I was already so nervous about this situation, and her wide eyes and parted lips made me want to snuggle her. She hadn't offered that, though, so I kept my fists on my thighs.

"I heard you're moving around a lot in there," I said, returning my attention to the adorable bump cradling my baby. "Maybe you could give me a high-five or something."

Millie made a noise and swayed a little. Not willing to risk her health, I wrapped my arm around her hips and tugged her legs against my chest.

"What is it?" I asked, looking up at her.

"N-nothing," she mumbled. "I just didn't… You're on your…greeting—ow! She punched me." Millie jumped, her eyes widening. "That was hard."

I chuckled as I moved my hands up and down the taut skin of her belly. "Do that again, baby. Daddy was talking to Mommy, so I didn't feel—there's my girl!" A tiny appendage rammed into my cheek, and I grinned like a loon. "She's strong."

"That's my bladder she's drop-kicking," Millie muttered, shuffling her feet like a preschooler told to wait. She squeezed her eyes and legs together at the next burst of movement from Bree.

I rose to my feet. "Let's get you to the bathroom."

"I'm not sure I can—put me down! You'll hurt yourself."

I chuckled. "I deadlift way more than this every day. Don't worry, Millie; you and Bree are safe."

I maneuvered toward the powder room off the living room. I

set her down inside the door. She shuffled forward.

"Need help?" I asked.

She inhaled sharply. "No! I can pee alone."

Her horrified tone had me backing up, hands raised in supplication. "Okay. Right. I'll just…be out here."

She shut the door, and I thought I heard her muttering something about hot, buff guys and panties, but I wasn't sure. I loitered, desperate to talk to her and feel my daughter move around more.

I ran my hand through my hair, leaving it standing on end. I was past exhausted, thanks to my inability to sleep more than a couple of hours on any of the three flights I'd taken to get here, but I was on a high now. I'd waited over two months to get back here, and seeing the swell of Millie's stomach, feeling the movement of my daughter, the pregnancy became more real.

I hadn't been sure about the plan Alyssa and I concocted when I'd first learned about the baby, hadn't decided if I should fly back to Colombo to make my play yet. Then I watched Cormac and Keelie at their wedding, saw how he interacted with his unborn kid, and I didn't have a choice.

Not that I'd ever tell him this, but Cormac was one of my heroes. He was an even better man than I'd expected, leading us with a cool head but also willing to lend an ear, a shoulder, hold a punching bag—whatever we needed.

So when I saw him rubbing Keelie's belly, head bent close as he talked to the baby, I'd known I needed to do that with Bree. I coveted the chance. So I'd changed my flights and come here.

Impulsive, just as Coach called me. I hadn't thought it

through…just known it was right.

And actually, Coach hadn't called me impulsive since I flew out here the first time. Oh, I'd felt the heavy weight of his stare more than once, but he seemed to be observing me, measuring my responses.

Seeing if I remained a good fit for the Wildcatters.

Considering Wildcatter management had recently offered Reece Hopper in exchange for an older left winger and a draft pick, I thought my first-line position might be safe.

Might being the key word.

I huffed a breath, letting the rightness of this choice settle into me. It had been a spur-of-the-moment decision, but Cormac was always telling me to trust my gut.

Exhausted and at risk of confusing myself, I shelved those thoughts. I'd tease them out later.

When Millie emerged from the bathroom, she'd changed into a maxi dress, and I marveled at how much Bree had grown since the last photo Millie had sent me. She'd started texting a weekly snapshot that I woke up early to see each Friday. I looked forward to that message more than anything.

"Bree's grown," I said. Much as I wanted to rub Millie's belly again, I didn't want to freak her out by pressing my face to her bump.

Millie nodded, a bit stiff. "I thought you meant me."

I saw the hurt in her eyes. "What? Why would you… *Oh*. I'm an idiot. I meant *her*. In there." I rubbed the back of my neck. "I came because I wanted to see you—both of you," I clarified.

Millie raised an eyebrow. "I figured that out. What with you being here and all."

"And I… I hoped I could take you to dinner—a date. You know, so we could, um, talk about us, the baby—whatever you want." I blushed and slammed my mouth shut, appalled by my less-than-smooth approach. But then, I supposed it was to be expected. There'd never been a woman who mattered as much to me as Millie—or would ever matter as much. Millie was the mother of my child.

Her lips kicked up in a smile and her eyes sparkled. "Luka Stol stammering. Who would have thought?"

Her computer chimed with an incoming video chat, and I clenched my fists. What if it was another man? I couldn't stand the thought of her talking to, let alone *dating*, someone else. I wanted to reach through the monitor and destroy any man who thought he was going to take Millie and Bree from me.

"It's Ida Jane. Hang on."

She slid onto a chair at the bar and enlarged the app's screen. "Idge!"

"Mil-bil! Oooh, who's there with you? Does Stolly know you have a man in your condo?"

My heart warmed at the censure in Ida Jane's voice. She and I had gotten closer during the weekly dinners she hosted. But it was our walk after I'd stalked her outside Maxim's place a couple months ago—when I was too far down the rabbit hole to think of another option—that had sealed our connection.

"Considering Luka's hovering behind me, I think he'll be fine," Millie said, her voice brittle with dryness.

"Hi, Ida Jane! How are you?" I asked, coming up beside

Millie. I laid my hands on her shoulders. She stiffened for a moment before her body went slack under my touch. I rubbed my thumbs back and forth on the delicate skin at her nape, and she huffed a little sigh.

"I'm good. We weren't sure where you'd gone after the wedding."

"I surprised Mille."

"He sure did," she muttered.

Ida Jane pursed her lips and nodded. "Good, good. So I won't keep you long."

"Why did you call?" Millie asked.

"Because Maxim and I are having a shindig at Cormac and Keelie's in a couple of weeks. I need you to be there, Mil-bil. Bad." Ida Jane's eyes widened, and her expression turned pleading. "It's *real* important to me."

Millie leaned forward, and I watched her as she assessed Ida Jane. "What aren't you saying?"

Ida Jane's smile turned sly, and her gaze flicked around the room. "Maxim's settin' up a marriage celebration party for us next month," she said. She rattled off the date—right in the middle of summer. "But the CATS, Mama, Daddy, and I are plannin' something even *more* special." She winked. "Something I think he's gonna like a tad bit better than a party."

I fought the urge to rub my hands together with glee. Oh, this was working out better than I'd hoped. I wouldn't have to talk Millie into flying back with me—Ida Jane would do it for me. I owed her for this—big time.

Millie laughed. "A surprise wedding, huh? That's too cute!"

"Come." Ida Jane looked around, then lowered her voice. "You have to be my maid of honor. I want to do it right this time."

"I…" Tension built in Millie's shoulders. "I don't know…"

"You can fly in and stay with Stolly. Your dad won't know you're here. It's one weekend, and it means the world to me."

Her father? That's why she'd moved so far away? What did a dad have to do to make his child take such drastic measures?

Millie remained stiff, but she sighed. "You'll send me the details? When you need me and everything?"

"Of course," Ida Jane said. "As long as you have a clean bill of health to fly…"

Millie perked up under my hands, and I knew she wanted to use her pregnancy as I reason to stay in Colombo. "I'll ask the doctor at my checkup tomorrow."

And I'd double-check with the doctor at the checkup. No way I was going to let Millie endanger herself or our daughter, but I wasn't letting her weasel out of this chance to get back to Houston—or for me to learn more about her past.

"And it won't be a problem with work?" Ida Jane asked. "I know it's kind of short notice…"

Millie hesitated again, but then she shook her head. "I have a generous vacation package, and I've been working a lot of weekends to speed up our process. My boss won't have a problem with me taking some time off."

She can't lie to Ida Jane. Interesting…

Ida Jane nodded. "That's great news! Oooh, I'm so excited you'll be here this go-round." Her voice was soft. "We had to get married so quickly before because of Maxim's visa issue—"

"And your stalker," Millie said.

Ida Jane made a face. "And that, but let's focus on me helping out Maxim, 'kay? You know having Daddy walk me down the aisle and you standing there with me were so hard to give up."

Mille's pulse pounded in her neck but she smiled into the camera. "Well, now you don't have to. I wouldn't miss your special day. I can't wait to see you." She clicked off and shut the laptop. Taking a deep breath, Millie turned toward where I was hovering. "I have to go to work," she said.

"All right." Disappointment niggled, because she'd just mentioned she could take time off. I wanted to ask her about her reactions to the mere idea of going back to her hometown, and I was dying to know more about her father. I *needed* to know about her father.

"Dinner?" I asked again. My gaze slithered down her maxi dress and the smart hip-length cardigan she'd paired with it. While Millie preferred pants, she'd told me, Bree didn't. So, Millie had taken to long dresses that flowed more easily around her expanding belly.

"Yes, I'll go to dinner with you," she said, tucking her hair back and staring down at the floor.

"Yes!" I fist-pumped, trying to break the tension that had crept back between us. "Hey, maybe I could I go with you? See your office?"

She nibbled on her lip. "How about you stay here, nap and shower? Unless you have a hotel—"

"I'd planned to ask you where I should stay," I said, a bit sheepish. I hadn't gotten to the rest of the details of this visit, like a hotel.

Millie pursed her lips. "Um, yeah, that'll be hard right now. There are a couple of big conventions…"

"I can sleep on your couch. No problem."

It was going to be a problem. When I was here last time, I'd noted that the couch was shorter than my six-two frame. But being close to Millie was more important than anything else. I needed to show her she could be comfortable with me. That meant not pushing back against her decision to go to work, and definitely not whining about the sleeping arrangements if she was letting me stay here. I didn't need Ida Jane or Alyssa to tell me that; I'd figured it out the first time I'd brought up Millie coming back to Houston.

My conversations with Ida Jane and Alyssa had helped me understand how to better engage Millie so we could come to some decisions as a team. I was used to working in that environment on the ice; so transferring it to my personal life should've been a piece of cake.

Except I was a selfish bastard who liked the limelight.

Yeah, I'd done some soul-searching during the last weeks of the post-season. And, as much as I hated to admit it, Coach had been right about me playing impulsively—making myself look better on ESPN clips instead of considering what was best for the team. I'd been working on that.

That hard pill still seemed stuck in my throat sometimes, but it had also gotten me nods of approval from Coach Whittaker and cuffs of appreciation from Cruz. If I could do it for my job, I could also be more methodical and present for my family.

Fuck me. Everything I'd ever wanted was in this room. I just had to convince Millie to stay with me when we returned to Houston. How, I wasn't sure. Mainly because I didn't know why she wanted to stay away.

Millie stared up at me, her eyes more gray than green as she rolled over scenarios in her head. She began to mumble. I leaned in closer, hearing "*methane is C-H-four.*"

I bit my lip. Millie was building molecular compounds to calm down. I recited player stats. "Bree's going to be an athletic chemistry nerd," I said with a smile. "Man, I can't wait to hold her."

"You—you heard me?"

I shrugged. "Yeah. Luckily, it was one of the compounds I remember from this global-warming podcast I listened to."

Her eyebrows rose. "You listen to science podcasts?"

"Love them. Always feel smarter afterward." I shifted. "Erm… okay?"

Her face softened into a smile. "*Definitely* okay. I love them, too. I'll be back around five thirty or six. But I have to warn you, I get tired, and evenings aren't my thing."

"Nothing new about that." I tapped her nose. "I remember you all owly eyed at dinner the other night."

He'd called just as I was about to eat. Not wanting to ignore him, I'd answered. Luka had settled at his kitchen bar and eaten a snack with me. It had been homey…nice.

"Can the doorman downstairs help me out if I want to see the sights?" he asked.

"Of course. There's a car service, and he can point you toward the local market or The Londoner, which has British food." She shrugged. "It's good but not Houston-restaurant level."

I narrowed my eyes. "You've been eating a lot of curries and—what was it called? Lam…lamp…"

"Lamprais," Millie said. She smiled. "I do enjoy the cuisine, but there are days I need an American fix."

I tucked that tidbit away. "Well, I'll grab some curry for lunch. Anything you want?"

She shook her head, her expression wary. Millie didn't expect me to be here when she returned from work this evening. I saw it in her eyes. I wished she'd tell me why her ability to trust was shattered, but she wasn't ready. I would not win her over in a night or two. I just hoped I had the stamina to wear her down.

"I'm sorry I can't stay…"

No, she wasn't. But eventually she'd see that I wasn't going to hurt her. Not now, not ever. I had a strong suspicion that knowledge would help Millie lower her walls and finally take us seriously.

I needed this plan of mine to work, and I needed to make at least some progress soon. I only had a few months off.

CHAPTER 6
Millie

I exited my condo building onto the street, the blare of horns and exhaust from old cars causing me to choke. I ignored my shaking hands as I began my trek down the street. *Luka is here*, in my home. He'd flown to Sri Lanka to see me. *Again*.

He'd spent two days on planes and in airports so he could spend five minutes with his cheek pressed to my bump.

I tried to ignore how warm my chest—and other anatomy—had become when Bree responded to him. The way his eyes lit up as told me the trip had been worth it for that alone.

"Who does that?" I whispered.

My hunky, crazy baby daddy, that's who. Engulfed by the heat, I crossed the busy street with its rushing cars and tinkling bike bells. The walk to my office was long enough that I would break into a sweat, but I needed the time to clear my head.

All these months after departing, I still missed the Houston summer. Houston was home; it was where Ida Jane was digging in roots. It's where my mother was buried, where Luka lived…

I gnawed on my lip, trying to process what his actions told me, what I *wanted* to believe they said.

I wanted him here because he missed me. Because he cared about me.

Because he wants a future with me.

I admitted my truth, and it left me lightheaded, my legs shaking as if I'd just completed an hour of jiu jitsu. I couldn't do much sparring now, but I'd tried to keep up with the drills so my technique and muscle memory stayed sharp.

I sucked in a breath, struggling to shove down the butterflies in my belly at the mere thought of Luka Stol. He was even more of a presence in person. I'd forgotten the sexy punch he packed. I placed my hand on a wall and breathed for a moment.

Stop it. Men betray your trust. You know that. You lived it and have struggled to recover from the fallout.

That's why I was in Sri Lanka. My father's cavalier attitude after Trent's treatment of me had cut so damn deep, though it shouldn't have surprised me. Chasten Jones wasn't an emotive man. He didn't hug, nor had he sat with me through the early bouts of grief when my mother died.

Maybe that's why I yearned to believe in Luka—not just with my baby and my future, but with my heart. I'd been desperate to share it for more than a decade.

~

The day passed with the tortuous slowness of a last day of elementary school before summer break. Each time I looked at the clock, I groaned to realize just minutes had passed. I couldn't focus on my data, and I had to redo my math equations multiple times because I kept daydreaming about a certain hockey player.

Thankfully, I'd set my team up with their assignments yesterday, so few of them needed any direction. I wouldn't have been capable of providing it.

The moment the clock struck the end of the workday, I rose

from my seat and walked down to the car I'd ordered. I arrived home in less than five minutes, breathless, unsure, excited...

I tiptoed to the door of my condo because part of me expected it to be empty, for Luka's sudden arrival to end with an equally sudden departure. Instead, I opened the door to a blast of delicious smells and cool air.

"What..." I began.

Luka strode toward me, gorgeous and intimidating in his T-shirt and low-slung jeans. He was barefoot—his toes long and elegant. His hair was disheveled, as if he'd spent the day running his fingers through it, and he had a couple of stains on his gray, V-neck T-shirt.

"I'm making you dinner, so we don't have to go out tonight. You know, because you get tired..." He trailed off and peered at me. "Unless you'd rather go out?"

I licked my lower lip, frozen with my messenger bag in my hand and the door to my place still open.

"You..."

He eased around me and shut the door. Then he took my bag and set it on the couch. I just stood there, staring at him. Luka had short-circuited my brain. That ability would annoy me if I wasn't so touched by the gesture.

He made me dinner.

No man had ever cooked for me—not my father nor Trent. It was such a simple thing, cooking. Providing sustenance for another person.

"Are you all right?" he asked.

I fell against his chest and struggled to hold back tears. I would not cry, not over something as mundane as a meal. He couldn't know what a huge deal this was. I wouldn't break down…

I shed a few tears into the stained cotton of his shirt. "Thank you." My voice warbled. I cleared my throat and lifted my cheek from his chest. His concern was palpable. I needed to be honest. "No one's ever made me dinner. Well, besides my mother, occasionally, and Ida Jane, but you get what I'm saying."

"Ahhhh." The worry in his expression waned a little. "Well, I'm not as good a cook as Ida Jane, so keep that in mind."

I snuggled against his chest, reveling in the warmth of his arms around me. *This.* I'd craved this intimacy, fantasized about it with an intensity that frightened me. I'd *never* imagined that Luka would want to share such moments with me. I took a deep breath as I silently admitted my mistake.

I'd expected Luka to treat me like Trent and my father had. Because my father had made me out to be a simpleton whose only purpose was to have the man of his choosing's babies, when he wanted them. Therefore Luka, who didn't love me and who was known for short flings, must see me the same way. Right?

I'd carved Luka out of my life before I even gave us a shot. I'd pre-judged him based on other people's commentary, and on my painful past. That realization was particularly difficult to swallow.

Luka's reputation came from fans, both ardent admirers and jilted women he'd brushed off. People who didn't know him well. People who made assumptions about him, like I had.

Why hadn't I realized that before?

I lifted my head and met his gaze. I offered him a tremulous smile. "I owe you an apology."

"For?"

I inhaled a shaky breath and exhaled on a shudder. "For believing what I read about you instead of focusing on how you treated me. I'm so sorry, Luka."

He cupped my face in his hands, and I leaned into him. Though I wanted to close my eyes and soak up the contentment, I kept my gaze locked on his. I needed him to see that I was sorry, that I understood and took responsibility for my actions.

"From now on, I think it would be best if you and I talked to each other rather than making assumptions," he said calmly, his eyes warm. "Okay?"

I hesitated. Whatever was on my face caused his expression to soften.

"I won't ask you to spill your every secret tonight, but we're connected, Millie. For life. I want to talk to you. To know you." He hesitated, and I desperately wanted to know what he'd chosen not to say.

He waited. I did, too. But how could I push him for his secrets when I wasn't ready to share mine?

"Okay."

"Good," he said. "Great. So…would you like to eat in tonight?"

I smiled. "I'd *love* to eat the meal you made."

A relieved grin blossomed across his face, and I caught my breath as his dimples peeked from his cheeks. He was just so beautiful. I touched his cheekbone, once again begging the universe to give Bree his incredible facial structure. I hadn't been able to discern much from the sonogram except that she had all her features and they were *perfect*.

Luka dipped his head closer, and his breath bathed my lips and cheek. With a faint shiver, I inched closer, pressing my belly into his. We both paused, my breath baited, as the enormity of deciding what came next hit me. I teetered on a tiny pivot; the direction I chose would impact Luka, Bree, and me.

If I pulled back, he'd let me. If I pushed forward, we'd both accept that I was acknowledging the chemistry between us and giving Luka at least a tacit agreement to pick up our sexual relationship.

He murmured in my ear, "Be sure."

"Are you?" I breathed.

"I wouldn't be here if I wasn't."

That sealed my choice—if it even was one. I lifted on my tiptoes as he bent closer, and his lips touched mine.

He felt better than I remembered. Gentle but firm—both his lips and his grip on the base of my skull, my hip. He made me feel safe, sexy…wanted. Never had I been so immersed in the moment; I always needed to catalog the world and its threats and verify potential escape options. Not right now. Not with Luka.

He held me as if I were precious. His fly rubbed against my belly, and I felt the growing bulge behind it.

His kiss, though chaste and achingly sweet, echoed that sentiment. I was surrounded by his desire.

The oven timer went off, and I startled, pulling away with a laugh. I'd forgotten where I was. Maybe that should have scared me, but it didn't. In fact, the ability to let go was exhilarating—something I'd need to study more, soon.

Luka brushed his lips over mine once more, gently, before he pulled away. "Do whatever it is you do when you get home. I'm going to finish up dinner. We'll eat in twenty."

I touched my fingertips to my lips. Already, I was right back under Luka Stol's spell.

CHAPTER 7

Luka

Stay. In. Control.

I repeated that mantra over and over as I took the meatballs out of the oven and checked on the sauce. It was Alyssa's recipe, one of my favorite comfort meals that I'd learned to cook once I moved to college. After I'd tasted what homemade food *could* be—not the frozen shit my parents left me—I'd asked her to teach me how to make her Sunday sauce, as she called it. While I'd never be a Michelin-starred chef, I could hold my own with simpler cuisine, especially Italian, which was Alyssa's staple.

But finding the ingredients here, in Colombo, had proven tricky. I'd needed the help of the doorman, a driver, and a chatty clerk at the supermarket to gather everything required to make this dinner.

I really hoped Millie liked it.

"Oh my God," she breathed from behind me.

Her breath puffed along my cheek, causing a deep shiver that ended with a pulling in my groin. I wanted this woman. From the first moment I'd seen her, I'd wanted her, but this wasn't mere sexual interest. I was infatuated—had been since the beginning. Being here, spending time with her, only made that bigger.

"Are those *meatballs?*" she asked on a whimper.

I turned to face her, once again putting us chest to hip. She felt good. Strong but soft. Supple, like a great leather jacket. Except Millie was prettier than any piece of apparel and more intriguing. Yeah, I shouldn't compare her to a coat. Jesus, I was a mess.

"Yep. I had a little trouble at the market, but I eventually found the ingredients." Understatement of the year. But Millie didn't need to know that.

She licked her lips as she met my gaze with her wide, wondering eyes. "I *adore* meatballs."

I grinned and winked. "I know."

She returned her attention to the cookie sheet and swallowed. "Ida Jane?"

"Ida Jane," I confirmed. "She said—and I quote—'turnaround is fun.' She told me you'd understand."

Millie glanced up with a shy smile. "I do. I helped Maxim when he was trying to talk her into the courthouse wedding in Nashville."

"You did?" I asked, surprised.

"Of course. He's a good man. He's got this look when he sees her." Millie's gaze dropped back to the meatballs, but not before I caught the longing she tried to mask. "When can we eat?"

"Hungry?"

She had to be. She was carrying around and growing an extra human; I'd live in a state of constant starvation if I had to go through that.

"Want one now and then more with the spaghetti and sauce?"

"God, yes." She moaned. Quick as a sprite, she darted past me and nipped a fork from her drawer. She poked a small, browned round of meat and nibbled at the side. She moaned again as she chewed. "So good." She licked her lips and attacked the rest of her treat, which had blood leaving my head and flowing straight to my dick.

Millie turned me on like no other woman. Ever.

Some of my teammates were vocal about their desire to only ever bed skinny models, but I was more liberal in my tastes. I'd always liked a woman who looked like she could take a pounding—no ultra-skinny chicks for me.

But Millie was more than her juicy ass and her bouncy tits that continued to tantalize me. She had a lovely hourglass shape that even her pregnancy hadn't diminished, at least from behind. She was also fit—strong. I still wasn't sure why she had those starburst patterned scars on her hands, ones that looked like she'd punched something or someone many times. Enough to have her skin split more than once.

We'd get to a place where she told me about those scars—and the ones she carried inside. I hoped.

I cleared my throat because my thoughts were turning decidedly X-rated as I watched her tongue swipe her lower lip. "Want to change before we eat? The sauce needs to simmer a bit more, and I'll start the water to boil now that you're home."

She paused from licking the fork, her tongue sliding back into the soft recess of her mouth. I gripped the counter behind me to keep from reaching for her and slamming my lips to hers with all the hunger pent up after months of missing her. "You should go. Now."

"I…sure." She turned and disappeared, looking a bit like a dog that had been kicked.

I heaved a long, harsh sigh. *Shit.* I had many questions, but I needed to let her open up at her own pace. It was frustrating, but it was also the best way to learn about Millie. And I wanted to know *everything.* Also, I was pretty sure I'd just failed to meet one of Millie's needs. Problem was, I wasn't sure which need it was. And that pissed me off.

Women were monstrously confusing creatures.

But *how* was I supposed to know what a woman needed if she didn't tell me?

Also, even if I could get to that point with Millie, I sucked at relationships. I knew this because I'd never had one for more than a week or two, max. Alyssa told me I'd never put any effort into getting to know a woman before. She said I was "*surface,*" which wasn't wrong but also pissed me off.

Things were getting better between Millie and me, now that I was here, but I had a long, slow, frustrating road ahead before I made the progress with her that I needed to. And plenty of chances to mess it up along the way.

Millie

I slunk into my bedroom and removed my cardigan and dress. In the bathroom, I washed away the sweat of the day and took off my makeup. Of course I had to pee, too, but that was par for the pregnancy course. Once I'd washed my hands and brushed my hair, I went back out into my bedroom to grab some lounge clothes.

"Millie…" Luka stopped talking and just stared at me from the doorway.

I fought the urge to cover myself—he'd seen me naked before, and this was his baby growing in my bulging middle. Whatever affection he might be feeling, I now knew he didn't want me sexually after he'd told me to back off a few minutes ago. Got that message loud and clear, so I might as well let him take in the changes his baby had wrought. I clenched my fists, struggling to keep my breathing slow and steady. I felt so exposed.

Unsure what to do next, I stood there, waiting.

"Can I…" He trailed off again. "Can I touch you—her? Skin to skin?"

"Sure." I shrugged like I didn't care, but my heart rate tripled as he came forward and laid his palms on my stomach. *This is about the baby.*

Bree kicked into his left palm, and he laughed, his eyes meeting mine. "She's active. And strong."

I nodded, a lump in my throat. He lowered his eyes to talk to my belly, delight dancing across his features.

"Oh, good one, baby Bree."

He was slaying me with his kindness. *Why* had I thought to deny him this—deny me this?

From the time I was a little girl, I'd dreamed of being a mother. Trent had torn that dream; I shouldn't have let him. I should never have let him seduce me with kindness…and touch.

I still craved touch. Luka's specifically. If only I hadn't been so forward with him. My cheeks burned with embarrassment.

Luka shifted his weight, crooning against my skin, causing me to shiver. Bree shoved hard, seemingly energized by his voice. Luka yelped and tumbled backward, and I laughed. He smiled up at me, sheepish. "She's active tonight."

I sucked in a breath, those words slamming into me, mending my most tattered edges. I'd been different since Trent's attack. Harder, yes, but also brittle. Scared to trust, scarred *from* trusting.

I placed my hands on my belly, enjoying Bree's movements. Enjoying this moment with Luka more than I could have imagined.

I would never have another child. I'd only needed one to ensure the future of the Jones fortune—something Trent had informed me that fateful night.

Now that I'd been with Luka—been lonely without him to share these moments, missed his sweet smile and the way his eyes lit up, the softness of his fingertips trailing across my skin—I couldn't imagine ever allowing another man to touch me.

And I'd made that impossible with Luka.

He'd go back to play in the NHL, and I'd be here—alone with Bree. That's what I'd wanted, yet now, seeing Luka on his knees, his bulk between our vulnerable daughter and the world, I had to wonder if I'd failed him, Bree, and myself by not giving him this chance from the get-go.

Luka

Millie's inattention during dinner gave me time to study her. Her thick glasses sat on her pert nose, and I had to resist the urge to boop it. She was just too cute.

Pretty.

Fresh and smart. The best thing ever to happen to me.

"Tell me about your job," I suggested, this time determined to actually learn what the hell she did for a living.

Millie looked up from her plate of spaghetti. "What would

you like to know?"

"What exactly do you *do*? I know you're a chemical engineer, but you've never told me what this position entails."

She stared at me for a long moment before she swallowed. "I—I'm sorry," she stammered. "I'm not used to people being interested in my work."

She meant a specific *people,* but I let that go for now. "Well, I am."

She offered a shy smile. "I mainly analyze the formation of rocks and oil reservoirs, but I'm here to improve our computer-based models for drilling."

"That's…" *Hard, intense, not something I totally understand.* "Cool."

She snorted. "I get it—it's boring. Nerdy. Possibly arcane." She waved a hand. "Environmentalists hate my job. They think I want the world to burn to a crisp."

I cleared my throat. "But you don't, right? I mean, that would be bad."

She rubbed her hands on her belly. "No, I don't. I wanted to be a petrochemical engineer so that while extraction remains one of our energy sources, we didn't have another massive oil spill."

I frowned. "That's noble."

"Thanks…I think. It didn't hurt that I also get to see the world and bring home a good salary." She set her fork down and focused on me. "What got you into hockey?"

"My parents."

She smiled. "Really? They're fans? Come to every game?" she teased.

"More like fans of me not being around." I winced. "Sorry. That's harsh."

She shook her head. "No, I get that." She was quiet a moment. "After my mother died, my dad told me to stop moping. When I couldn't get out of my *"funk"*—as he called it— he shipped me off to boarding school."

I made a sound of disapproval deep in my throat. Then I told her the painful truth I hated sharing with anyone. "Hockey took up a lot of my time as a kid, whether I wanted it to or not. My parents liked that aspect of it."

Millie gawked. "*What?* Your parents made you play a sport you didn't like so they didn't have to..." She trailed off, clearly uncomfortable with her train of thought.

I shrugged like it was no big deal, but I also clenched my hands into fists, no longer hungry. "I was active—too active, according to my teachers and parents. Getting me on the ice for hours each week was supposed to tire me out, as well as to keep me out of their hair. Plus, they were mostly just following their noses to the next exciting activity, and my schedule got in the way."

Millie's eyes went soft with sympathy. I waved her off before she could comment.

"I ended up loving it. Best decision they made for me."

I wouldn't share with anyone how good it had felt to find a place to finally *belong*.

Millie seemed to think we were different—too different. But we weren't. In fact, with each tidbit of her past she let slip, I realized just how similarly loveless our childhoods had been. That's probably why we were both so excited to be parents ourselves.

Shifting so I could see her bump, my breathing slowed as contentment washed over me. I wanted our family. I wanted to be a family—more than I knew how to express to her.

The meal was low-key, perfect to show Millie being with me didn't have to be a high-stress, fame-in-the-way situation. I insisted on cleaning up, though Millie kept me company. But once she started yawning, I shooed her to bed.

"Are you sure you'll be okay out here?" she asked, her dubious gaze swinging to the couch.

There was no way I'd fit on my back with my legs straight. Why did people insist on buying furniture that didn't fit them? Well, in fairness, the couch fit Millie fine. Just not my extra ten inches.

"Yeah. It's fine."

She pressed her lips together, shifting back and forth.

"It's fine, Millie. *I'm* fine. Go to bed."

Three hours later, I groaned as I flailed, barely keeping myself from landing cheek-first on the floor. I knocked my foot into the coffee table, stubbing my toe.

With a low curse, I rolled over onto my back, one of my shoulders hanging off the couch's cushion. My back ached from the hunched position, my muscles too tight.

"My twin bed at my parents' house was more comfortable," I muttered, running my palms down my face. But I must have slid back into sleep because the next thing I heard was the water running for the shower. I blinked open my bleary eyes and squinted at the morning sunlight hazing through the gauzy drapery over the sliding glass doors. Jet lag and too few hours of sleep caused my head to pound.

With a grimace, I hauled myself off the torture device and limped to the kitchen. Caffeine would help my fuzzy head. Stretches and a workout would eventually loosen my muscles. By the time Millie came out, I'd finished half my cup of coffee and folded the sheets and comforter into a nice, neat pile in the corner of the couch.

She tucked her hair behind her ear. "Morning. Sleep okay?"

"Great." The word spilled from my mouth because I was still caught on her lips. They were so soft and pink. I wanted to run my thumb over the bottom one. She'd open for me, caress the tip with her tongue. I cleared my throat, yanking my mind from the fantasy. "Want some?"

She shook her head. "No caffeine while pregnant. I'll just make some herbal tea. Then we can head out to my doctor's appointment."

I nodded. Right. No caffeine. Cruz had mentioned that. I glanced at my bag, which held a list of pregnancy books I wanted to read. Problem was, I hated reading. The words swirled around, dancing, making it hard to concentrate.

Cruz knew about my dyslexia, so that fucker had bought me a pile of picture books—for younger siblings—that explained the changes happening inside a mom's body.

I'd never admit it, but I'd pored over those books, memorizing most of the images.

"Sounds great. Can I make you breakfast?" I asked.

She nodded. "I'll make it. You good with fruit and yogurt?"

In a smoothie that typically went along with a couple of eggs and toast, yes. But I nodded instead, because if Millie wanted to make me something to eat, I was going to enjoy it.

We arrived a few minutes early to the appointment, where Dr. de Silva measured Millie's belly and I once again heard Bree's heartbeat. That sound never got old.

"And it won't be a problem for Millie to fly to the States in a few weeks?"

"When are you planning to travel?" Dr. de Silva asked.

"In about a month," Millie said.

She studied the chart. "I should see you a couple of days before you depart to make sure you're healthy enough to do so, but right now I don't foresee any complications. You should still be good, timing wise."

I'd learned my lesson, so I didn't ask to join Millie at work when the appointment was over. Instead I contented myself with walking her to the building and kissing her cheek goodbye in the air-conditioned cool of the lobby.

That morning set up a routine we followed for the following couple of weeks: Millie and I had breakfast before she spent the days at her office and I poked around the city and came up with dinners for us to share, as well as indulging in the hours-long secret I kept from her.

After I nearly fell off the couch multiple times the second night, cursing and wincing, I took to napping in Millie's bed while she was gone, desperate for a few hours of decent shut-eye. At night, between attempts at poor sleep on the couch, I listened to an audiobook I'd found on raising an infant—much better for me than trying to power through the printed version—and that kept me awake for even more hours.

"They shit *how* often?" I whispered into the dark one night.

With a shudder at the idea of wiping up bodily fluids—not something I handled well, truth be told—I turned off the book and took out my headphones, pushing my heels into the end of the couch, as if that would stretch the fucker out long enough for me to lie on it with ease. I seriously considered buying a bigger couch, but Millie had commented on how comfortable this one was when she'd settled onto it earlier, so I couldn't do it.

Instead, the next day I stumbled into her bedroom after my early lunch at a small dumpling shop down the street from her place. My head hit her pillow, and I inhaled her scent, moaning at the pleasure of stretching out fully...and Millie. Her scent wrapped around me, slithered through my nasal passage and into my blood, causing it to thrum.

I flipped onto my stomach, pushing my hips into the mattress to ease the growing ache in my dick even as my heavy eyes slid shut. I woke four and a half hours later, refreshed and giddy that Millie would be home in an hour. I made her bed carefully and exited her room—after I squeezed her pillow to my chest and inhaled that citrusy scent one last time.

Millie had been tightlipped about the upcoming second wedding between Ida Jane and Maxim since the video call right after I got here. It had taken me weeks to tease out more details, but I now knew the wedding would be at Cormac's house, and the CATS had thrown themselves into planning it.

Millie had agreed to attend, so I was escorting her home for a wedding. Just not *our* wedding. Not that we were ready for marriage, or that I wanted to get married…did I? I wasn't sure. I just knew I didn't want to be like my parents, and committing to a partner through marriage had to make it easier for the kid, too.

The realization that Millie would be horrified if I asked her to marry me disappointed me for days. I'd seen that in Cormac and Maxim. They were both grounded in a way that Naese and even Cruz weren't.

Cool fingers brushed hair off my forehead as I inched out of a deep sleep and into another type of wonderful dream. Millie never balked at me talking to her belly, but since that first night, when I would have *sworn* she was flirting with me as she ate that first meatball, she'd been reticent—almost standoffish about me touching her.

But now her hip was next to mine, her body leaning over me, that soft lilac-and-grapefruit scent I loved surrounding me. I wanted this forever.

"Ah, Luka, I *knew* you were too big for the couch," she murmured. "Are you really one of the good ones?"

This question was so softly spoken, I knew I wasn't supposed to hear it, let alone answer. It took everything in me not to yell that *yes*, I was, in fact, a great one, and she should give me a real chance, not continue to keep me at arm's length.

"You scare me," she continued.

Why? Ah, hell… What had I done?

Her fingers danced along my cheekbone before settling on my lips.

"Oh, how you scare me. You make me yearn… You deserve a woman who isn't afraid to love you." She ended the sentence with a hitch of her breath.

Thank fuck! I thought I'd actually made her afraid of *me*. But no, she was afraid of what I made her feel. That I could work with. I opened my eyes and took her hand in mine.

"Why don't you let me decide what I deserve? And what I want."

Millie's eyes widened, and she pulled away, so I wrapped my other arm around her hips and slid my head across the pillow until I was nose to bump.

"Hi, baby." I kissed Millie's stomach, as I did every time she returned. I liked the opportunity to talk to my kid—and the soft smile that always curved Millie's lips when I showed our Bree affection. Rolling onto my back, arms still cinched around her, I met her troubled gaze.

"Hey, stop that. You don't need to worry, not about this— me." I glanced at the clock and frowned. "Why are you here?"

"Because I have a doctor's appointment in half an hour and thought you'd like to come."

My confusion deepened. "I thought that was tomorrow."

Millie smiled, her eyes alight. "It was, but it got moved to today. You still want to join—"

"Hell, yes." I scrambled around her, out of the bed and into the bathroom. "Give me two minutes."

I washed my face and brushed my teeth, a twinge of longing hitting me when I returned my toothbrush next to hers in the holder. I wanted *this*. I wanted Millie to remain in my life, in my condo, *us* together.

I hadn't brought it up again, not after I caught the wonder

and fear in her eyes every time I cleaned up after dinner or brought her a cup of herbal tea, like I had yesterday morning when she was feeling lousy.

I exited the bathroom to find Millie still standing next to the unmade bed. She lifted her head, and her expression held a longing so intense I stumbled. Righting myself, I settled on the balls of my feet, waiting for her next move. She dropped her gaze, but not before I saw fear in her eyes.

"You should sleep here," she said. Her voice shook. She cleared her throat. "Tonight."

"I'm not kicking you out of your bed," I scoffed. "Especially not with us traveling tomorrow." I scooted around her, nudging her so I could pull up the sheets and comforter. Then I went to the living room to grab the shoes I'd left next to the couch.

She inhaled sharply. "I was, ah, thinking we could both sleep here."

CHAPTER 8
Millie

"So, it's no problem to travel as long as we watch her water intake and move every hour between naps?" Luka asked Dr. de Silva.

He was determined to make sure Bree and I could fly safely tomorrow.

She shook her head, a slight smile on her lips. "That's correct. They're both healthy, and she still has ten weeks before she's considered full-term." She aimed a pleasure-filled grin my way. "I'm guessing that as a professional hockey player, he takes workouts and hydration seriously."

I gasped. "You know who he is?"

"Love hockey," Dr. de Silva answered. "I was miffed when Stolly missed a game last season, until I met him in person." She winked. "Move," she told me. "Your ankles will swell because of the altitude. And remember, absolutely no air travel if you have complications or after thirty-four weeks."

Luka and I nodded our understanding.

"Great! You kids have fun. And win the Cup next year, okay?"

"I'll do my best," Luka said, his expression grave.

We exited the doctor's office and headed down the street for an early dinner. I was hungry. These days I was either starving or too full to eat another bite, nothing in between.

As we ate, my mind continued to replay Luka's expression

when I'd asked him to sleep with me tonight.

"I'd like that."

He'd like to sleep in bed with me so he doesn't need to nap all day, I told myself. *So his back won't hurt.* Yeah, I'd caught his grimaces.

Or did he want to sleep in the bed with me because he wanted to hold me?

I desperately wanted it to be the latter, but I couldn't let myself hope like that. I just couldn't. I'd thought I was in love with Trent. He'd paid me attention; he'd opened doors and looked deep into my eyes and kissed me so sweetly.

And he'd shattered my heart into tiny pieces the night I left his place for the last time.

In some ways, I was reliving that sweet wooing with Luka, and his gentlemanly ways drove me bonkers. In fact, I wanted to rip out my hair almost as much as I needed to kiss him.

At least he'd let me treat him to a meal he didn't make or clean up himself. Now that I'd paid the bill, though, he came over and helped me from my seat. I didn't need the help—yet—but I enjoyed his touch and the admiring looks I received from women nearby.

"Thanks," I said, smiling up at him. Could he see the pulse pounding in my neck? Did he know how nervous he made me?

"Let's get you home," he said, slipping a proprietary arm around my waist.

The buskers played on most street corners, creating a lovely musical backdrop to the soft breeze and spiced air. We strolled down the street, and I smiled at the familiar melody.

"Wait! Is that John Denver?" Luka asked.

"Sure is, hockey man. They love playing that song." I hummed along to "Take Me Home, Country Roads," thrilled by the beauty of a night in Colombo. I liked this city, mostly because I felt safe—something I didn't always feel in Houston, even though I missed the city's frenetic pace and dual down-towns. Mostly, though, I missed Ida Jane and, yes, Luka. A pang hit me hard as I realized we'd be separated again soon.

After the trip back to Houston for Ida Jane's wedding, I'd be alone.

My hand went to my belly. Not alone. Just…not whole. And that was my fault. I should tell Luka why I was so against returning. I really should. Yet I didn't want to ruin the happy bubble we were in here, now.

Soon.

I snuggled closer to his side, forcing away those difficult thoughts as we walked another block. A group of people gasped and pointed, and Luka stiffened, his arm tightening around my shoulder. But I simply smiled. He was about to find out just how much both locals and tourists from other parts of Asia liked Americans.

"They want to take a photo with you," I murmured.

"I noticed. Is that okay with you?" he asked.

Warmth flowed through my chest at his question. He'd ignore them or tell them *no* for me. But I didn't want to say no; I wanted Luka to get the full experience.

I nodded, and Luka was a good sport, smiling as he stood behind the group of five. Another group came over and then another. I took the photos for all of them, biting my lip to keep from laughing as Luka became more and more shocked.

"I had no idea the NHL was so popular here," he said.

I barely held in my laughter as another group trotted toward us, waving exuberantly. "It's not. They just like you because you're big and blond."

He gawped. "Not because I'm a professional athlete?"

I shook my head, biting back the giggle that crawled up my throat. "No. You look American. They like *that.*"

His eyes went wide. "Are you sure?"

I nodded. "Oh, yeah. Hear what they're saying?"

"American," a few people crowed, pointing.

He grabbed my hand and marched me through the crowd.

Luka

I was *such* an idiot. I growled, hating that I'd shown myself to be the bumbling, self-aggrandizing ass I clearly was.

Millie hadn't laughed at me, but amusement had lit her eyes. And I was the father of her child. She had to be questioning that, too. I was so full of myself that I assumed everyone in the world knew my face and name?

Finally, unable to stall in the bathroom any longer, I opened the door and padded across the airy, cool space of her condo.

"Are you okay?" she asked, her voice tired.

"Yeah, sorry. I was…" *Flagellating myself.*

"It was an honest mistake," she said. "You are quite popular in the States and Canada, Mr. Hockey Man."

"You should sleep," I said, trying to deflect.

I lifted the sheet and duvet, my heart thumping as hard as it did when I skated sprints. I'd slept in Millie's bed for days, but never when *she* was in it. The difference was enormous. We were getting closer—she was sharing more of her space, *herself,* with me. That was good. Great.

Except things were about to change again, as we flew back to Houston tomorrow. And tonight she'd witnessed my overinflated ego slowly wheezing out its air. *Gah!* Heat suffused my neck, ears, and cheeks. I hated feeling foolish because that led to remembering the humiliation of waiting for my parents to show up for my pee-wee championship. I'd been so excited, had already told my friends my parents would be cheering the loudest.

Instead, they'd gone to brunch and picked me up an hour late. I'd had to wait with my impatient coach's family. That day I learned how badly others could make me feel—if I let them.

And until Millie, I hadn't let anyone. Except Coach Whittaker. He got to me because disappointing him meant I could be traded—not because I cared about his opinion of me as a player or a man.

Of course not.

And Millie, well, she'd ditched me, after all.

"Bree's up," Millie said. "I think she's waiting for you to tell her goodnight."

Those soft words, her willingness to share, slowed the trickle of negative thoughts in my mind. I settled on my side and slid in close enough to Millie that I could rub my palm on her belly. My hand, splayed out, covered the entire side of her stomach.

"Good night, little Bree," I crooned.

A thump and a swirl met my words. Millie was thirty-one

weeks pregnant, which meant Bree was the size of a pineapple. And according to the doctor, she was close to the three-pound mark. If she came now, she might not even need intensive-care interventions for her lungs.

"She seems to know you," Millie said. "She's been more active since you arrived. It's clear she enjoys spending time with her daddy."

I continued moving my hand over the undulations of Millie's belly, relaxing into the beauty of the moment. I inhaled that grapefruit scent of Millie's shampoo, the warm lilac of her lotion from the curve of her neck.

The moment eased my embarrassment. Contentment filtered into my chest. I held Millie and my child in my palm.

I had a family.

Millie shifted. "Sorry. My back hurts."

I eased away but kept my hand on Bree's movements.

After a moment, Millie released a tired sigh. "I'm so glad you came, Luka. I can't imagine how hard that was. I wouldn't have had the courage."

I took a chance and moved in to spoon her from behind, glad she couldn't see my face. My contentment grew, along with gratitude that Millie was sharing not just Bree but herself.

"Will you tell me what you're worried about?" I asked after a moment.

She sighed. "You deserve to know, and I'll tell you more, I promise. But, for now suffice it to say that my dad and I don't get along."

And there it was—what I'd been worrying over for months.

Millie's father had hurt her. I clenched my hands into fists, wishing she'd tell me what the bastard had done.

"And also, you've been with a lot of women…"

"Not that many," I scoffed, still focused on my all-consuming desire to slay Millie's dragons, namely her father.

Millie tensed, and I realized that wasn't the right thing to say. She was trying to talk to me—connect.

"I'm sorry. I'm not dismissing your concerns, I promise. It's just… There's an…aura, I guess, about being a professional athlete. If there are pictures taken, they always show me with women."

"Because you're surrounded by them. Beautiful women."

Ah. Millie worried about how she measured up appearance-wise. If she only understood me better, she'd know I worried about how I stacked up for her in every other category. I wanted to be more, much more, than a great lay.

"That makes me feel inadequate," she breathed. "Like you'll always compare my imperfections to those other lovers."

She whispered the last so softly; I knew she'd never have the courage to say it in daylight.

In that moment, seeing my life from Millie's perspective, it felt like someone had scraped my soul with a dull spoon. She saw the women, the dating, and all the sex she imagined as a huge barrier, whereas I'd always viewed it as a journey. I'd hoped to find a woman I wanted for more than a night, a week, or hell, even a couple of months once or twice. But those relationships had fizzled quickly because I'd always been searching for more.

For forever.

I wanted the commitment and surety of being together. I wanted love.

And that *need* had made me feel weak and antsy and… fucking stupid.

But it's what I wanted, desperately, because I'd watched Alyssa share that with Bob until his death, and I'd envied their son Mike for his sure-footed knowledge that he belonged to something important. To people who loved him, quirks and warts and all.

"I don't think you understand how much *this* means to me," I said.

Millie flinched, drawing away, but I held her to me—not tightly, just enough so she knew that's where I wanted her to be. She relaxed back into me slowly, like a skittish cat that expected the hand to pat too hard.

"Being here with you, holding you and our daughter…" I cleared my throat as emotions bombarded me. There wasn't a way for me to allay Millie's concerns about my past—not completely—so I focused on what I could change: our future.

Her hand drifted down to squeeze my wrist. "Because of your parents?" Before I could respond, she said, "We have that in common, you know. My dad truly doesn't care about me as a person, just as an object that can benefit him. That's why I moved here."

More pieces of Millie's life and personality fell into place. "To get away from him."

"Yes. He's proven I can't trust him."

Bree's movements had slowed. Millie's voice was thick with sleep. I'd guess she was close to slumber, yet she continued to engage me. I swallowed the emotion squeezing my throat. We were a pair, she and I.

"Having you and Bree in my life, it's a chance to have a *family*," I told her. "I've always wanted a family. To belong."

"But what if we don't work out? That scares me." Her words were tight, as were her muscles. Sleep had faded as she faced a monumental fear.

I nuzzled into her neck, holding her close. "Me, too. But you know what?"

"No."

I smiled. "I'm willing to give you and Bree my all. Not just because of Bree, but because of the connection we made at that restaurant."

"You were—are—every woman's fantasy," she mumbled. Once again, she softened toward sleep.

"I only want to be yours."

"You're so perfect, Luka. No wonder I dream about you."

I kept my knees up and my hips back, not wanting Millie to freak out at the enormous erection I couldn't shake. This constant state of arousal annoyed me, but I couldn't seem to prevent my dick's desire to get closer to her. It loved her scent. It loved the softness of her skin, her laugh, her raspy morning voice, shower gel, and the way she sometimes sighed and relaxed when I touched her, as she'd done just now.

"'Night, baby girl," I said, running my palm from the top of Millie's bump around the side to her hip. I repeated the caress over and over. Bree calmed. So did Millie. Soon, both my girls were asleep.

Peace permeated my bones, drew into my chest, and settled there.

I lay awake, my arm wrapped around her middle, enjoying the closeness. Until this moment, I'd never known what it would be like to be truly intimate with another person. My teammates were awesome, but I didn't share all my feelings—not like Cormac and Cruz. Even Maxim had begun to.

I'd assumed the best course of action was to hold it all in, like I did my fears and uncertainties about hockey—especially my fears and uncertainties about having a deep, meaningful relationship because I didn't know what to do or how to do it.

I hadn't realized the sheer joy of resting together, of being close simply because I enjoyed Millie's company. I hadn't known because I hadn't seen such connections growing up.

More thoughts about family and intimacy raced through my mind until my eyes grew heavy and I slid into sleep, only to be screeched awake what felt like mere seconds later.

"We are so late!" Millie squealed.

"Wh…?"

"I forgot to set the alarm, and we need to be at the airport like *now*."

I jumped from the bed, adrenaline pumping. "Okay. Okay. Bathroom, then clothes."

I darted toward the door, only to skid to a halt and turn back to Millie. "Um, do you need to go first?"

She giggled. "I do. Thanks for asking. And thanks for the show."

I looked down, realizing I had a raging hard-on pressing

against my underwear. Millie sashayed by me, trailing her fingers across my stomach as she went, which caused me to shiver and my dick to jump. I flattened her palm to my stomach.

"Keep that up and we'll miss our flight," I growled.

Her lips parted, and her eyes widened. She dropped her gaze to my pulsing erection. Her cheeks flushed. "Ida Jane needs me."

I let her go, but I couldn't stop my sour response. "So do I."

Millie slid the bathroom door shut as she mumbled a response. All I made out was "*don't really think* I'm *sexy*."

I scratched behind my ear. Millie thought I didn't find her sexy?

Well, shit. That wouldn't do. I was going to have to up my game. No way in hell was she allowed to think she wasn't the only woman on my mind—and the only woman I *wanted* on my mind.

We made it to the airport and onto the plane, but I couldn't help but worry the stress of our hurried arrival had been bad for Millie and the baby. I seemed to spend all my time worrying about the two of them, and I wasn't sure I liked the feelings my concern generated.

Like, I wasn't good enough for Millie. Like I'd be a terrible father to Bree—how could I not be? My parental examples were shit. Except for Alyssa. And maybe Coach, who pissed me off with his high expectations and disappointed head shakes.

Once we touched down in Houston, I sent Alyssa a text, letting her know Millie and I were back in the States. She responded with: *Hell, yeah! Hard part's done. Turn on the charm!. I'll expect a call once you're settled.*

I shook my head at her enthusiasm. That was the thing about

Alyssa; she expected me to succeed at anything I put my mind to. I texted her back.

When are you coming to visit? I'm ready to buy your ticket.

She didn't respond immediately, but I'd cajole her later. She didn't fly much, and the idea of getting on a plane frightened her. While I understood, I couldn't get back to see her as much as I should have—because of my hockey schedule but also because of the unhappy memories held by my parents' house down the street. I'd been working on getting Alyssa out of the neighborhood, but so far, she'd dug in her heels, enjoying her role as elder stateswoman. She'd also paid off her home, which was an enormous deal.

I pushed my phone into my pocket.

"You ready?" I asked once the seatbelt sign dinged off.

Millie looked at me, and the trepidation in her eyes took my breath away. Something was wrong. Very wrong.

"The baby?" I asked, panicking.

Shit. *Shit.* I knew twenty-six hours of travel was a bad idea.

Millie dropped her lashes, then her chin, hiding her face from me. "No. She's fine. We're fine."

"Something is *not* fine, Millicent," I said, my tone stern. "I *need* you to talk to me about your dad—what happened before." The emotion was too intense for her to hide. Did Millie think I only cared about our kid? Something told me that yes, she worried I only cared about her because she was carrying our daughter.

She sucked in a slow, shuddering breath that I somehow felt in my shoulders and neck. "I just don't like Houston much."

"Bullshit," I snapped, probably much more harshly than I needed to.

Her gaze shot to mine, the fire I loved burning brightly. "You don't get to tell me how I feel about this city—"

"I'm not telling you how you feel. I'm calling crap on that being the reason you looked like I was about to shiv you. *What's going on?*"

She licked her lips.

"Sir? Would you two please deplane?"

The flight attendant smiled at us, but I could tell she wanted us gone. She'd interrupted the moment, anyway. I helped Millie up and out of our row—I'd splurged on first-class tickets so she'd be comfortable.

I grabbed her large tote and my duffle bag and walked behind her as we exited the plane. Each step she took added to the tension in her neck and shoulders, which made me tenser as well.

I knew that look, which was why I was worried. Millie had the same body language as some of my friends did the last time I saw them—right before they went into the known gang territory out in our area.

They never came back.

Millie

I exited the gate, and tension continued creeping up my spine. This was so different from Sri Lanka. The people, the smells, even the quality of air and light in the terminal felt different. Like home. My heart squeezed as I realized how much I'd missed Houston.

With a painful swallow, I admitted that I needed to explain my reasons for leaving this city…for running away from Luka and Ida Jane. But how did I bring up my father and Trent to the one man I wanted to see me as sexy and desirable? No man wanted another's castoff. That's what my father had said.

"Go back to Trent. He's the best you can hope for. No man wants another's sloppy seconds."

My father had said that to me. My *father*. He'd followed me to my apartment the morning after Trent found the mutilated engagement ring just to say that to me. I'd moved shortly thereafter so neither of them would know where I was.

No, no! I shut those memories down. But I wasn't fast enough because, as if the universe wanted to prove a point, I heard Trent's voice right after we stepped out of the gate's seating area and into the walkway.

"Well, well, well, if it isn't Millicent Jones."

My world tilted and my body quivered, but I turned my head with regal dignity—I hoped—away from Trent and walked toward the exit. Luka was a half-step behind, but Trent was in front of me. And the leaner, shorter man reached out, snagged my arm, and squeezed it.

"It's been a while, and I see you've been busy. Don't you *dare* try to ignore me."

Luka dropped his bag as he stepped forward, fists clenched, aggression pouring off him. He snarled, clearly ready to hurt Trent, but I'd already turned my arm around and over Trent's, breaking his hold on me. Then I went further and gripped his thumb, bending it back at an awkward angle.

"You don't touch me without permission," I hissed. "And I'll *never* give you permission to put your disgusting hands on me."

Trent's jaw clamped down, hard, as he worked not to cry out. I pushed his thumb farther, watching whiteness creep around his eyes and mouth.

"I'll take care of him, Millie," Luka rumbled.

I shook my head. I would not let Luka get arrested for assault. Trent wasn't worth the impact that would have on Luka's life.

"I have this under control," I said.

"Ohmigod, it's Luka Stol," came a high-pitched cry. And a moment later, we were surrounded by probably ten teenagers who crowded close, oohing and ahhing over Luka as they asked for selfies and autographs.

"Hey, guys," Luka said, strain obvious—at least to me—in his voice and expression.

"You're *so* much bigger than I thought," one girl gushed. "Isn't he big?"

"But fast," a boy chimed in. He rattled off Luka's stats.

"Millie…" Luka said again. He was hyped, ready for a fight, but I'd read the opportunity in Trent's eyes. He'd sue Luka, try to destroy him financially. That's what Trent understood. Money. Power.

He'd used his against me.

"No," I snapped. "*I've got this.*"

An older woman being pushed in a wheelchair moved past as I spoke. She put her foot on the ground and held up her hand as she noted the stand-off between me and Trent. Her chair stopped, and Trent tried to shuffle backward, so I put more pressure on his thumb.

Luka inched closer. I could feel the heat from his body against my back and side. He said nothing else, just anchored me. Gave me support. But even now I could feel the question in his gaze, his self-control threatening to snap.

Luka was a doer. Standing by, letting me handle the situation my way wasn't in his make-up.

"Allow me to offer some help." The older woman set the dog from her lap on the ground next to Trent's foot.

"Potty time," she sang. Her attendant protested, but the woman waved her away.

"If that dog urinates on me—" Trent began, but he winced when I bent his thumb back more. He tried to smack at me with his free arm, but Luka maneuvered in closer, a snarl slashing his mouth.

"Better here on this sick bastard than some poor soul on the plane," the woman said.

"Let me go," Trent howled.

"Why?" I snapped. "You didn't listen to me when I asked."

We were drawing a crowd. People were murmuring, probably taking pictures of me gripping Trent.

Luka shifted his large body to partially shield me from Trent, which also put him in my way. *Dammit. I have this under control.*

My jaw clenched as I shot Luka a fiery glare. His expression tightened before a mask fell into place, shielding his thoughts and shuttering his eyes.

"That is ancient history, Millie," Trent said. "We were just… messing around. You gotta let bygones be gone and all that."

"Two years isn't enough time to forget or forgive," Millie murmured. "There isn't enough time."

"Doesn't seem the young lady agrees with your assessment," the elderly woman said. "It's okay, Gus. You go right on ahead and do your business."

I laughed, giddy with pleasure when Gus lifted his leg and let out a stream of urine over Trent's suit-clad leg and into his shoe. Trent cursed and tried to kick the pup, so I applied more pressure to his thumb.

"You don't kick animals. Just like you don't force your will on people who are smaller and weaker than you," I hissed.

"Good dog." The white-haired lady nodded, and when Gus hopped back onto her lap, she waved the attendant to push her forward again. The teens were no longer paying attention to Luka. My standoff with Trent had become more captivating, *especially* because he was now cursing and dancing, clearly disgusted by the wetness on his ankle and in his shoe.

That was not good. *So* not good. Dammit. I wanted to break Trent's thumb—break *him*.

I pressed harder for one more beat, enjoying the last of Trent's squirming before I flung his hand away from me.

The weasel straightened his suit even as he winced. Then he glared. "I'll be sure to tell your father you're in town. He'll be thrilled to know he's getting the grandbaby he always wanted."

I held it together until Trent passed, refusing to breathe in his cologne—I detested that scent. But once he was down the terminal, out of reach, I swayed. My breath pumped nearly as fast as my heart. Luka wrapped his arm around me, trembling slightly.

He'd hated standing by. I could hear the frustration in his voice when he spoke to our audience.

"Sorry, guys. My girlfriend isn't feeling great."

I let him lead me from the terminal and out to the parking lot, my ears still buzzing and my legs feeling stiffer with each step. There would be pictures of me posted online. Luka had been right beside me, called me his girlfriend. My father would sniff those out with ease. So much for staying under the radar. I hadn't even made it out of the airport before I ran into one of my nightmares.

But I'd survived that interaction—not only survived but proven my ability to take care of myself. My breathing turned a bit ragged. Trent might be my personal hell, but he wasn't my biggest threat. My father was, and Trent had probably already called and told him everything.

"What the fuck was that?" Luka asked. He'd stopped walking and stood rigid, jaw tight, eyes flashing.

The air was muggy, and it settled over me like a comforting blanket. Sure, it was smoggy and hot, but it was right. I'd missed this. So much.

We stood in front of an SUV. It wasn't new, but it wasn't old either.

"Where's your car?"

"I sold the Corvette after you told me about Bree. We need something safe for her, something that can hold all her gear."

I swallowed. He'd sold his Corvette, his "*favorite toy*," I remember he'd said, and bought our baby a car.

"This one's a couple of years old. I got it because it has the best reliability and safety rating on the market." He shoved his fisted hands in his pockets. I heard the faint rip of a seam. "I wanted to make sure it was really the safest one."

Still, I remained silent, too taken aback by his thoughtfulness—by this huge step forward in parenting that left me completely…

In love.

I was so in love with Luka Stol.

He cleared his throat. My gaze flashed up to his, my heart kickboxing my ribs.

I was in love with him.

Irrevocably.

I'd have to see him, often, while we raised our daughter…

"You need to explain that scene to me, Millie."

I did. I knew I did. The shaking got worse. So much worse.

He deserved to know about my past, about those videos that made me sick to my stomach, but—but I couldn't stop thinking about my future. After I told him, Luka would find a woman he wanted to be with, and I'd be alone.

Again.

More alone than I'd been after I left Trent. Because my heart would have lost something vital.

There was no way Luka would stay mine once he learned the truth, but I had to tell him to protect Bree. I pressed my fingertips to my pounding temple, staving off the worst of the pain.

No, not the worst. That was my heart breaking.

"Millie?" Luka's tone shifted from frustration to concern.

I blinked back the grief and panic, forcing myself to meet his concerned gaze. He didn't know about the bomb blowing up in my head, my chest. And I wouldn't tell him.

"He's going to cause problems," I whispered.

"I assumed that." Luka's expression was neutral, but his eyes burned with questions, still hyped from the interaction. "Want to tell me why?"

No.

"Yeah, I can see you don't want to." He ran his fingers through his hair, his expression worried. "I'm going to insist on this, Millie. I need to know what's going on."

He did. He deserved to know. I steadied myself. Much as I wanted his touch—craved it, needed it—there was no way Luka would want me once I told him this story. I needed to prepare for that. Somehow.

"That was Trenton Cox," I began with a shudder. "My former fiancé."

My throat closed as Luka's expression changed to one first of hurt, then anger.

"And?" he snapped.

Perceptive. Luka had great social intelligence. I might spend time in my head working through a complex chemical problem, but Luka could suss out an interaction in mere seconds. The problem was he was too aggressive, too quick to throw a punch rather than study the situation or retreat.

"My father chose him for me," I whispered. "I… Trent never asked me…"

Luka's brows tugged lower, and his eyes seemed to harden. "What aren't you telling me, Millie?"

I wrapped my arms around my middle, below my breasts and above Bree. I was cold, so cold, even in the muggy summer heat of the Houston airport parking garage. Cars drove past, their tires squealing against the hot concrete. Fumes tickled my nose.

"He…"

Luka's palms slid up my arms. His touch was warm and centering. I opened my eyes and forced them to meet his.

This was it. This was the last moment I had with Luka. I studied his face, inhaled his scent, and let go of all my dreams.

"No, Luka. Trent didn't rape me."

CHAPTER 9
Luka

My lungs seized and my vision tunneled as Millie's words replayed in my mind, an endless loop of her shattered voice and shadowed eyes.

"What *did* he do?" I asked with a measure of calm that came from some source I hadn't known I had.

Ida Jane had told me Millie had been hurt. She'd hinted that it was assault. I'd thought I was ready to hear those words.

I wasn't. And my relief that he hadn't raped her made me feel shitty. I gritted my teeth to accept what she'd just told me.

"We were engaged, see…"

She'd mentioned that—as if it made whatever happened next okay. I swallowed, not liking where this was going.

"We'd been…together for a while. It was a slow seduction, one I didn't have any defenses for." She cleared her throat and looked at me, pleading with me to understand. "That night… when I left…he…" She shivered.

I need to know, Millie. Shit, I need to know! I cupped her elbows, trying to give her my support, and if she needed it, my strength.

"He threw away my birth control pills. He said he was going to fuck a baby into me."

"Why?"

Her smile was sad and angry and filled with loathing. "To ensure his portion of the Jones billions."

The words didn't translate into my mind for a long moment. When they did, I felt as shattered as she looked. "He knew you didn't want that, I assume."

She bit her trembling lip and nodded. "I wanted a career…"

"He tried to take your choice from you, Millie."

"I, I know."

I cupped her chin and looked deep into her eyes. "It was about power and force," I whispered. The words seared us both, made my hair follicles sizzle.

She licked her lips. "Y-yes."

"Millie, sweetheart, I'd like to hug you," I said, my voice as ragged as my emotions.

She didn't refuse, so I tugged her into my arms, holding her against my chest. So much made sense now.

That slick-haired douche had betrayed my girl, hurt her emotionally—to her soul. Used her with plans to break her.

And she'd just ninja'd his hand, nearly dropped him to his knees right there in the terminal *with ease*. She'd smiled faintly when that old lady's dog took a piss. That had been awesome—something I would have laughed about with the guys if not for the background Millie had just shared.

She'd faced, with poise, the man who was supposed to love and cherish her and had betrayed her instead. She hadn't let me wade in and pummel the slick-suited jackass like I'd known he'd deserved.

Millie amazed me. Right now, though, she was

vulnerable—like her guts were outside her body and she might not survive her next breath.

That reined in my aggression. Some, not all. The need to beat Trenton continued to hound me.

She shook her head, sniffling. "Just go, Luka. Leave. I know you must want to."

"No, sweetheart. I'm going to hug you for another minute," I said, my voice as gentle as I could manage. "Don't shut me out now. We both need this." I thought—I *hoped*. I was in so far over my head with Millie that I wasn't sure how to keep breathing as the waves continued to crash, hauling me down.

No wonder she'd ghosted me. I couldn't fault her for wanting to protect herself from another man—from another betrayal.

Because there were more. She hadn't told me yet about her father, not directly and not enough. But I'd already figured out that he was the real villain in this story.

She nodded, but she still felt stiff—fragile. I held her close and slowly, her body relaxed. She whimpered and then she went limp. Glancing down, I noted her eyes squeezed shut and her mouth in a tight line.

Yet she settled against my chest as if she'd been made specifically to fit there. I closed my eyes, trying to ease the tension pulsing through my muscles. Now wasn't the time to fixate on Millie's past. Right now, we both needed comfort. I rocked her gently, enjoying the feel of Bree's movements against my abdomen.

This woman.

"We're going to have to talk about this more."

"I know. I need to tell you my father's part."

And I needed to know. I was going to hate the details, but I couldn't protect her without the knowledge.

"Just *please,* not now."

I kissed the top of her head. "Not here."

I needed to get her home and fed and *safe.* I needed time to think through what she'd said, and what that meant for me, to me. Ida Jane had warned me not to go after Millie unless I was serious, and I'd spent some time thinking over my options before I got on that flight to Sri Lanka.

Millie was such a series of contrasts. She cuddled closer, her hands gripping my shirt, her nose buried in the space between my pecs. Her body was soft but strong, lush with my child.

Millie was mine. Not because I needed to own her, but because she owned me. I'd already given her my heart; I'd given her my future and my happiness.

She just didn't know.

Millie

Even after Luka led me into his condo and brought up our luggage, even after we'd both showered and eaten, he continued to fixate on Trent.

I knew this because I did, too.

His fists clenched and released, clenched and released enough for me to realize he was fantasizing about hitting the guy.

I'd wanted to also, but that wouldn't have solved my problems. Assault would have only increased them. But Luka wasn't me—there was still so much I didn't know about him, his history. Still, I had the sense that he lived by a code Trent never would.

Solving matters with his fists, having a code of honor were things Trent couldn't fathom. Keeping those two apart became paramount; no way could Luka lose his future, especially not because of my past.

"Are you tired?" Luka asked.

I felt drained. In fact, I spent a good portion of most days exhausted, thanks to the human growing inside me.

"You can have the bed," Luka said. There was a rasp to his voice—an off-ness to him that worried me.

I'd known he wouldn't want me once he learned I'd been unable to protect myself. Too young, too naïve, too weak to realize Trent was using me...

"Stop." Luka was in front of me, his hands loosely caging my wrists. "Come back. That place—wherever you went—I don't like it. I'm pretty sure it isn't healthy."

My lower lip wobbled as I looked up at him. "I..."

Luka dropped his gaze. "Let's get you to bed."

"I don't want to go," I exclaimed. "I mean, I'm tired, but we need to talk—"

"Not tonight," Luka said.

"Don't tell me not tonight," I snapped back. "I hate when people decide for me!"

All the tension from the airport swirled around us. But it was more than that. I was so aware of him, his beautiful eyes, his plump lower lip, his hard-angled jaw. I wanted him. Desperately. I needed him to want me, too. To show me that Trent's actions meant nothing—that he was still attracted to me.

I shook my head. No, that was foolishness. I'd check into a

hotel in the morning. And the moment Ida Jane's party ended, I'd get back to the airport—go back to my lonely, sad existence in Sri Lanka.

"I'm hanging on by a thread here, Millie." Luka groaned.

"What? Why?" I asked, blinking up at him.

"Because you're mine, and I can't stand the idea of another man touching you. It's driven me crazy since you left my bed all those months ago. And now you're telling me that…that…" Luka vibrated with anger. "I want to rip his dick off and shove it down his throat so he chokes on it."

A laugh bubbled out of my mouth. "Crazy how we've both had the same fantasy."

Luka shook his head. "I don't know what I'm doing with you. I wanted to give you time to realize I was a better man than you expected me to be—"

"I know that, Luka." I placed my palms against his cheeks. "You deserve better than me—"

"Stop. Right fucking there. I want *you*. I've wanted you from the beginning. Nothing's changed there."

"Um…" I looked down at my bulging midsection. "Pretty sure a lot's changed."

"I hate when people decide what's best for me," he snapped, parroting my words. Anger quivered from his lips, his muscles. "And I hate being told what I should think or feel. I'm me—I know."

I sucked in a breath. "Of course, Luka. Of course." I leaned so my forehead touched his. I wasn't aware yet what caused him to respond so vehemently to my words sometimes, but Luka had a past that haunted him, too. That much was obvious.

"I want to take you to bed and brand you as mine all over again," Luka said.

His tone remained clipped, his words coming too fast. He was worked up, no doubt from the altercation with Trent, but also from whatever demons rode him.

"I want to fuck you so hard you're hoarse from screaming my name. *Mine.* Over and over. I want to make you so drunk with pleasure, so boneless from orgasms, you can't think or feel or remember anything but me."

"That…" I swallowed. My pulse thrummed in my neck and my core warmed. "Sounds amazing."

He pulled back, so I clutched at his collar.

He frowned. "But I need to leave you alone, let you recover from our trip, from seeing that—"

"No, Luka. Don't do that to me now. I get to decide for me, too, right?"

He paused, eyes searching as the silence drew out between us, taut. Delicious. I shivered, leaned in, and pressed my lips to his.

His breath crashed over my mouth, heating it and causing me to shiver again. This man was *potent.*

"Are you sure?" he asked against my lips. Not pulling back, not taking space from me.

"I'm so sure," I murmured.

"Fuck," he groaned out before he sealed his lips to mine. Our tongues and teeth dueled for supremacy—though I planned to lose the fight. Luka's dominance excited me, but more, it made me feel safe, protected.

Maybe that was fucked up—I was a little or a lot messed up from my time with Trent—but Luka felt right. He gathered me in his arms, and I was home.

Safe.

Cherished.

I never wanted to leave.

Luka

She smelled like heaven—grapefruit and lilacs—and tasted divine. I'd missed the softness of her skin and the breathy little moans that slipped past her lips as she grew more and more turned on. I did that to her. I knew because she whimpered my name.

Biggest fucking turn-on of my life.

I swooped back in for another kiss, the passion drugging us both. Her tits were bigger, heavy against my chest, her nipples hard little points that speared against my sensitized skin. I slid my hand to her nape, tipping it back so I had access to her neck, which I nipped and licked and sucked and kissed until we were both writhing with want.

"I *need* you, Luka."

The. Best. Word. She *needed* me. Well, there were three I was desperate to hear from her lips, but Millie needing me was pretty good.

I smiled against her neck before I gently bit at her pulse then laved the sore spot with my tongue. Millie whimpered my name. I growled hers as I slid my hand down her back and gripped her ass in my hands. Millie had one of the best butts I'd ever seen. It was round and firm from her jiu jitsu but lush enough to bounce when she walked. I had a mighty big thing for her butt. I ground my pelvis against her belly to get some much-needed friction.

But then I stopped, my eyes wide as a thought crossed my mind. "Will Bree know?"

"That you're rubbing your dick on my belly?" Millie's eyebrows shot up. "No. She won't. People have sex all the time while pregnant, Luka."

"I don't want to traumatize our kid…"

"You're traumatizing *me* right now," Mille snapped. "I haven't had sex since that night with you, and before that, I'd never had an orgasm with a man. Let me tell you, penis-stimulated orgasms are the best. I want one. Now."

I bit back a laugh, struck by the humor and worry of this situation. "I'm not sure I can do it."

Millie growled. "No. Sex. In. Eight. Months."

"I know." I nodded. "It's been quite a dry spell."

"Wait, wait…hold up. Are you telling me you didn't sleep with another woman?" She gaped at me.

I stepped away from her, offended. "No."

Her eyes widened so much I worried they'd bug out of her head. "You…"

"I was faithful to the woman I wanted," I clipped. "Who wouldn't give me a fucking chance."

"Luka." She breathed my name like a prayer. "Really?"

Anger sizzled over my skin and through my veins. "Why is it so damn hard to believe I could be devoted to you?" I turned away, only stopping at the sting of her nails against the flesh of my forearms and the wild look in her eyes.

"B-b-because you're *beautiful*," she said. Her voice was raw, a little shaky—as if the answers were yanked from her very soul. I stilled, barely breathing, desperate for her next words.

"You're fun, funny. You really listen, not just pretend to. You put me at ease with a smile. And you're so damn sexy. And... and you make me come harder than I thought possible. I saw stars last time."

My dick and my ego rose to the metaphorical stroking.

Millie

So many words had exited my mouth. Words I hadn't been able to control or keep inside. My cheeks burned, my throat ached, and my body thrummed with awareness.

Wanting Luka the way I had—*did*—left me slightly crazed. He was everything I dreamed of in a man, but always outside my reach thanks to my sheltered upbringing, my innate shyness, my issues with Trent.

His eyes smoldered as he heaved a breath, then another one. "We're connected already, you and I, forever." He laid his hands on my belly. I bit my lip as I nodded.

"But this is more than our love for our daughter—you understand that now?" He eased closer to me, his big body sheltering mine.

With Luka, I *always* felt safe. Now wanted. Maybe one day loved.

I licked my lips, noting his eyes tracking my movement. My breath stilled, my heart pumping. "Luka. *Please*."

I wasn't sure, exactly, what I was begging him for—to ease the tension between us, to show me he cared, asking him to take me, flaws and all, and hold me forever.

"I got you, Millie." His eyes sparkled. I loved how he brought us back around to our first meeting. His hands flexed on my belly and slid upward to cup my breasts. I whimpered as I pressed more firmly into his hold.

"We got this, together." He bent his knees, bringing his face closer to my level. His gaze searched mine, eyes filled with emotions I couldn't process. "You and me and Bree. We're a team. The most important team."

He flicked his thumbs over my nipples, and my knees turned to water. I didn't worry, though. Luka would hold me up, keep me safe. That's what he was promising right now, and I desperately wanted to hand him control—not just of my body but of the craziness that was my life.

"Yes," I whispered.

Again, I wasn't sure what I was trying to tell him. I took a deep breath, holding it for a long moment as his hands worked their magic over my body. I tried to clear my head and think about what I wanted to tell him—what I needed to say. What we had, what we were building was important. For Bree, but for and to me. I wanted him to feel the same…wanted him to know how I felt about us. I licked my lips more slowly this time, enjoying the power of my femininity as Luka watched, his own breath catching.

"I want you," I said.

"Just now?" he demanded.

I shook my head, not breaking eye contact. This moment was

momentous—an alteration for us in a relationship of shifts. "I wanted you then, always, but I thought you'd..."

He growled, and goose bumps exploded over my skin. He was dominance, power restrained. At least with me.

"I wanted you then," I said more firmly, "and I want you now. More because I know how thoughtful and decent you are. I'll *always* want you."

"Good." He kissed me. Like his earlier kisses, this one was fierce, possessive, and it lit me up. Until Luka, I'd assumed I was too assertive to be interested in offering myself to a man.

But his kiss incinerated those beliefs. Luka had proven himself worthy of my trust, over and over. Even though it went against his instincts, he'd allowed me to fight *my* fight. He'd given me the respect and space I needed to feel confident enough to open up to him.

I tilted my head, giving him better, deeper access to my mouth. He flicked my nipples again, causing me to arch into him. He sucked my lower lip into his mouth, gently tugging, nipping at the soft skin there, and once again making my knees weak.

"I'm going to fuck you now." His lips remained against mine.

"Yes. Please."

Without lifting his head to break the kiss, he scooped me up. I looped my arms around his neck and held on, knowing he'd easily manage the added weight from pregnancy. He lifted his head, and I nipped at his chin, his earlobe, anything I could reach.

"Shh... I need to make sure I get you two on the bed safely. Just a minute, Millie."

But I was burning with need. Months of repression went up

in flames. I was so hungry for skin-to-skin contact, desperate for the connection, the bliss Luka brought me.

He elbowed into his bedroom, moving something from his pillow—a baby doll in a pink onesie?—and settled me in the middle of his bed. I stared up at him as he knelt next to me, shifting my body so I wasn't lying fully on my back. His hands skimmed the side of my breast, my ribs, my hip.

"Why do you have a doll?" I asked.

"To practice diapering and holding." He nuzzled my neck.

Oh. Oh, my heart melted all over again. How could I not fall for this man? He was thoughtful, loving…perfect.

And I'd tried so hard to push him away.

He looked down at me. "You are a sight lying here. Like those Renaissance paintings. Fucking gorgeous and lush. What I'm going to do to you?"

"Luka."

"Shh… I got you, sweetheart."

He'd keyed in on how much I loved that phrase. Now he said it to me when I became agitated. "I got you."

He slid to his side and kissed me again. I loved his kisses—was addicted to his taste, the firmness of his lips, the sweep of his tongue. I inched closer, my fingers deep in the material of his shirt, twisting the fabric.

He helped me remove my leggings and oversized shirt, taking special care to peel off my socks. Then he slid off his T-shirt and scooted onto the bed beside me, his hands on my belly. I arched into him, wanting more. He obliged by moving his warm palms over the taut skin to cup my breasts. My nipples, which were already sensitized and hard, tightened further.

"I need…" I began. The words died in my throat when he rolled my nipples between his fingers.

He bent his head, the beautiful hair sliding with a silky weight between my fingers, as I pressed him closer to my chest. He kissed his way around my areola. My panties grew wet as he lavished attention on the sensitive skin.

"Your breasts are so beautiful, Millie. You're beautiful."

"More," I moaned.

That sexy smirk flittered across his mouth before he peeled the other bra cup out of his way and kissed, plucked, and suckled that nipple to a firm peak. My hips shifted, restless from the need for friction.

"Luka."

"I'm right here, pretty girl. I got you."

"I need to come. So bad."

"You will. Soon."

He spent more time loving and nuzzling my breasts. Each time he sucked one of my nipples into the warm recess of his mouth, arousal trickled from my folds. I'd never been this wet—this turned on. He took me to the brink of orgasm…from breast play.

I teetered there, my breath caught in my throat, waiting, needing, desperate…

His sleek, blond head slid downward. My bump obscured him, but I felt his hands cupping my butt, his warm breath against my damp panties.

"Someone's excited," he said, satisfaction lacing his tone.

"I might explode."

He chuckled as he slid his index finger under the gusset of my panties and glided it over my folds. "Mmm... Wet, warm, soft. Perfect."

"Luka," I gritted my teeth, my body humming. I wanted to scream, I wanted to cry. He moved his finger forward and rubbed a circle over my nub. That caused my hips to buck and my breath to catch. He did it again with a little more pressure.

Luka

The orgasm crashed over Millie hard. Her entire body shivered and convulsed as she screamed her pleasure. I shifted my hips so they were parallel to the bed, seeking some friction for my aching dick.

Watching Millie fall apart from my touch was the single hottest moment of my life. Nothing else came close. She continued to whimper and convulse, causing me to grit my teeth.

"Ah," she whimpered. She sucked in a breath, blinking, her expression dazed and relaxed. "Oooh."

"You're so pretty when you orgasm."

She turned toward me. I slid my hand under my head, propping myself up so I could see her properly. She bit her lip and shook her head.

"What?" I demanded.

"You. Saying *orgasm*." She giggled.

"That's what you did," I said, confused—maybe because most of the blood was still in my crotch. My dick throbbed, desperate for its own orgasm.

"You weren't so proper the last time we were together," she said, smiling. But the smile slid from her face and her pretty eyes darkened. "You won't change, will you? You won't think of me only as a mother, right? Because Elvis did, and that seemed really weird—"

"I do not know what you're talking about, but I think I've already changed since I found out about Bree. For the better." I leaned closer and kissed her lips, taking it slow. I tasted her pleasure and her hunger.

This was so different from anything I'd ever experienced before. With Millie, everything was richer, more vibrant. As much as my balls ached and my dick scraped uncomfortably against my zipper, I was content—no, I was fucking *ecstatic*—to be in bed, kissing my woman.

When she popped the button on my jeans, I moved to stop her. She bit her lips and glanced up at me, vulnerability in her eyes. *Right.* She seemed to think I didn't find her attractive. If she only knew how many times I'd jacked off as I thought about her rounded with my child…

Alyssa had told me to open up—be honest. So easy to say, so fucking hard to do.

"You are so gorgeous," I said. Her smile lit up her face. When she slid her hand into my pants, I groaned, pressing myself into her hand. She worked my pants and boxer briefs down my hips and tugged them off before caressing her way back up my legs. I panted, lightheaded from her touch.

"Fuck, Millie. Fuck! I want you so bad…"

She straddled me, her breasts and belly brushing my chest and abdomen. She kissed me, then kissed me again. And again. Those drugging kisses I'd become addicted to. When she sucked my tongue into her mouth, I had to grab the base of my dick to keep from shooting my load.

"It's been so long," I muttered. "I'm desperate to be inside you, but I'm worried I'll come too fast…"

Millie smiled against my lips. "I want to make you feel good. No, I need to." She pulled back and stared into my eyes. Her face was soft, open, her expression so trusting. This honesty thing was *freaking* genius.

"Is it okay like this?" she asked as she hovered over my swollen tip.

"Yes. Please. I want…need…inside…"

She settled over me, her supple, warm flesh running along the sensitive underside of my shaft. I wanted to piston up into her, but instead, I took her hips and waited. And waited, as my breathing turned ragged and sweat sheened over my chest. Finally, she slid down, taking my rigid length inside her.

We both gasped as she settled her hips against my pelvis.

"Luka," she mumbled as I blurted, "So fuckin' *good*."

She lifted, then slid down again. I wasn't sure the sensations could get better, but they did. She rose and let gravity bring her down over and over, until we were both covered in a layer of sweat. Her movements grew less fluid, no doubt because of the baby. I toppled her gently, so we were facing each other, still joined, and I worked my hips in and out. She hitched her knee higher, giving me deeper access, and I pistoned, over and over, doing my best to bump against her clit with each stroke.

Millie's breath stuttered and her cheeks flushed more, her eyes glistened. Then she stiffened, her body wound so tight, and released. As her inner muscles undulated around my shaft, I pushed into her once more, groaning and cursing as I emptied my aching balls deep inside her.

The great thing about being on my side was I didn't collapse onto her. I studied her as I caught my breath, taking in her parted, kiss-swollen lips, her rosy cheeks, and her glistening eyes with the lids at half-mast. Her hair was a halo of tangles that lay over her cheek and neck.

"I love you, Millie."

Millie

My gaze flashed up to Luka's, my heart pounding against my ribs even harder now, but for an entirely different reason.

"You…" *Can't.*

I'd *used* Luka—ghosted him. Now he knew how I'd been duped and betrayed by a man looking to better his financial situation. *I* was like Trent—my treatment of Luka, out of fear, was the *same.*

I shook my head, frantic to break free from the vise of terror his words created within me.

He frowned. "What are you thinking?"

I dropped my gaze. Why the hell was I naked? I mean, I knew why, but now that he'd said those words, I felt raw, exposed…so much more *naked* than I'd been when we were banging. I gasped. "You…"

Luka's warm palm slid against my cool skin, shocking me back into the moment. I gasped again, my gaze locking to his. The worry had settled in his eyes; his lips tugged down at the corners.

"I've got you, Millie," he murmured.

My heart raced, my breath broke, and I was crying, clawing at his back—trying to get away, trying merge into his skin.

All the while he held me, making *shh* sounds, letting me fall apart in the safety of his arms while he kept my parts from flying away into the ether.

Eventually my sobbing slowed, and mortification built. I ducked my head.

"Stop putting up so many fucking walls," Luka growled. He rolled onto his back, releasing me, and I shivered. So cold, so lonely.

I didn't know what to do.

He couldn't love me. He *couldn't*.

I wasn't worth his regard. My father had told me as much. Many, many times.

I crawled toward Luka, desperate for his comfort, his touch... his love. He let me settle against him, but this time his embrace was begrudging. He didn't want me there.

I'd ruined the moment. Worse, I worried I'd ruined the fragile bond Luka had been working so hard to build.

I must have fallen asleep, because I woke ravenous enough to gnaw my arm from my body and nauseous enough to vomit anything inside my stomach. Luka wasn't in the bed, and from the cool feel of the pillow when my hand drifted across it, he hadn't been there for quite some time.

I stood, winced, and waddled to the bathroom. I nearly jumped at the sight in the mirror, my crazy hair and my red, swollen eyes.

I groaned as the heat from the shower eased the tension in my shoulders, at least somewhat, and hissed when the water poured over the slightly raw skin on my face.

After a ridiculously long time, I turned off the taps and wrapped a towel around my hair, another around my body. Luka wasn't in the bedroom or the open-concept kitchen, living, and dining room.

In fact, I realized he wasn't in the condo. And I had to get ready for Ida Jane's wedding today. I'd booked a hair and makeup appointment at my favorite salon. I turned to the clock on the microwave. I was running late.

I crammed my body into a clean pair of leggings and a tunic and grabbed my purse and phone, unsure what to think about Luka's absence.

We needed to talk. In order to talk, he needed to be here.

He wasn't here. Ergo, he didn't want to talk to me.

I knew that wasn't totally rational. That was the thing about the mind—it led me to fucked-up conclusions I knew were wrong, but somehow eased the tension in the rest of my body when I accepted them.

My hunger warred with my nausea as I called a rideshare to drive me to the salon. I left the condo with one last, forlorn look, wishing I'd handled last night better, wishing I had more to eat than the crumbly snacks I'd packed for the flight.

Wishing I knew if I was coming back to the condo, and if Luka could forgive me for not responding with my own three important words back.

Words I'd been desperate to say since my mother died.

CHAPTER 10

Luka

Millie's text message chimed on my phone, pulling me out of my zoned-out running. I glanced down at the machine in the building's gym and grunted in shock. I'd been on the thing for over an hour and run more than ten miles.

My knees wobbled as I turned it off, and I barely got off the machine before my legs collapsed under me.

I hung my head and breathed hard, sweat pouring down my face and further soaking my already damp T-shirt.

A large metal water bottle filled my vision. I squinted at it before I tipped my head back and met Cruz's concerned gaze.

"Drink. It'll help with the cramps you're going to have."

I took the bottle from his hand and uncapped the lid. The water was cool, but not too cold, and it slid down my parched throat like a freshly sharpened blade through butter. I sucked back half of it before my lungs protested. I lowered the bottle, panting.

"Back with me?" Cruz asked.

That caused me to frown. "What do you mean?"

He gestured toward the machine.

"I've been trying to talk to you for the last twenty minutes. I was about to unplug the thing because I knew you were close to your limit."

I offered him my hand, and he clasped it in his larger paw,

yanking me up with an ease that made me feel like a toddler being hauled from the pool. He slid his palm from mine and supported my elbow as I struggled to maintain balance. I was going to pay for this workout tomorrow. "Thanks, man," I said.

"Want to tell me why you were punishing yourself like that?"

I blinked, mouth open. Was I? My shoulders folded in, and I stared down at my feet. "I told Millie I loved her."

"And?" Cruz prodded.

"She had a stuttering fit or a panic attack or something, then ugly cried all over me and passed out."

Cruz grunted, seeming unsurprised. "Damn, I didn't want to be right."

My eyes narrowed. "About *what*?"

He heaved a sigh before he bent down and grabbed the water bottle. Once he'd shoved it into my hand with a stern admonishment to *drink*, he motioned for me to follow him.

"Where are we going?"

"My place. I need to show you something."

My phone chimed again. I pulled it out of my soggy shorts pocket.

I'm heading over to my hair appointment. I'll meet you at Cormac's this afternoon.

I gritted my teeth as I shoved my phone back into my pocket, slamming the edge of the damn thing into my thigh. Millie needed to stop with these damned dismissals.

"Millie?" Cruz asked. At my curt nod, he sighed. "Putting up walls, running away?"

I couldn't decide if I wanted to gawk at him or punch him for being an oracle of Millie's reactions. "Yes," I snapped.

He dropped his chin to his chest. "Let's go."

I followed him like a duckling after its mama. Except we weren't going to a pond.

"Wait—I thought you were in Austin, getting a retired K-9," I said.

"I was. Got her. Came back for Maxim's wedding."

I smirked, loving that Maxim was getting married—rather *re-married*—today and didn't know it. We'd get to razz him for months. It would be epic.

Once we left the elevator and entered Cruz's apartment, he walked over to a large German Shepherd who was curled up on a new dog bed.

"How's it going, lovely?" he crooned. "Shh. Don't bark at Stolly. He's sweaty, smelly, and gross, but he's having a rough time."

I glared at Cruz but couldn't disagree with his assessment. "What's her name?"

"Belladonna."

"How long is she here?"

"Just until I find her former handler."

I nodded. Cruz finished petting the dog and came into the kitchen, where he washed his hands. After pointing to my usual chair at the breakfast bar, he filled a glass with my favorite smoothie and pushed it toward me.

"Drink up while I get my laptop."

I did because I was ravenous, but something inside pinged an internal warning.

When Cruz brought back the computer and I saw the screen, I understood why.

Millie wasn't just an engineer. She was the daughter of one of the wealthiest real estate moguls in the state. I set the glass down with such force, I was surprised it didn't crack.

"Her father disowned her when she ditched that piece of shit?"

Cruz crossed his arms over his chest, looking like a massive bouncer. "Yeah, and it gets worse. I'm pretty sure this is why your girl is running so hot and cold, man. She's been fucked." He winced and shot me an apologetic look. "Found out why Gunnar was meeting with Coach, and it has to do with her father. He wants to buy in."

"What?" I asked.

"To the team. Seems like the offer was pretty sweet," Cruz said.

"How do you know?" I asked.

He turned a little cagey. "I maybe overheard the conversation when I went to visit Coach the other day. He was talking to Paloma about it. For the record, Coach didn't like the idea."

"I guess that's something," I muttered.

"And Millie's dad's a shit bag."

"So is the ex."

"Slick-haired douche. Saw the photo of y'all in the airport."

I dropped my forehead to the counter. "It's everywhere?" I asked.

"Yep."

I cursed. Belladonna rose from her bed and crossed over, pressing her body against my leg. I petted her ears, wishing she could take away the worry gnawing at my insides.

Millie

I pressed my hand to my pronounced belly, wondering if I had the strength to walk into Cormac Bouchard's house for Ida Jane's wedding. Her *second* wedding to Maxim, but the first one for her family and friends.

Needing to watch my bestie pledge her life to the man of her dreams was a given. However, facing Luka revved my anxiety so high, I worried I'd pass out.

"Just get it over with, Millie. You've already lived through the nightmare. This is just some roadblocks."

"Why are you out here talking to yourself, hon?" Loreen Barlow, Ida Jane's mother, asked from my shoulder. She had her hands full of flowers, and I lifted a bouquet from her arms. "Ida Jane needs you inside, darling."

"I'm coming. Just…steeling my nerves."

"I can understand that. I used to think the boys' football friends were a good-looking bunch, but these hockey players are in a whole different league." She chuckled, her eyes twinkling. "And that Luka of yours? He's what my mama would have called a tall glass of water."

I couldn't help the giggles that burst past my lips. Partly nerves, partly the idea of Luka as a thirst-trap—because he was most *definitely* that for most of the female fans. And supposedly, he loved *me*.

Me. Unlovable Millicent Anne Jones, whose own father had tried to litigate into behaving his way. When that didn't work, my former fiancé had ruthlessly expressed his interest in my fortune—and disdain for me.

Tch. As if.

I didn't even have a fortune anymore. My father had cut me out when I refused to make up with Trent. He'd chosen a man he'd met two years before over his daughter.

"Come on, Millie. You need to get in there and do the maid-of-honor stuff—like tell Ida Jane she's beautiful and fuss over her bouquet and all that jazz."

"Ida Jane doesn't need fussing, and of course she's beautiful," I countered. "Have you seen how radiant she is now that she and Maxim are going to be officially official—not just legally official?"

Yes, I had envy. No, I wasn't happy about my feelings, but Ida Jane seemed to walk on air these days. Air Maxim provided. They were adorably, disgustingly in love. Something I hadn't thought I wanted until I saw her joy and excitement…and until Luka's reappearance in my life.

"I love you."

No. Don't think about that now. Not now.

"I admit, I had some concerns, what with the way they went about hooking up early on."

I hid my cringe at Loreen's words as I walked through the front doors and into Cormac's beautiful house. Luka was nearby, and there was no doubt in my mind that he wasn't happy with me for running away this morning.

He hadn't been there when I woke.

But still, I'd run. He and I both knew it.

He'd tire of chasing me, if he hadn't already.

"They had an unconventional start, sure, but she's happy, Mrs.

Barlow," I said.

"I know it," Loreen agreed. "Maxim's such an attentive spouse. My Ida Jane really did *good*." She grimaced. "Especially after that, that *dud*. Ugh. Daddy and I were worried about her head for a while there, but she came to her senses."

"Dillon wasn't Ida Jane's best decision," I muttered. He'd hurt her, scared her, tried to control her. What kind of sad sack of shit needed to do that to another person?

At least he was now in jail, hopefully getting some of his own treatment from the other inmates. That was my dream, anyway. I hadn't gotten that type of closure with Trent.

She turned toward me and smiled. "You did, too, hon." Her lip curled. "That ex of yours was cut from the same cloth as Ida Jane's. I'm so glad you girls got sense and dumped those losers."

I nodded and made an encouraging sound. Mrs. Barlow was right. Ida Jane and I had spent our college years and after with really terrible men. Maybe it had been youth or naivete or—who knew? But Ida Jane had definitely moved up in the world.

I had, too. Luka was a good man.

What was I supposed to say to him? I couldn't tell him no one had said they loved me since my mother's death when I was twelve. Well, besides Ida Jane. But no one in my family.

"Since you're already holding your bouquet, hon," Loreen said, "would you give this one to Ida Jane?" She pushed a lusher one into my hands.

I buried my nose in its sweetness, enjoying the beautiful scents and soft petals. For something made up of ninety-five percent hydrogen, oxygen, and carbon, flowers were pretty amazing. So many different textures, shapes, scents—all from five percent of their molecular makeup, what they absorbed from the ground.

I'd absorbed my father's unloving disinterest, then Trent's. Was it possible that I could uproot myself and resettle in Luka's garden? Find a more nourishing environment?

Did I deserve that chance?

I hadn't told him I loved him back. Because I was scared…and still too afraid to have my heart crushed again to admit my feelings.

That didn't mean they weren't there.

They were, and I swallowed down the weight of the words, of my emotions, with every single breath. I'd been alone for so long, fighting one battle just to be a person, and another to claw my way back from terrible mistakes, all because I wanted someone to love me.

Luka did. So he said.

I yearned to believe him.

But I *couldn't*. Not fully. Because my father didn't, and my mother had said she did, but then she left me. Trent's only reason for proposing marriage was to get his hands on my family's money—the hard reality was he'd never, ever wanted *me*.

I'd been unwanted since I was a kid, and it was a terribly lonely feeling.

Sure, I had Ida Jane, and Bree, …and Luka. I might not think I deserved him, but he was part of my life now. Always. Because of Bree. I gathered the bouquets in one hand so I could place the other on my belly, caressing my daughter. She'd changed so much of my life.

The flowers trembled in my hand. I hated Trent and my

father. Detested them. Never wanted to share space or give them a chance to hurt me again.

But neither Trent nor my father would be here at Cormac's today, and I could slip back out of town before my father tracked me down. Tonight. I'd leave right after the wedding.

One day, Luka would forgive me.

I hoped.

CHAPTER 11
Luka

Millie's hip brushed my leg and her luscious breast rubbed against my arm as she walked gracefully across the grass toward the arbor Keelie and the other wives and girlfriends, which the Wildcatters called CATS, had set up.

I was so fucking angry with her I could barely see straight, but that didn't stop me from noting her voluptuous beauty.

"What's that?" Millie asked.

"I said you look stunning. I thought it before but didn't say it."

"Thank you," she whispered, staring down at her bouquet.

She was like trying to milk a grain of rice. I turned away. Cormac's backyard looked like a flower shop had barfed across it. The decorations were abundant, perfect for an outdoor wedding, especially the fairy lights around the trees.

I liked it, and despite my current anger, I hoped Millie did, too, because the two of us should definitely have a similar ceremony, and soon.

I nearly tripped over my feet when I realized where my thoughts had turned. *Marry Millie?*

For a man who'd been hell-bent on never developing a deep, lasting relationship with a woman, I'd managed a one-eighty. Maybe there was something in the water here in Houston, or the other Wildcatters were giving off contentment hormones or some shit.

That woo-woo explanation made as much sense as me fantasizing about my wedding. I shook my head, marveling at my shift. But Cruz's research had solidified the need to make Millie legally mine. Together, the two of us would be a stronger, more united unit against any of her father or ex-fiancé's bullshit. And we'd have the Wildcatters players and organization at our back.

"We need to talk," I said.

Millie sighed. "Of course. After?"

Well, we couldn't talk *now*. "Sure."

Millie's breast bobbled and brushed against my arm again, causing the muscles in my gut to clench. She worried she wasn't the same fit hourglass she'd been when I'd fucked her into a near-coma all those months ago. That was true, but she was lusher, more beautiful now. Never in my life had I considered a pregnant woman sexy, but Millie pulled it off and *then* some. Which was why I knew she was the only woman I would ever want in my life forever.

She had me by the fantasies and the balls. And I'd be much calmer about that once she admitted I had the same hold over her. Well, similar hold because she was ball-less.

I needed to get out of my messed-up head.

We reached the end of the aisle, and Millie glanced up at me, her expression filled with something that looked like regret.

Ah, hell no. She would not bail on me. I understood the whole fight-or-flight response—I'd lived it for years. Without thinking, I leaned in and dropped a kiss on her lips.

"The fuck, man?" Maxim muttered. "It's my wedding!"

"Your *second* one," Naese said.

"He's just staking his claim to the hot maid of honor." Because Cruz said that, in solidarity with me, I didn't need to bash in heads.

I leaned closer to Millie and whispered, "I'm not letting you out of my sight. And I know about your shit-bag father disowning you."

She stiffened, her inhale sharp, her face turning pasty.

"He's doing a damn poor job of wooing her," Cormac muttered.

"That's karma not liking him horn-dogging on my wedding day," Maxim snapped.

I squeezed Millie's elbow and pressed another kiss to her hairline before moving to my spot on the opposite side of the altar.

"Really?" Maxim asked, eyes narrowed in a glare.

"Shit's going down," Cruz muttered. "And your girl's gonna want Stolly on it to keep Millie safe. Which is what he's doing… weirdly and possibly poorly. Now, quit bitching. Here comes your wife."

"She is the most beautiful creature," Maxim breathed, completely overcome by Ida Jane. Her timing was perfect, too, because Maxim no longer remembered I existed.

The range of emotion that flitted across his face fascinated me. Longing, gratitude, joy, and love morphed into a sappy expression I'd never believed Maxim could achieve. It was a good look on him, one I hoped continued for all the years of their marriage—and one I wanted captured in a book for us to show Bree and her siblings one day.

Millie

An opossum interfered with my half-assed, partially baked plans.

A rodent made up of fur, teeth, and a ratty tail. Why? Because they loved Houston. Also because *fuck my life*.

Nothing was easy, yet I refused to admit the universe was trying to tell me something epic. Important. Life-changing.

After the ceremony Blade, Ida Jane's large guard dog, sat between her and Maxim as teammates gave their speeches. The poor pup panted heavily in the early evening heat. He wasn't designed for Houston's mugginess, but I knew he wanted to be there based on his blissed out, hooded eyes and his grin with lolling tongue. He also had a personal mister blowing cool air into his face.

Blade knew he'd soon be back in the coolness of Cormac and Keelie's place with a bone. He had a cozy bed he shared with Keelie's cat, Slippers, when he came over. The cat sat at the glass door, tail twitching as she watched her canine friend outside.

I stared at the officiant, trying to ignore the feel of Luka's stare, which sat heavily on my cheek. The man was the star of the hottest sexual experience in my life—two of them, actually, now that Luka had loved me up so well last night. But wait, reliving them, as I was, at my best friend's wedding reception was far beyond taboo.

Yet I couldn't concentrate on the speeches because I kept returning to last night. Goose bumps exploded over my skin in a ripple of awareness and an echo of that pleasure. He'd manipulated me so easily, flipping me this way and that. He'd kissed and licked while he dragged his fingertips in feather-light touches over my heated, sensitized skin, making me quake and moan.

I'd never known I was a moaner. I hadn't known I was a lot of things until Luka—like my ability to multitask by deep-throating him—new skill—while he feasted on my drenched folds. I'd never known I could orgasm three times in an hour, and that each would be successively deeper, releasing a tension from my very core and leaving me boneless.

But I'd found that out the first night we'd spent together all those months ago.

I shifted so I couldn't see Luka's all-too-knowing eyes. He knew I wanted him, and he knew that scared me. I wasn't sure which was worse, and I didn't want to think about him, my father, Bree's future, any of it.

I sighed as I rose.

"Where are you going?" Luka murmured.

"Bathroom."

He nodded, aware of my near-constant need to pee. I crossed the expansive yard toward the pool deck.

A cheer went up, and I looked back in time to see Ida Jane and Maxim kiss. A hiss at my shoulder startled a yelp from me. I turned to stare into gleaming dark eyes and twitchy whiskers. The opossum must have snuck into the tent for food, and I was blocking its escape route out of the yard.

I reacted without thought, by smacking at the opossum. With my bare hand. It assumed I was attacking it—fair—and growled low, paws clutched tightly around its treat. Was that *an empanada*?

Blade must have heard the commotion because he was immediately at my side, leaping toward the rodent as it lunged toward me a second time. The Newfoundland used my leg as his launchpad, propelling himself through the air. He nearly caught the now-retreating opossum's tail. Blade landed in a heap on the pool deck while I flailed, thanks to my shifted center of gravity and my heels.

My calf hit a lounge chair, and I reached out, planning to stabilize myself just as my foot tangled in my gown and I pitched forward.

The collective gasp drowned out my faint yip. I wrapped my arms around my middle as I closed my eyes and scrunched my face, trying to prepare myself for the painful collision with the ground. I twisted as much as possible, hoping to take the brunt of the fall on my buttock, not my hip—as far from Bree as possible.

Which was how I found myself sprawled, spread-eagled and panting, in Luka's lap, staring out at a tent full of shocked wedding guests.

The rookie wolf-whistled, bringing the rest of the guests back to themselves. Ida Jane rushed over.

"I'm all right," I said, stopping her before she could bend down and muss her beautiful dress. "I'm all right, Luka."

"That was the freakiest thing," Ida Jane said on a gasp. "A possum—oh my—Blade! *Maxim*, Blade! He's not getting up."

Maxim rumbled a response, and Blade wagged his tail. Ida Jane dropped to her knees nearby, and Blade licked her wrist.

"Who's a brave boy?" she cooed.

"Ask him to stand up, Ida Jane. We can see if we need to call the vet," Maxim said.

I realized Luka hadn't moved. He hadn't breathed. I turned to look at him and realized he was gritting his teeth.

"What—" I managed.

"Landed...on my..."

"Oh!" I tried to shift.

He groaned and held me tightly. I stilled, cheeks flaming with mortification.

"Didn't realize weddings were a contact sport," Naese joked. He stood next to me but squatted at Luka's head, concern etching his brow line.

"Direct shot?" he asked.

Luka managed a brief nod, sweat beading his brow.

"Hell of a save, though. Adam will be jealous."

"Not...of...my nuts," Luka ground out.

Naese slapped his shoulder as he chuckled. "We'll get her up and that'll ease some of the pressure."

I gasped. "Did you just call me *heavy*?"

Naese rose, eyes wide. "N-no. I mean, you're pregnant. There's a baby in you. You're...you're...beautiful...glowing..."

"A delicate rose who ninja'd the fuck out of that possum. Cool trick," Cruz said as he joined us. He shot Luka a sympathetic glance. "I'll lift you on three."

Cruz picked me up, and Luka curled into a fetal position, panting and cursing with each exhale.

"Trainer will be over in a sec," Cruz said. "I caught that on video. You were magnificent, diving in under Millie, breaking her fall."

"G-great," Luka muttered. "I think I have splinters in my ass."

"Not possible on the pool deck, but maybe abrasions from

the concrete. They're trophies," Naese said, trying to keep a straight face.

"Fuck off," Luka growled.

I tried to dart away as mortification began to burn my super-heated flesh from my body.

"Nope. You need to stay here," Cruz rumbled, almost as if he knew my plan was to keep running through the house, out the door, and back to my condo in Colombo. He snapped his fingers and the rookie stepped forward, looking slightly awkward but determined.

"Get her some water and a chair," Cruz barked.

The rookie nodded and hastened off. Cruz kept his bear paw on my arm. I sagged into him, wheezing.

Luka touched my arm. I glanced over, blinking back tears of embarrassment. "You okay?" he asked.

"I should ask you that! Are you?"

Luka grimaced. "I'll be okay."

"Dick shots are the worst," Naese said.

"Shut it," Cruz muttered.

Naese met my eyes and rolled his lips into his mouth. "Er... are you okay?"

"Yes," I said through clenched teeth. Better to be angry than to show anxiety or fear. I knew that all too well. I snatched my arm from Cruz. "Thank you," I said to the bear of a man at my side.

He nodded, but I couldn't see much of his expression, thanks to his bearded cheeks.

I looked down at Luka, who sat up but still looked pale. He'd pressed his lips together, and the skin around his eyes was taut. His gaze never left mine. I felt a bit like a mouse under the benign eye of a roly-poly cat who was too full to do more than watch its next prey.

How did my brain come up with this drivel?

"Th-thanks, hockey man. Um, I…"

"Let's get you inside, checked over," Ida Jane said, coming to my side. Blade was in the house now, his bulk visible at the sliding windows.

Ida Jane was the *best* of friends. I squeezed her fingers and let her lead me away, trying not to limp as I put pressure on my left leg.

I looked back in time to see Naese slap Luka's back. "Fucking *epic* how you dove in."

Luka's attention on me never wavered, not even as he took Cruz's hand and rose to his feet, wincing.

CHAPTER 12
Luka

Millie limped off with Ida Jane.

"A possum? Dude, who knew they were even out here?" the rookie chortled.

What was his name? Something douchey… Marcus Waters, maybe. I didn't know—didn't need to know yet. That was Cormac and Maxim's problem. I'd waved off the trainer—no way I was dropping my pants to have him poke at my dick, particularly at a social engagement.

Still, my groin throbbed in a not-so-friendly way when I finally made it into the house, and I couldn't find Millie. Her disappearance made me more anxious than anything else. I knew she'd try to pull some stunt; she was good at ghosting.

I caught her tiptoeing out of a guest room, headed toward the front door.

"And just where do you think you're going?"

She whirled, once again almost toppling over. Millie had always been so graceful—balanced and aware of her body. Clearly, the added bulk of our baby in front was throwing off her game. I strode across the space, getting my palm under her elbow even as she righted herself.

"I…I…"

I closed my eyes—briefly, because I couldn't take my eyes off

Millie. She glowed and her eyes were luminous, drawing me in, but she was treacherous, too. With that devious mind at work, I never knew what she'd do next, except that I wouldn't like it.

Her gaze dropped to my crotch, her cheeks blasted with pink, and she averted her gaze.

"You can look," I said, sidling in closer. "After all, you did more than look before." I paused. "Just last night."

Her cheeks turned an even brighter red. Damn, I loved teasing her.

"Luka," she breathed.

"I like it when you say my name, Millie. I love it more when you scream it."

"I'm eight months pregnant," she snapped, breaking the sensual haze I'd been trying to weave around us. "I'm sure you noted the stretch marks. I'm not for you. Not anymore."

Her words smacked me in the face but also in my chest, burrowing into my heart. "You think I was only with you because of your tight body?"

She looked up at me, furious. But underneath her gritted teeth and anger, I saw the vulnerability. Millie was afraid. Of me.

Correction: of me not wanting her anymore because of the way her body had changed *while carrying my child.*

Of me dropping her like her father had.

Like the douche Trent did when Millie refused to play their twisted game. Ida Jane's words came back to me, Maxim's words: "*She's been hurt.*"

Millie's emotional wounds might well be deeper than mine, and I was going to spend a lot of time teasing them out, like a viciously tight knot.

I stepped closer, using my free arm to cage her in, pulling her near. "I want you to listen to me, and I need you to hear me," I murmured into her ear. "You know what the most sacred thing is to me?"

Her breath caught as she slowly shook her head. But she kept her eyes on the far wall, the stubborn woman.

"*Family*. That matters more than anything," I told her. "I mean *anything*—money, my job, your job, where we live… Anything. I know it because of how I was raised: without one. Because it's what I've craved my *whole* life. And Millicent, you and Bree are *my family*."

She inhaled sharply, tilting her head back, her eyes flashing up to mine. "Luka."

"I adore the way you say my name. Like a prayer and a wish all wrapped up together. I can promise you this, sweetheart: I'll be that for you."

She stared at me, expression open, longing building in her eyes. Her lips relaxed. She lifted her hand to cup my cheek. I nuzzled into her palm, kissing it. Bree started rolling and pushing against Millie's stomach, and I dropped to my knees to press my cheek to her belly.

"Hey, Bree. It's Daddy."

Millie tried to back away, so I wrapped my arms around her hips.

"I think you're going to be a gymnast with all that rolling around," I said. I could feel the faint ridge of Millie's belly button against my upper lip. My image of Millie from that night at Naese's party appeared in my mind. Her stomach had been flat and smooth, her belly button a sweet indentation. Now, it popped outward, like a turkey timer.

"More like a martial artist," Millie said with a wince. I pulled back just as a foot or elbow slammed against the skin.

"Let's get you to the bathroom," I said, rising. "Then you and I need to talk."

Her demeanor changed, becoming colder. "I *can't* stay, Luka."

"Well, you can't go anywhere tonight except to bed."

"You don't understand." She pressed her hands to her belly protectively.

"Then explain it to me," I snapped.

She shuddered, and I didn't think it was because my baby had drop-kicked her organs. Millie's face contorted with fear. "My father is here," she whimpered.

"So?" I asked. "You don't have to see that prick if you don't want to."

"It's not that simple," she said. "He's Chasten Philip Jones IV."

"I know."

"Then you know he'll try to take Bree from me," she said.

Millie

"Over my dead and rotting corpse," Luka snarled.

"You don't understand. My father is controlling."

"That's a nice way of saying a douche gargoyle shit bag," Luka snapped. He inhaled and then blew the breath out through his mouth. "Look, I get the guy has money falling out of his pockets, but you're Bree's *mother*. I'm her *father*. We're raising our kid."

"He has the best lawyers—ones I can't afford, especially after he cut me off from my bank accounts. And he wants to punish me."

"For what?"

I tucked my arms tighter around myself, glancing around, desperate to break this conversation. Bree rolled, and my belly contorted to the right, bulging before resettling.

"I need the bathroom," I squeaked as I hurried back down the hall toward the powder room.

After a few minutes I came stumbling out, more unsteady than when I'd gone in.

Luka leaned against the door, all leopard grace as he shifted his bulk and rose to his full height. His eyes were worried. "Tell me, Millie. Why is your father going to punish you?"

"We…we have bigger problems than my dad." I opened my mouth, shut it, opened it again. "I'm bleeding."

Luka's gaze dropped to my stomach, eyes widening with horror. "Bl-bleeding? From *Bree*?"

I tried to march toward the door, but Luka's arms banded around me. He slid one under my knees and picked me up with ease. There was something so sexy about a man being able to lift me. I felt safe, and that made me uneasy. I knew better.

Yet in that moment, I couldn't help but sigh with relief. I was so damn tired of always trying to think three steps ahead of my father, trying to be strong. I was scared for my baby.

I'd been strong when I'd walked out on Trent and when I'd blended up my engagement ring and couriered it back. I'd been strong when my dad pitched his epic tantrum and issued his ultimatum: I get back with Trent or he'd cut me off and cut me out of his life.

I didn't want to be strong now. I wanted to curl into Luka and let him carry me, carry the burden of my fears. But that wasn't fair, and I refused to do it for long. Yet I needed a minute to orient to the fact that Luka already considered us a team, that he planned to fight for our daughter, for our family. For me.

I heard Ida Jane and her mother asking about me. Luka responded, worry lacing his tone, which had me pressing my nose even tighter to his shoulder. He smelled good. Of course he did. But he also smelled safe.

I was safe with Luka.

He settled me in the car, and we made our trip to the ER in silence.

The middle-aged woman who greeted us with a friendly hand-shake and serene smile got me into a room with shocking speed.

"I'm Dr. Lopez. Keelie called me. I'm her obstetrician. She asked if I could examine you tonight. Luckily, I was on call, and I'm more than happy to help that lovely lady out."

"Keelie's great," Luka said, his voice tense. When I couldn't seem to find my voice, he summarized my health history. Dr. Lopez nodded along.

"Well, let's get you checked out," she said. With a lifted eyebrow, she turned to Luka. "And would you like some ice for your testicles?"

He shifted in his chair, his face a flaming red, so I was surprised when he nodded. "Pretty sore," he muttered, shooting me a look.

"I bet. Quite the heroic move." Dr. Lopez smiled as she pulled one of those crunch-activated ice packs from a drawer. She handed it to Luka, who laid it on his crotch. "You got yourself a good one," she told me.

I met Luka's gaze over her head as she pulled out a paper gown. *Is he mine?*

He'd said he wanted to be, but I'd been such a brat today. And we still needed to talk. He deserved the full story about my family and my history, not just dribbles I let slip because I couldn't hide them any longer.

I just couldn't believe in his goodness. He seemed surreal. Too good to be true.

Especially given his past.

Especially because he was a professional athlete.

Especially because I wanted to find fault, so I didn't have to put myself out there.

"I love you."

I closed my eyes as I laid down on the exam table.

Dr. Lopez checked Bree's heart—"Great!"—that caused my muscles to go lax, and I opened my eyes, meeting Luka's gaze. He reached out and squeezed my hand. I exhaled a trickle at a time, so thankful for his support.

Dr. Lopez wheeled in the cart for another sonogram. "All is well with the baby…" Dr. Lopez stopped and showed us the intact placenta. "With your bleeding, we're concerned about a tear, but the lack of amniotic fluid is very positive."

I understood why Keelie liked this woman. She took her time, making sure we understood each new revelation, each health-re-lated question, before moving on.

"Ah…"

"What does that mean?" Luka asked, panic leeching the color from his face.

I fumbled over, grasping his hand, squeezing it, trying to let him know he wasn't alone. That I loved him, too. I was simply too chicken to say the words.

"Give me just a moment," Dr. Lopez said.

After a pelvic exam, she scooched her chair back and Luka helped me sit up. He threaded his fingers through mine, and I nearly cried at the comfort of his touch. A fleeting thought of how I'd avoided touch for years tried to snag my consciousness, but Dr. Lopez finished typing and met my gaze.

"So, I have good news, which you already know: Bree is healthy. In fact, she's great."

My breath whooshed out in a gush of relief.

Dr. Lopez's lips twitched. "I also have some maybe not so good news." She peered at me, her expression stern. "You can't fly. In fact, you really need to be on bed rest for the duration of your pregnancy."

"What? Why?"

"Because your placenta is thinning and your blood pressure is elevated, which puts you at high risk for preeclampsia. That could be from the fall or from other stressors, but bottom line: getting on a plane, doing anything more than growing your baby, puts her and you at risk."

"But…" I searched for something grounding, something I could break down and reconfigure like I normally would, but my mind was too chaotic to concentrate on the molecular structure of anything in the room. Instead, I stared at my shaking hands until Luka settled his fingers over mine. He wiggled his way in and linked his long fingers between my smaller ones.

My breathing slowed, evened out. I could focus again. I shuddered out a breath as I held on to Luka's hand.

"Can you go over what bed rest entails?" Luka asked.

He pulled out his phone and typed notes as Dr. Lopez offered advice, suggestions, and orders. Luka asked questions, but I couldn't follow them.

Somehow I was at a crossroads that led in both directions to potential doom: stay to keep Bree safe or leave because that was the only way to keep Bree safe, and risk her health.

I remained quiet as we exited the hospital and headed back to Luka's condo. Once we stood in his place, a million thoughts bombarded me all at once.

"My job—" I said, my voice unsteady.

"Will be there when you're ready to go back," Luka said in a calm tone that didn't match the frustration in his eyes. "I'll even fly over there with you. Just don't shut me out. Don't count me out. Okay?"

"O-okay."

"Good." He huffed a breath. "I thought I'd have to argue with you more."

"I'm too tired to fight."

"Then let's get you in bed and tucked in."

"Luka?"

"Yeah?"

"Thank you."

He seemed to deflate even as he kissed my forehead. "You're

not alone now, Millie. We're a team."

"A team. I like that." My lips curved upward. "I've never been part of a team before."

"Well, you are now." Luka winced. "I need to ice my nuts some more."

"Bruised?"

"Yeah."

"I'm sorry—"

"I'm not. Making sure you and Bree were safe was worth it. But that doesn't mean I want it to happen again."

We shuffled through the week—and I mean *shuffled*. I took everything easy because I was worried any sudden movement would pop Bree out of me prematurely. Luka shuffled because of his bruised balls.

But by the end of the week, he moved with his normal effortless grace, whereas I was growing to scary-large size and could no longer bend over to put on my shoes. Not that I needed shoes often.

Luka enjoyed pampering me. In fact, he seemed to revel in the opportunity. He bought a big cookbook filled with healthy recipes, and he'd sit with me after his morning workout with Cruz to develop the day's menu. I found out he was good at cards, especially canasta. That was a game my grandmother had taught me—and Alyssa had taught Luka.

He always gave me time to make my work calls. I was still working, but I knew my bosses weren't happy about my move to America and my lack of ability to be in the office now that drilling had started.

I was seeing Dr. Lopez every week, and today was the second visit since my trip to the ER.

"You both are doing well," Dr. Lopez said with a grin. "While I expect baby Bree to show up early, the bed rest has bought us time to get her lungs more developed and add some much-needed fat to her little body. If you manage another three weeks, Millie, we'll consider Bree full term."

"At thirty-seven weeks?" Luka asked, clearly skeptical, though I remembered Dr. da Silva had said the same at my last visit with her. "I read that before, but why do you push for forty, then?"

Dr. Lopez offered us a breakdown of the baby's growth rate, which Luka studied with fierce concentration, as if willing Bree to stay inside me longer.

He drove us back to his—*our* condo. It was strange to consider that I once again lived in Houston, though for the first time with a man.

He helped me into bed, fiddling with the sheet and gnawing at his lower lip. Finally, he settled his hip on the edge of the bed and stayed there, with me, until I fell asleep.

Luka was attentive and sweet, but I felt more and more an impostor. He'd shown me nothing but love, and I didn't know what to do. Most of the time I wanted to throw myself into his arms, but I worried Luka didn't truly want me. The others hadn't.

We were getting ready for bed about a week later, and my mind chased itself around in circles. But as much as I wanted to talk to Luka about these worries, I couldn't.

Rather, I didn't know how.

"Millie?" he asked as he settled next to me.

"Hmm?"

"If I were to, say…want to make our team more permanent. What would you think?"

I turned so I could look at his face, my brow puckering. "What?"

He cleared his throat. "I, er, I…well, marriage," Luka blurted.

"Marriage." I blinked up at him, mouth fallen open in an O. "You want…you think *marriage*?" I squeaked.

"So that's a no," he said.

I could feel him withdrawing, emotionally, but also literally. Luka rose to his feet and moved away from the bed.

"Is this because of the money?" I asked. My voice cracked.

"What money?"

"My father's money," I said.

"I don't give a single flying fuck about that money. In fact, far as I'm concerned, your shit bag of a father can keep it. Hope he chokes on it," Luka spat.

I struggled out of the bed.

"Why are you getting out of bed?" Luka asked. "You just got in…"

"Because I can't lie there and worry and not see your expression." I stood, my hands on my belly, my eyes growing wider and wider. "Oh…"

"What?" Luka turned and his gaze slid over me, still annoyed until he came to the puddle at my feet.

I wiggled my toes and scrunched my nose at the mess.

"Um…"

"Labor," Luka breathed. He flapped his hands as if trying to calm himself, making a hell of a sight in his boxer briefs and bare chest. But his eyes were wide and his mouth slack, and shit! Shit! He wasn't breathing.

Then I wasn't breathing because the pain in my torso had begun; I wanted to pass out. Before I toppled over in a moaning, sobbing heap, Luka's arms were around me, sheltering me. Holding me.

He was *always* holding me. And I loved that. So, so much.

Dammit. I wanted to finish our conversation about marriage, but I also couldn't breathe. Licks of flame seemed to shoot out of my torso and straight up to my scalp.

Luka murmured into my hair. I had no clue what he said, but the kindness in his deep voice was enough. I latched on to that.

"Okay, sweetheart. You're doing great. Breathe. That's it. Breathe just like we learned. In slow, out slow."

I collapsed against his chest as the last of the tension ebbed from my body. Holy hell. This was labor? It fucking *sucked*.

"I'm going to pick you up—"

"I'm too heavy. Just, just help me to the shower."

"Millie…"

"I don't want the amniotic fluid on my feet. It's sticky. And gross. Plus, labor can last twenty-four hours, so we have time."

Luka paled and swayed a little before he set his jaw. "You will *not* do this for twenty-four fucking hours."

I giggled as I patted his chest. "Bree will come when she's ready. We don't control this show. She does."

He mumbled something that sounded suspiciously like *the fuck I can't* just as another contraction caught me off guard. This one slammed into my belly and wrenched a startled scream past my lips.

"Two minutes and fifty-eight seconds. Holy shit. *Shit.* Hospital! Now. Go bag. Need the go bag. After. I'm holding you. Rubbing your shoulders. Are you breathing? Millie, breathe through the contraction."

I would have laughed at Luka's predicament if my insides weren't trying to push out through my skin. I didn't like labor.

"Keys, bag, wallet, flip-flops for Millie. Call Cormac and Keelie. No, first, call the doctor."

Luka called my obstetrician as he held me, swaying slightly. His obvious care brought tears to my eyes. Even now, in the intensity of this moment, Luka somehow managed to give me everything I'd dreamed a life with him could be. Another contraction seized my body, and I dropped into a squat, trying to find a position that eased the unbearable ache in my hips, lower back, and belly. Luka dropped his phone as he sought to soothe me.

"Dr. Lopez will meet us at the hospital. We just need to get you there." He repeated that over again.

Someone pounded on the door just as the last of the cramp eased. I froze, shock and fear searing through my system.

"Who?" A terrible thought crossed my mind. "Trent?" I squeaked. We hadn't heard from him since the airport, and I'd been waiting.

Luka stared back at me, wide-eyed, still shirtless and in his underwear. "I don't know. I'll get it—"

"Don't leave me," I squealed, clutching him tighter. Rational? No way. But Luka was my security.

"Okay. We'll go together. Can you move?"

"Y-yes." I stepped forward, but it was more of a shuffle, made even more inelegant because I was clutching Luka's arm. We eased our way slowly toward the door, and I flinched when another round of pounding rattled the locks.

"I heard Millie crying," Cruz rumbled. "You okay?"

"It's Cruiser," Luka mumbled. "See? All good. Just let me grab the door. I won't let go, Millie. I have you…"

Luka leaned forward and gripped the door handle with his fingertips just as Cruz flung it open, nearly catching Luka's nose. He stumbled back with a yelp that sent him—and me—against the back of the sofa. Luka cradled me gently as he glared at Cruz.

"The fuck, man?" Luka began.

"She's in labor?" Cruz asked, no nonsense.

"Yes," I said. Another contraction ramped up. "I don't want to do this anymore…"

"I got you, Millie. You're doing so well with your breathing," Luka cooed. But his eyes were wide.

"*You* breathe, hockey man. And have this baby," I gritted. "I don't want to!" The last ended in a shriek.

"Definitely labor," Cruz said. "I'm grabbing her bag—"

"And her flip-flops," Luka said.

"And flip-flops. Then you should put on some clothes so we can get to the hospital. I'll drive your car so you can sit in the back with her."

"Solid plan," Luka said.

It was. Once Luka dressed and I had my flip-flops, I walked down the steps by myself, and we only had to stop once for another contraction. We settled in the car, and I heaved a sigh of relief.

"Twenty minutes," Luka said, stroking my hair away from my sweating cheeks. "Then you'll see your doctor and get an epidural, and—shit! Millie, I need my fingers. Not so hard, sweetheart."

CHAPTER 13
Luka

I wiggled my fingers, wincing at the fierceness of Millie's grip as Cruz made a deep growly grunt that meant trouble.

"What?" I asked, looking up and out the window at the Houston gridlock. Ahead, barely visible, were blue and red flashing lights.

No! No, no, no, no. Not now. Millie needed the hospital. She and Bree were counting on me to make this right.

"Accident," Cruz said. His teeth flashed for a moment as he grimaced. "New, by the looks of it."

"Well, *do* something."

"And just what would you have me do?" he asked.

Millie whimpered as another contraction hit her. She pressed her palms against the sides of her belly and panted. I murmured to her, trying to calm my desperate heartbeat. I wasn't good at this shit. I needed a plan I could attack—boxes I could tick.

Millie needed care.

"Two choices, man: either go along the shoulder until you can drive up on the feeder or come sit back here, hold Millie's hand, and let me do it."

"Man," Cruz whined. "Those options suck."

"You wanted to drive," I reminded him.

He shot me an evil look before easing out of the line and onto the shoulder. "If I get a ticket, you're paying for it."

"Deal. Now get us to the hospital. The contractions are closer together."

Millie's cheeks flushed. Between contractions, she was great, but these seemed intense. And Bree was early. *Five weeks* early. That couldn't be good. Babies needed time to add fat and finish their lungs. That's what Dr. Lopez had said last week at our visit.

So, yeah, I was freaking out, replaying every word I'd read about preemies as I held Millie against my chest to reduce the bouncing.

Cruz floored the SUV up a slight embankment…and directly at a police cruiser. The cop stood out front, arms akimbo, sour expression pronounced even behind his sunglasses.

Cruz cursed and rolled to a stop. Millie stiffened, whimpering, seeking my hand to crush. I winced but kept my mouth shut since her body was the one trying to push out a baby.

The officer swaggered over and Cruz rolled down the window as I walked Millie through the *e-e-e*s and *oh-oh-oh*s from the videos we'd watched.

The officer leaned against the window frame, confident in the law. "You realize you're in violation—"

"I'm in fucking labor," Millie screamed.

The officer rolled back on his heels, fingertips gripping the window frame. "Ma'am…"

"Unless you plan to escort us with your lights flashing and sirens," Millie growled past teeth clenched so tightly I heard them squeak. "I suggest you move your ass."

"Um…" Cruz gave the officer an apologetic look.

"She's not normally so feisty," I added.

"I'll show you feisty," Millie screamed. She gripped my fingers even harder.

"Shit! That hurts," I said. "Stop trying to rip them off."

"Um…" The officer lost his swagger and turned pale. "Yeah, so…maybe you, you should, um, follow me to the hospital."

"You got it," I said, flashing him a smile. "The faster the better," I added.

Cruz heaved a massive sigh and gave me another dirty look in the rearview mirror. "She is too feisty."

"I'm right here," Millie shot back. "Shut your face and drive the car."

Cruz raised an eyebrow but did as he was told. By the time we arrived at the hospital, Millie had had six more contractions and now sobbed softly between them. I hated seeing her like this, and the impotency of being unable to relieve her pain broke something loose in my chest.

The officer had rushed in and grabbed a wheelchair for us so that by the time I helped Millie out of the car, she could drop right into it.

"Thanks, man, for escorting us. I gotta go in with my… Millie, but I will send you some signed gear."

"I'll take care of this," Cruz said, shooing me off.

Much as I wanted to bolt forward, I couldn't risk Millie, so I settled for a sedate pace. The good news about active labor? You don't have to wait in the waiting room. Another good thing about active labor? The staff puts your woman directly in a delivery room.

The really terrible thing about active labor?

"No drugs," the doctor said, a hint of regret settling over her features. "But this will be over soon."

"Now," Millie gasped. "I want her out *now*."

Dr. Lopez had helped get Millie out of her wet pants and underwear as I washed up. They draped Millie in a sheet, over her bent knees, as I took position by her head. I gave her my right hand this time, unsure my left one could take any more squeezing.

I kissed Millie's temple. "You're doing so well."

She looked up at me, her green-gray eyes filled with hope and worry. "She'll be okay, right, Luka?"

I smiled at her. "You both will."

"Okay," Millie whispered. Her face contorted. "Oh, God… another one."

"You're dilated to nine centimeters," Dr. Lopez said. "My guess is this girl is coming soon."

"Now," Millie said. She chanted again and again: now, now, now.

One nurse smiled at me before she turned to offer Millie advice about her breathing.

"Then you do it," Millie snarled at her. Her name tag read Olivia, and when she looked at me with hurt in her eyes, Millie tried to crawl off the bed to get at her.

"He's mine, Olivia," Millie yelled. "Mine! I've loved him forever, and no one else will ever love him like I do." As I reeled from that statement, Millie turned toward me, eyes wet with tears. "For the love of God, Luka, am I going to chase women out of my delivery room?"

"No, sweetheart," I said. "Of course I'm yours. I love you, too."

A thrill rippled over me, the hairs on my arms standing on end. Yes, that was right. Even if Millie had told me she loved me for the first time while wrestling a tiny human from her body.

"That did it, Millie," the doctor announced. "You're fully dilated, so you can push with the next contraction."

My moment on cloud nine faded as Millie pushed and strained, panted and screamed. No wonder this was called *labor*. I'd worked hard my whole life to get in the shape to play professional hockey at an elite level. But never had I seen anyone work as hard as Millie did to bring Bree into the world.

Worry settled in as Millie turned toward me. Her eyes had lost their sheen, her hair was plastered to her head from sweat and tears, and even her lips were pale—nearly bloodless.

"I can't do it anymore," she whimpered.

"Yes, you can," I said. I sent Dr. Lopez a frantic look. "She can, right?"

Dr. Lopez's expression pinched with worry, but she nodded. "The baby's in the birth canal. I can see the top of her head. We just need a couple of good pushes to get her out."

"You can do that, sweetheart. I know you can."

Millie was already shaking her head. "I can't. I really can't. Oh…ohh…" Another contraction hit her. Olivia pressed on Millie's belly, just under her breasts.

"That was good, Millie. The baby's crowning," Dr. Lopez said. But I heard the unease in her voice and saw her glance at the monitors. Millie slumped back, tears of exhaustion leaking from her eyes.

I toed off my shoes and clambered up on the bed. I levered Millie upward, as I'd seen in some of the birth videos, and let her head rest in the crook on my shoulder, brushing Olivia's hands off Millie's belly.

"Tell me when to push," I said to Dr. Lopez.

Millie inhaled, a sure sign of another contraction. Dr. Lopez gave me a nod. I pressed both hands downward against the hard ball of Millie's stomach.

She screamed.

I grunted.

Bree slid out.

Dr. Lopez crowed.

Millie slumped back against me, her body trembling. I was shaking, too. *Intense.* There was no other word for this experience.

"She's not crying," Millie whispered.

"Bree?" I asked Dr. Lopez, clutching Millie to my chest.

"Just need to clear her nasal passage…"

The sweetest wail rose above our broken breaths.

"Oh, she's got a good set of lungs," Dr. Lopez exclaimed.

"What's her APGAR?" I asked, biting on my lip.

Dr. Lopez gave me an approving look—like I gave a fuck if she was impressed that I knew that test's name. I needed to know my daughter had passed it. "Nine. We'll check her again in a couple of minutes, but she's strong and healthy. Congratulations, you two!"

"Our girl, sweetheart," I whispered, kissing Millie's hairline, her cheek, her neck. "You did it."

I bet she'd really scored a ten but the doctor didn't want to tell me that, what with the room for improvement and all. Still, I was sure Bree was a ten in all ways. She was mine and Millie's kid, so of course she was perfect.

"I want to hold her," Millie said, her voice shaking.

"After we cut the cord. Dad?" Dr. Lopez handed me a pair of scissors, and Olivia steadied my hand enough for me to cut the umbilical cord.

The nurses huddled around, oohing and ahhing. Dr. Lopez checked her another time, then beamed at me. "A perfect ten APGAR."

I fucking knew it.

Dr. Lopez laid Bree on Millie's chest, her tiny body against Millie's soft, pale skin. Goo covered our baby that caused her dark hair to stick to her tiny skull. Her fingers were long, her nails smaller than anything I'd ever seen. She blinked her blue eyes, frowning at the lights. I cupped my hands over Millie's, thrilling all over again at the perfection of this moment.

I had a daughter.

Millie loved me.

Life was perfect.

Millie

I'd known Trent would tell my father I was in town, and pregnant.

What I didn't realize was just how callously my father would make his possession of this knowledge known. I had Bree at my breast—we'd been in the room barely three hours—when a man walked in. He wore an expensive suit and a predatory expression.

"Millicent Jones?"

I remained silent.

"Who's asking?" Luka demanded.

The man smirked. "I represent Chasten Jones. He asked me to deliver these."

I clutched Bree, my heart hammering.

"And just what are those?"

The man's smirk turned into a full-blown grin. I wondered if he'd ever lost a case. Probably not. I shuddered.

"Mr. Jones is seeking custody of his grandchild, considering Ms. Jones' clear lack of capability."

Luka vibrated with rage. "That's my child."

The attorney shrugged. "Is it, though? Ms. Jones has a… history."

I didn't bother to listen to more. I stared down at my baby, my vision going black at the edges.

My father planned to dredge up my high school years. I wasn't proud of those, but I'd needed a connection. And boys had offered a short-term one.

The smarmy attorney strolled out of the room.

"You had a baby *four hours ago*, and he thinks now is the time to bring up a custody battle?"

"Welcome to my world," I said with a long sigh. "This is what I was trying to protect you from."

Luka considered me for a moment, and I could tell he was working something out in his mind. "I'll be back."

He was gone.

"How did your father find out about Bree so quickly?" Ida Jane asked as she sashayed into the room. Keelie followed, her baby bump still in the adorable stage. She took in the room and me before she dropped her packages in a chair and strode toward my bed, peering down at Bree.

"Oh my gosh. She's tiny! May I hold her?" Keelie's eyes begged me.

"Of course. She is. And beautiful," I beamed.

"Adorable," Ida Jane said, coming to stand next to Keelie, a soft, lovely expression on her face. She'd always wanted kids. Me not so much. We'd both expected her to have a baby first.

Ida Jane pursed her lips and narrowed her eyes. "Did you know there's a blond nurse out there flirting with the guys—even *our* guys? Maxim doesn't like her."

"Is her name Olivia?" I asked.

"Yep."

"Mmm... She was flirting with Luka while I was in labor."

We all shook our heads. That was one of the hardest parts of being with a professional athlete. They had constant female attention—and it was like we, their significant others, didn't exist. Why would women treat other women that way?

"Leave that to me," Ida Jane called over her shoulder as she twirled around, heading right back out the door.

A shocked gasp followed by, "Oh, hell no!" had me scrambling from the bed.

I'd already wrapped myself in the robe Luka had bought me, so I tottered toward the door, shocked by the ache in my hips and the instability in my legs.

"You go back inside there with Millie," Ida Jane said to Luka as she glared daggers at Olivia, who seemed to shrink into herself. "I'll deal with this...this..."

"What's going on?" I asked.

Keelie peeked over my shoulder. Bree nestled in her arms.

"I caught Olivia propositioning—"

"I said no, but she was relentless," Luka said, his eyes pleading. He was desperate for me to believe he hadn't stepped into the hall to be with another woman as I recovered from childbirth.

"I should have brought my golf clubs," Keelie muttered.

Ida Jane continued to speak, telling me about Luka's hands above his head and his face turned away. I never took my eyes off of Luka. He held my gaze, the love he'd proclaimed for me shining in his eyes and outward, toward me, keeping me warm.

He'd told me before, but I hadn't believed him. Even when he'd told me earlier today while I was screaming and raging, I'd been sure he was humoring me. But now I was sure.

Luka *loved me*.

I burst into tears. He moved toward me, and Keelie backed into the room, making shushing noises to the baby.

"Now you've done it," Ida Jane said, her tone dark. "Oh, I am going to unleash—"

"No unleashing those, Fists," Maxim said, coming up behind Ida Jane. "Cormac and I found the doctor and had a talk with her."

Dr. Lopez stood between the men, eying Olivia like she was rotted cabbage. Olivia tried to dart away, but for a tiny thing, Ida Jane was quick. Came from having so many brothers.

"I'd never," Luka began. I clutched his T-shirt, pulling him toward me, needing his warm arms around me as I nuzzled into his chest.

"I know," I sobbed. "But how *rude!*"

More hospital staff crowded around. "She showed me pictures of him," another nurse piped up, pointing to Luka. "That she took in L&D."

"She *what?*" Dr. Lopez snarled, stalking toward Olivia like a tiger to its prey. "Well, that's not just inappropriate, that breaks HIPAA."

And the pieces clicked. I gasped. Luka looked down at me in concern.

"That's how he knew, Luka!" I turned toward Dr. Lopez. "I need to know who Olivia shared those pictures with. And if she contacted my father, Chasten Jones."

Luka's growl was too soft for anyone but me to hear. His arms tightened around me. "I'm calling my lawyer."

I tipped my head back and frowned. "You don't have one."

"He does now," Maxim said. He and Cormac glowered at Olivia. "I called Lance Colleson about this."

"Good," Luka said. "We'll have him come to us." He kissed my temple.

As if you simply requested one of the most sought-after attorneys to make a house call. I guess in this situation, you did. I swayed, and I wasn't sure if it was from having Bree or from the weirdness that had become my life.

"Until this is sorted, Bree doesn't leave our sight," Luka said.

Cruz, who'd just made it to us and held a cup of coffee from the cafeteria in his hand, stepped into the hospital room, no doubt to stand sentry over Bree.

"You really think he'd kidnap a newborn?" Ida Jane asked.

I looked over at Olivia, noting how pale she'd become. "I think that's exactly what he planned, and I believe we'll be able to prove it once we get her phone."

Olivia whimpered, twisting her hands. Maxim and Cormac seemed to puff as their need to protect reared up. They towered over her, their disapproval radiating.

The rest of the staff murmured.

"Show's over," Luka said. He clutched me to him as he headed back into our room.

Keelie still held Bree when we entered, her slight frame hunched over our baby while Cruz stood, legs powerful and spread wide, in front of her.

"He's right. I'll take Olivia straight to HR," Dr. Lopez said from behind us. "Where I'll call the police." She turned toward her. "Don't even think about touching your phone."

Luka edged me toward the bed. There, he cupped my shoulders and bent his knees so we were at eye level.

"Okay?" he asked.

"Too much happened today." My lower lip quivered. "I want to go home."

"Soon, sweetheart." Luka scooped me into his arms and lowered me into the waiting bed. "As soon as you're cleared, I'll take you and Bree home."

When he moved back, I clutched him tighter. "Don't leave me."

"Never." He kissed my forehead and rearranged so he was in the bed with me. "Bree okay?"

"She's perfect and still asleep," Keelie said, but she made no move to lay Bree back in the bassinet.

If my friend hadn't been holding her, I would have snatched her up. But I was so tired. I inhaled as I tried to stop the tremors pulsing through my body. But nothing could shake the chill of just how far my father would go to get his way.

He wanted Bree—except he didn't care about *her*. Not at all. He cared about what she represented: billions of dollars. Power. Status.

And I couldn't let my father near my daughter. I never, ever wanted her to meet the man.

Arriving back at Luka's apartment the next day was a relief, even as the anxiety—and fear—of being responsible for a tiny, sweet little human overwhelmed me.

I couldn't care for an infant. I took in the moment, trying to think—that had become harder and harder, even before my father's full frontal assault on my parental rights to Bree. Warmth spread across my back as Luka wrapped his arms around me and the sleeping bundle I couldn't seem to let go.

"I'm scared," I whispered.

"I am, too."

I tilted my head up to look into those mesmerizing sherry eyes. "Of what?"

Luka stared down at me for a long moment. Our breathing meshed, and I leaned against him, trusting as I'd trusted no one since my mother's death, or since Ida Jane came into my life. She'd be over tomorrow to snuggle Bree while I showered or napped or whatever else I was supposed to do. Something else to learn.

"Of failing you. Not being a good father. Of somehow

hurting or neglecting her. Your father taking her from us." His throat seemed to seize, and he made a choked sound.

I inched away from him and laid Bree in the crib. Luka had pushed to finish the room early, and I was so glad now. Because of his motivation, we had a completed nursery to welcome our baby girl into, even though she'd come a month earlier than expected. The sheet was cool, and she looked so tiny, bundled up in her blankets and wearing a cap atop her fuzzy head. The baby doll Luka had bought once I told him I was pregnant sat on the shelf next to a stack of diapers. Our daughter would need more toys, but none would be as special to me as that doll.

The pang I felt melted as I turned, wrapping my arms around Luka. I swayed with him as I had with our baby.

"You'll be the best daddy," I said. Again, that noise. His fears ran deep—his demons brought on by disinterest, neglect. Not that different from my own, really. I rolled up on the balls of my feet and kissed his chin. His stubble abraded my lips, but I didn't mind. "I know that because of how you cared for me—us—in the hospital. By the way you look at her when you hold her. By the way you've transformed your condo into a home for her."

"For you both," he corrected.

I smiled even as I tightened my arms around him. "For us."

We were quiet. Bree's breaths pelted the air like tiny butterflies. I relaxed into the sound because I knew she was close. She was safe.

"Would you marry me, Luka?" I squeezed my eyes shut so tightly that the pressure caused them to ache.

"Are you proposing?" he asked, amusement in his voice.

My breath stuttered. "If I am? I mean…to protect Bree."

He gathered me closer, dropped his cheek against my hair. "Stop that. Just stop, Millie."

"S-stop?"

"You don't have to protect yourself from me. I want what you want: to make sure Bree's safe. But also to make you happy—to make me happy. So, if you're asking me to marry you, I'd say yes."

I blew out a breath and leaned into the fear eddying around me. Luka was the giant boulder keeping the swirling current at bay. Unmovable, stubborn, beautiful man.

I slipped from his arms and dropped to my knees in front of him. He smirked even as he petted my hair back from my now-burning cheeks. I didn't want him to change. Ever. I loved his mischievousness. I loved his sly innuendo. His stamina. His wonder in us.

"I…" I began, my voice clear in the quiet. The room's shadows enhanced the bubble effect. It was just us and Bree. She was here for this unplanned but perfect moment. "I love you, Luka. And I want to make you mine. Forever."

Luka's gaze softened, and he shifted, as if to settle on his knees, too. I shook my head, planting my palms on his thighs to hold him steady. His grin turned devilish, but his eyes remained full of emotion. He opened his mouth, but again, I shook my head. My heart pounded in the hollow of my chest, blood whooshing in my ears.

I stared up at him, dizzy from nerves. "Will you marry me?" I whispered.

His thick thighs shifted as he dropped down, still towering

over me, his palm cradling my skull while the other captured my cheek and chin.

"I'd be so fucking honored. And I've been yours, *just* yours since I sat across from you at that restaurant. You're mine, Millicent Anne Jones—soon to be Stol. I can't wait to make it official."

Instead of kissing me as I expected, Luka leaned back and laughed. It was a deep, joyous sound. He collected me closer, pressing my cheek to his chest.

"I get to be the Bridezilla," he crowed. "Man, I'm going to love ordering Cruz around."

I clutched his shirt as I giggled at the image of Cruz's hulking mass in a pastel bridesmaid dress, his massive paws clutching a bouquet. Luka must have had the same image because he guffawed, tipping backward, taking me with him so I lay atop his big body. I shifted my hips as the bulge in his pants grew.

"Fuuuuuuck." He dragged out the word as his hands slid from my nape, down my back to cup my hips. Somehow, someway, Luka Stol made me feel sexier than any other woman alive with a newborn in the crib mere feet from us and me in maternity leggings.

That was the moment I knew I didn't just love Luka Stol; he owned my heart.

I'd broken my promise never to let another man inside. But Luka Stol wasn't just in my heart. Like our daughter, he'd imprinted on my soul.

~

Luka's phone rang the following morning. I only knew it was morning based on the light coming into the condo. Multiple diaper changes and attempts to breastfeed had punctuated the dark hours.

I groaned and Luka searched for his phone, too tired, it seemed, to even raise his head.

"Hello?" he finally mumbled.

"Luka, Mom's in ICU."

He must have put the phone on speaker because I jolted first at the deep voice, then at the words.

Luka sat up. He rubbed his eyes. "Mike, slow down. Alyssa's in the hospital?"

"Yeah. She's…well, she's bad, man."

"Millie had our daughter yesterday…"

"You're going to be with her, Luka," I said. I settled my hand on his thigh, right above his knee, and squeezed. There was no give—his muscles were clenched tightly. "She needs you."

"You need me," Luka snapped. "After what your father tried at the hospital, not only do you need me, but we also need a freaking army—"

"Is that Millie?" Mike asked. "Hey, Millie. I've heard a lot about you from Mom."

"Erm…hi, Mike!" I said, nerves skittering through me. "I'll make sure Luka gets on a flight to see Alyssa." I glanced over, wondering if I should tell him Luka had asked that Bree's middle name be Alyssa. Luka hadn't mentioned it, probably because he was busy glowering.

"I'm not leaving you," he growled. "I don't want to miss—"

I leaned forward and ended the call. Luka grunted but didn't seem overtly angry with my decision.

"I know how much she means to you," I whispered as I turned toward him. "At least I think I do. You talk about her a lot—way more than your mother."

He flinched. "Alyssa *is* my mother—at least the closest thing I had to a real one."

I clutched his hand. "Right. Which is why you need to be there with her. You'll regret it if you're not there."

"But you won't come with me."

I cupped his cheeks with my hands. "I don't think it's smart for me to take a two day old on a plane. But I can give you these last moments with her. Please, Luka. Please go to her. I don't want you to regret not seeing her…"

His frown deepened. "The way your voice broke—you're thinking about your mom."

I nodded. "I didn't get to see her at the end. My dad wouldn't let me go to the hospital. I never got to say…" I inhaled, exhaled slowly. Closed my eyes and waited for the threat of tears to dissipate enough for me to lift my head and meet Luka's gaze again. "I was thinking about how excited she'd be for us. To meet Bree."

"Alyssa's been psyched about having a baby to spoil."

A poignant bubble burst in my chest. I wanted that for Luka, for Bree. I rested my head against him and squeezed my eyes shut. "I'll miss you."

"Give me the other words," he said.

"They're hard for me," I whispered. "I haven't ever said them to a man."

"That's why they'll help me get through our separation."

I inhaled, trying not to think about the boys I'd fucked to

finally feel closeness. "I love you, Luka."

His arms banded around me. "I love you, too. And I'm psyched as hell to get married."

I smiled. "Dr. Lopez said I shouldn't have sex for at least two months."

"I know."

"Do you want to wait for that? I mean, for a wedding night?" My cheeks burned.

"Do you?"

"I…"

"We've had a glorious night of sheet-ripping passion," Luka said. "I can wait a little while for another one."

"When?" I gaped. "Did we *really* rip the sheets?"

His lips twitched, but the sadness in them remained. "Don't worry. I bought Naese new ones."

"That doesn't make me feel any better," I mumbled.

"Should. It's mighty hard to tatter up five-hundred-thread-count imported cotton."

I took a deep breath. "Okay, so wedding soon."

"Yes to the wedding soon." He looked at me a long moment and raised an eyebrow. "But don't decide we have an expiration date while I'm away."

CHAPTER 14
Luka

"What do you mean?" she asked.

"We'll have to figure out what happens when your maternity leave ends," I told her. "Then you'll take my daughter across the world, right in the middle of the season, so I have no chance of seeing her?"

Her face fell. "I don't know. I can't—Luka, don't ask me…"

Her expression appeared tortured, but I was being tortured. If she still intended to leave Houston, to take Bree away, I'd miss weeks, possibly months of her life. Dammit. I didn't want to leave her. Not now. We had to sort this out. Plus, I was worried about her health and Bree's, but I was also selfish and wanted to bask in the affection she offered me, keep her close so she wouldn't think about leaving.

I needed a minute to collect myself before I did something utterly stupid like drop to my knees and beg, or threaten something I didn't mean. Now wasn't the time to make those kinds of decisions anyway. I headed down the hall, trying to clear my mind.

Millie and I weren't as different as I'd thought. She was starved for love, just as I was. With Bree, we'd be a *family*. Stronger together. I needed to get Millie to see that. And I needed help. Millie's father would keep trying to take Bree from us. I chewed on my lip, considering my options.

I needed to call Coach. He was my best plan. My only plan, really. Looked like I was going to swallow my pride. I clenched my jaw. For Millie, for my precious daughter, I'd eat as much humble pie as Coach forced down my throat. That didn't make placing the call any easier. But as Alyssa used to say, "*Doing right isn't always the same as doing easy.*"

I nearly dropped the phone as I found his contact. My hands were sweaty as I paced through the living room, too agitated to sit still.

"Stolly, I'm glad you called," Coach said when he answered. "How are Millie and the baby?"

I didn't waste energy on wondering how Coach knew so many personal details of my life. "That's part of what I wanted to talk to you about." I rubbed the back of my neck as I explained Millie's situation, and Alyssa's.

"Mmm… So you need to go out of town and are worried about Millie's father and his threats?"

"I am." My heart pounded.

"I'm sure Paloma and the CATS can set up a rotating visitation sheet to help Millie out while you're in Detroit."

I blew out a breath. "That'd be great. I don't want her to be alone." I hesitated. "I think it may be best if there were a couple of CATS here…or a player." I headed toward the bedroom and peeked inside, pleased to see Millie asleep. A pang hit me. I wouldn't get to hold her tomorrow night. I'd miss out on Bree's constant diaper needs. The days were slipping past, and I couldn't catch them, hold them tight enough. "But I'm not sure that's enough," I murmured.

"Why not?"

I crept back to the living room and into the laundry area, I closed the door and leaned against the machine to avoid waking Millie.

I didn't want to have this conversation, yet I had to see it through. Millie's happiness, our future, depended on it. "I heard Gunnar's been considering selling part ownership of the team to Chasten Jones. Millie's father."

"I can't confirm that," Coach said.

"Well, I can tell you it's a shit idea," I snapped.

"You're worried about what?" Coach countered. "Nepotism?"

I gritted my teeth. "Actually, I'm worried because he's suing for custody of my *kid*. I thought you might have some advice on how best to ensure that doesn't happen, especially since you went through something similar with Trixie. Clearly, I was mistaken."

"That's a hell of a thing to say, Luka—"

I hung up before I said or did something stupid, like chew out my coach. Shoving my phone into my pocket, I rested both hands on the washer and dropped my head forward.

After a bitter string of curses, I straightened, intending to look into a flight to Detroit. I knew Millie was right, and I'd regret not doing my utmost to see Alyssa again before… It took just a few minutes to find a flight that left later today.

I entered the bedroom quietly and went into the closet. I shut the door and turned on the light. I packed enough clothes for a few days.

Millie was still asleep when I tiptoed to the bathroom to grab my toiletries. I'd just finished throwing those into the suitcase when I heard a knock on the door.

I shut the bedroom door before I strode down the hall. I rolled my eyes when I saw Coach standing in the hallway.

"What do you want?" I asked as I cracked open the door.

"First, to apologize," he said.

Well, that wasn't what I expected. I opened the door wider and ushered him inside. He glanced around, seeming surprised to find the place tidy.

He shoved his hands into the pockets of his khakis. "Cruz sent me copies of the documents the lawyer dropped off at the hospital." He paled, his lips pressed into a disapproving line. His gaze darted down the hallway. "Is she okay?"

"With what?" I asked. Exhaustion hit me hard. I walked to the couch and settled on the edge.

"All of it…"

I glanced up at him. "I doubt it. She didn't want to be here."

Coach settled into the armchair. "I can understand why."

"Clearly, her father's willing to take her child away. And we had a run-in with that piece-of-shit ex."

He nodded. "At the airport. It was on the socials. *That's* the guy her father wanted her to marry?"

"Yeah. Hand-picked. He's being groomed to take over the business."

Coach pursed his lips. "I'm going to make sure Gunnar knows."

I met his gaze, willing him to answer when I asked. "Why would you tell the team owner?"

Coach hesitated, then looked away. "He should know, that's all."

I sighed, giving up on that for now. "Okay, but my bigger concern is making sure Millie's safe while I'm out of town."

Coach clasped his hands between his spread knees. "You don't have to worry about a thing there, Luka." His expression was earnest. "Paloma's already working on a schedule so one guy is always here with her. If that can't happen, we'll move her into our guest room. No way will we leave her alone. She's a Wildcatter, same as you."

I took a deep breath and met my coach's eyes. "Not sure I want to stay one if Gunnar plans to sell even a portion of the team to an asshole like Chasten Jones."

Millie

I clutched at the neck of my T-shirt. When I went to the bathroom and found Luka's toiletries missing, I'd panicked. Now, though, I wondered if I should have stayed in bed, preferably with my head buried under the pillow.

A shiver rippled down my spine as I stood in the hallway, setting the hair on my arms on end. They were talking about my father—the man who had photographic evidence of the guys I'd slept with during and after high school. Ten. I'd tried ten different times to find someone to love me. I'd failed not just at relationships, but at sex. That was the reason I'd slept with Luka. I'd just thought he'd give me fireworks. Instead, he gave me everything I ever wanted.

And my father could take it all away by showing everyone my mistakes. I laid my hand against the wall, woozy.

"Not sure I would either," Coach Whittaker said. His distaste was obvious. "Which is why I'll bring this up to Gunnar first chance I get."

Luka's eyes rounded as he jumped off the couch, moving toward me with the speed of a professional athlete. "Why are you out of bed?" he asked. His warm palm engulfed my elbow.

"I heard voices…" I looked up at him, my heart still thundering. *What have you done, Luka?*

"Millie, this is Silas Whittaker, the Wildcatters head coach. Coach, this is Millie." He beamed a smile of pride toward his coach.

"What's…what's going on?" I asked.

"A pleasure to meet you, Millie," Silas said, his smile and tone pleasant. "Paloma plans to be here later."

"Okaaaaaay." I drew out the word, confusion and possibly exhaustion making me slow to understand.

Luka led me to the couch, where he cuddled in close. "I'm packed and have a flight out in a couple of hours. Cruz is in the building in case you need anything. Then Paloma's going to organize the CATS and players, so you're not alone while I'm gone."

I nodded slowly. "I appreciate that. Having help with Bree…" I swallowed. "What does that have to do with my father?"

I caught Silas' flinch from the corner of my eye. He strolled forward and perched on the edge of the armchair. "When Luka called me earlier, I wasn't the listener he needed or deserved."

Luka's shock reverberated from his hand and up his arm. I leaned in closer, offering a modicum of the comfort he seemed to always be offering me.

"I came here to apologize, and he mentioned your father. I

don't like what I've learned, Millie."

I flinched, my heart rate escalating. Luka wrapped an arm tighter around me.

Silas raised his hands, palms out. "Not about *you*. Your father. What he's done to you…" He smashed his lips together, his nostrils flaring. "I have a daughter. I cannot imagine ever, ever treating her like…"

"Like my father treated me."

Silas gave a stiff nod.

I looked at my lap. These two men held much of my current situation and future in their hands. In some ways, I hadn't carved out the independence I'd been so desperate to achieve. Not even by moving to Sri Lanka. I still relied on men to help me navigate my world. While only half the population, men in my life held higher-paid and higher-level positions than me or most of my female friends.

I was so damn tired of not being able to stand on my own two feet.

"I understand if you'd like to ask me questions."

"Me? No." Silas shook his head. He caught Luka's gaze. "But Gunnar may have some."

"The owner of the team?" I asked.

Silas nodded.

"I don't want him badgering her," Luka said.

"Understood."

"But I meant what I said before," he added. "I know it may not matter that much, but I won't play for a team that takes money from a man like Chasten Jones."

Silas dipped his head. "I heard you loud and clear—and I get where you're coming from." He glanced at me before meeting Luka's eyes again. "Completely."

Again, Luka jolted. This conversation was so full of emotion, and I wasn't at my best to tease them out.

Silas cleared his throat. "I'll let you two get some rest. Cruz will be here before you head out, Luka."

Luka gave my shoulder a gentle squeeze, then rose. "Thanks, Coach."

"You got it, Stolly."

Silas offered me his hand. "Nice to meet you, Millie."

"You, too."

Bree's cry split the moment of silence after the door closed behind him. Luka headed toward the nursery, and I followed.

"What just happened?" I asked.

Luka's brows tugged together over his nose. "I'm not sure."

"If I understood that, you requested a trade rather than play for a team that might be owned by my father."

"Yeah, I did."

I bit my trembling lip, but shivers had taken over my body. " My father's never, ever shown any interest in sports. Ever. What does that *mean*, Luka?"

He slid his hands under Bree's tiny body and moved her to the changing pad. "Exactly what I told you before. I got you. You and Bree and me—we're a team. The most important one."

Once Bree was in a fresh diaper, he handed her to me and I settled in the rocking chair.

While the baby nursed, worry ate at me. Because Luka was

ready to give up his life here, knowing I'd not relinquished my life in Sri Lanka.

That didn't make us partners. Not at all.

Luka left for the airport later that morning, and good to Coach Whittaker's word, Paloma showed up just after lunch, relieving Cruz from babysitting duty. He'd only been here an hour or so, but the poor man seemed way too strung out for his own good. He promised to come back by that evening with dinner, and even as I thanked him, I was strategizing about how best to get him to spill the tea on his unhappy vibe.

Paloma shut the door behind him and looked at me. "Would you like me to hold your sweet pea while you take a nap?" she asked.

"You're welcome to hold her, but I'd prefer to stay on the couch."

Paloma nodded. "Oh, I get it. I wouldn't let this little peanut out of my sight either. Aren't you precious?" Paloma murmured to Bree. "It's been a long time since I've handled a newborn." Yet she held Bree with confidence, which helped me relax into the cushions. "Care to tell me what's going on with Lennon?" she asked.

I frowned. "Cruz's first name is *Lennon*?"

Paloma nodded, her eyes dancing.

"Oh, my… That's freaking *hot*," I whispered.

She settled in the chair her husband had sat in last night, resting Bree's tiny weight against her chest. Bree went boneless in a way that told me she would soon be asleep. "I know! It's almost too much…until I tell you he can *sing*."

"Get out." I gasped. "Like, well?"

She patted Bree's tiny, diapered butt. "Dreamy."

"That's a lot of potency," I murmured.

"Don't let Stolly hear you say that."

"He's potent, too," I said.

"They're professional athletes. Goes with the territory." She adjusted her position. "So, what did he tell you about why he's so stressed? I've never seen him like this."

I nibbled my lip. "He mentioned a woman bothering him about the dog he just rescued."

Paloma raised an eyebrow.

"An Army veteran who worked with Belladonna, too. Not as her main handler."

Paloma's smile grew slowly. "So she's young."

"And she has pretty eyes when they're not shooting fire at Cruz," I added.

Paloma leaned back in her seat. "Interesting…" She waved the thought away. "We'll deal with Cruz's love life later. What do you want to do this afternoon?"

"Not worry about the baby or Luka or my father," I said.

"I have just the thing," Paloma said with a smile. "Are you into mysteries? I've been saving one to binge."

"Sounds great," I said as I tossed her the remote.

I'd been dozing on the couch sometime later, after I'd fed and changed Bree, when Paloma rose to answer a knock at the door. She whispered quietly with the person on the other side, who, though I craned my neck, I couldn't see. She shot an apologetic look over her shoulder and stepped back.

A large man—a human version of a grizzly—stepped inside. His bulk might well be more than Cruz's, and he had deep-set brown eyes under blond brows. The rest of his features were straight out of a Nordic catalogue—not Ikea. He was too upscale in his bespoke suit and silk tie. His blond hair was tamed back but curled over his collar.

"Hello," I said, breaking the staring contest.

"Hello. Do you know who I am?" he asked.

"Gunnar Evaldson, the Wildcatters owner and Luka's boss."

His lips tipped up. "And you're Millicent Jones, daughter of Chasten Jones and former fiancée of Trenton Cox."

I swallowed and looked over at Paloma, who was texting on her phone. "Would you mind sitting down, please?"

Gunnar stalked a few steps to the chair and lowered himself to the edge. "I'm assuming you know that Trent and your father have shown an interest in buying a stake in the Wildcatters," he said. His light brown eyes were direct.

"Yes," I said. "Are you considering it?"

"I hadn't intended to part with any portion of the Wildcatters organization. But I have to admit, the offer's tempting because it revolves around adding to the team's outreach efforts, which would do a lot to help people in the city."

Outreach efforts? My father was truly shameless—and manipulative. He didn't care about helping others; he wanted a way to control Luka and me. I balled my fists and swallowed the bitter acid on my tongue.

"But I've heard things about Trent," Gunnar continued. "Things I don't like—about his treatment of women, specifically."

My jaw tensed, and it took everything in me to remain in my seat. "And you want me to clarify those for you."

He dipped his head, but it wasn't in acquiescence. He was *deigning* to listen to my story.

"You don't have to talk about that now," Paloma said.

She'd pocketed her phone and set her hand on my shoulder, shooting daggers at Gunnar, who didn't bother to look at her. I kept my gaze focused solely on this man, who seemed just like my father—a man who didn't care about the people who worked for him or surrounded them. So long as he got his money and the organization remained successful, the rest of us were just chess pieces to move and throw away.

"Trent slid a ring on my finger and *informed* me we were getting married. Later that night, he pinned me to the bed and *informed* me that I was getting pregnant, regardless of my feelings or goals, so I ended our relationship. Before that moment, I would have sworn he loved me."

I tucked my lips into my mouth. This was why I'd given up on men. Trent was the last in the string of men I'd dated—and slept with—who'd failed me. He went right along with my father's plan to try to tie up my life and choices in a conservatorship.

"What does that have to do with your father suing for custody of one of my players' kids?"

Right. Gunnar Evaldson had an agenda. I met his gaze.

"After I left Trent, my father sided with him, explaining that it was my job to keep my husband happy—and that no one else would want me after Trent, anyway. He threatened to set up a conservatorship because I wasn't in my right mind to turn down Trent."

"Your father threatened you with legal action if you didn't marry Trenton Cox?" Paloma asked. She'd turned a sickly shade of white. "Holy crap!"

I nodded. "I left this city after my father sent me a series of videos of me with other men. He'd been documenting my dating life and told me he'd use it against me in court."

"To force you to marry the man you didn't love or want?" Gunnar asked.

I nodded. "You don't get far or have much freedom when those two men intend to make you suffer."

Gunnar's eyes narrowed, and he steepled his fingers. "I'm going to be honest with you, Ms. Jones—"

"Millie. Just Millie." I wanted nothing to do with my father. Ever. I'd been so excited when Luka mentioned me taking his name. There was nothing I wanted more.

Gunnar inclined his head. "I talked to your father earlier. He painted you as too flighty to handle his business and fortune. He insinuated drug use and mental illness."

I laughed, but choked on the emotion in my throat. "I was on antidepressants after my mother died. Pills he insisted I needed."

Now I understood why: my father had been building the case against me, even then. He'd planned to force the conservatorship on me, force me to bend to his whim and will.

The door banged open and Cruz strode in, much like an angry bull, ready to fight.

Neither Gunnar nor I flinched. I was too busy sorting

through the details of my father's betrayal. I swallowed and plotted the molecular formula of a sodium oxalate, a complicated ion made up of sodium, carbon, and oxygen.

"Your father seemed concerned for Luka and your child, worried that you'd destroy his career and cannot provide a stable home for your daughter," Gunnar continued.

"Oh, for goodness' sake!" Paloma cried. "That's ridiculous! She's an attentive, wonderful mother." Her mouth twisted. "And it should *never* have been questioned."

"You're here," I said. "To test my intelligence and my story."

"*Seriously?*" Cruz growled.

Paloma gave a curt nod in agreement.

"You're leaving," Cruz said. "Not sure what I'm most mad about—that you showed up knowing Luka wasn't here, or that you interrogated a woman who just had a baby about a merger."

"My timing is intentional, and I have a few more questions." Gunnar's tone remained mild. I would never underestimate him.

Again Cruz made a sound—almost inhuman—as anger radiated off him like heat.

"Too bad," Paloma snarled.

Oh no, she'd gone all mama bear, too. I stared up at two people I really didn't know well—two people who were defending me from their boss. "It's okay, Paloma, Cruz. Really. I'm okay."

"I'm not," Cruz said, fisting his hands and moving in front of me. I had to crane my neck to see around his bulk. Gunnar appeared perturbed for the first time. Clearly, he wasn't used to Cruz's anger.

"You have no right to ask these questions," Paloma snapped.

"And it's doubly insulting because no man would have to answer for his personal life choices."

She settled next to my hip with Bree cuddled against her chest. She patted my hand, glaring at Gunnar.

"No one has a right to the details of my private life, but I'm willing to answer the questions one time." I gave Gunnar a look that should have cowed him. It didn't. *Of course* it didn't. The man was a bloody billionaire, and he owned a professional sports team.

But he did sigh. His gaze flicked to Cruz's and Paloma's before returning to mine. "You're correct. I apologize."

Those words hung in the air. No one moved. A heaviness settled over us as Gunnar and I continued our face-off.

"I made a misstep in my comments," Gunnar said. "I want you to know that I believe you, Millie, and I know Chasten is…"

"A ragged trash heap of a man who only finds joy in using others and gathering more wealth to pad his bottomless ego?" Paloma offered.

Gunnar's lips shifted upward into the faintest of smiles, but his eyes glowed with humor. "Yes. That. Best way I've heard him described. Let me leave it at this: I'm not a fan of your father."

"Makes two of us," I said.

He pulled a thick pile of papers from his briefcase. "This is your mother's will. I'm guessing you've never read it," he said, handing the packet to me.

I frowned. "I… No. She died when I was young."

Gunnar's eyes had gone colder than the Arctic. This was the brutal businessman that had clawed his way to the top of the oil business in a foreign country.

"And Chasten never offered you any details."

I shook my head.

"The key piece of information is that *your mother* brought substantial wealth to the marriage."

"*Not* my father," I said. I inhaled, realizing what he was telling me. "And I'm my mother's beneficiary, which means my father can't really disown me from wealth that was never his."

Gunnar's smile was as cold as his eyes. "Indeed. I highlighted a few parts I think you'll find enlightening—and helpful."

I gripped the papers so tightly in my hands, I worried about paper cuts. "Would you be willing to recommend an attorney that deals in family and wealth litigation, Gunnar?"

Humor crept back into his expression. Maybe because I'd used his first name—a deliberate attempt to put us on more even footing, which we clearly weren't.

"I'd be delighted to. In fact, I made you an appointment for next Monday morning."

That was in three days. Would Luka be back then? I didn't want to go alone.

I didn't want to *be* alone.

I wanted Luka.

"Nine a.m. Perhaps Cruz and the rest of the team would like to join you." Gunnar flicked his fingers at the corner of the pages. "Once you read through this and talk to Jonathan Dresden, you can tell me if you agree with my logic: cornered, injured animals are at their most dangerous. One thing about the Wildcatters, we don't let *our people* take unnecessary risks."

I struggled forward, my lingering belly still making it difficult for me to rise. Cruz was there to help me—and so, it seemed, was Gunnar.

"Thank you," I said.

"Don't thank me yet. And I'm going to recommend that Luka take a paternity test."

This time, it was Paloma who made the guttural sound. Gunnar's eyes turned sad as he looked her direction, but his expression remained neutral.

"Noted," I said through clenched teeth. That was smart; something I should have suggested. I wished I had because then I wouldn't have this gaping pit in my chest, making me wonder if Luka would hear the mere idea of a test and run away.

"You need to leave," Paloma said. Her hands remained fisted and her face flushed, matching her hair.

"Luka's a phenomenal player. Let's sort out this mess." Gunnar stepped toward the door. He towered over me, the debonair, inscrutable billionaire. I'd lived with my father's belittling, invasive tactics, but never had I felt as powerless as I did in that moment. And this was a person who intended to be on my side.

With a curt nod of dismissal, Gunnar left through the door Cruz held open for him.

CHAPTER 15
Luka

I clutched at my hair as I listened, through the speaker of my phone, to the conversation between the owner of the Wildcatters and my Millie.

I wasn't there. How the fuck was I supposed to prove to her that she could trust me, lean on me, be with me, if I wasn't there for her when she needed me?

Instead, Cruz and Paloma and even Coach were standing in for me.

Part of me was glad they cared enough to be there for my woman. But another less-confident part—the little boy who'd gone to his mother in tears over a skinned knee or a slight and been rejected—worried Millie would reject me, too.

"You hear all that?" Cruz asked as he closed the door behind him.

His voice rumbled through the air, into my ear, and through my body.

"Yeah, man, I heard. I need to get back for that meeting."

"True." Cruz paused. "By the way, Millie doesn't know I had you on the phone—that you heard all that, and maybe that's a good thing." He blew out a long breath. "You should also do the paternity test."

Shock flared white-hot through my chest. "Why would you

say that?"

"To give Bree protection, in case Chasten manages to Britney Spears your girl. Your child can't get caught up in *that*, man."

He was right, but the idea seemed mercenary, like I didn't trust Millie. But I had to pursue my options with a clear head.

"How's Alyssa?" Cruz asked into the silence.

I swallowed hard. "Dying."

I was losing my damn mind; I didn't have a clue how to solve the problem that was my life. Although I needed to be in Houston with Millie, I couldn't abandon Alyssa, the mother I'd always wanted.

"None of that now, son."

Alyssa's voice froze every muscle, and I couldn't take a breath. She never called me son—that moniker was Mike's, the child of her body. "You're a good boy, Luka," she added, patting my face when I met her eyes. "A good boy."

"Gotta go," I told Cruz. "I'll figure out how to get there for that meeting—and I'll call Millie in a few."

"You got it. Chin up."

I closed my eyes. That was a near impossibility in this situation.

"Love is hard," Alyssa rasped after a moment. "Until it's as easy as breathing." She reached up, her hand shaking. I took it in mine. "The secret is letting go, son. You gotta let all that other shit go."

"What?"

The door had creaked open as she spoke, and I lifted my gaze to Mike's.

"The details about her past, your past—they don't matter, not if you want each other," Alyssa continued. "Not if you want to be great parents to that precious baby. I raised you right, enough to be an even better partner than you already are."

"He's been a better son to you than me, Ma," Mike said, taking up position on the other side of her bed. "Giving you a grandkid earns extra points."

"Different, honey. Not better. Luka, see, he knows what it's like to go through life without a mother's love. Except you both have mine, and I did a mighty fine job of raising you both."

Mike's lower lip trembled, but he nodded. "You did, Ma. You did."

"My only regret is that I didn't find you a good woman, Mikey. Luka sorted himself out. His Bree is the cutest, and he's going to marry an engineer. Can you believe that?"

Mike shot me a testy glance, likely irritated that his mother was singing my family-man praises.

I pressed a kiss to her leathery cheek. "I'll give you two a minute." I needed to touch base with Millie.

Maybe the Wildcatters would call me in to fire me or trade me, not wanting to deal with the drama surrounding Millie and me. That actually brought a shadow of relief through the sadness. I'd hoped to be a career Wildcatters player, but I refused to leave Millie scared and uncomfortable for the rest of my professional years. So we'd have to move. Maybe her company had a location in another state. Or she could get another job with a different firm. Or stay at home with our daughter. I wasn't sure what Millie wanted, but as long as we were together, I'd do my best to make it happen.

I strode down the hospital hallway, looking for a place to make a phone call as thoughts swirled through my mind. I stepped into an empty waiting room, and Millie picked up on the third ring. "Hey, Luka."

"Will you tell me why Gunnar Evaldson came to see you today?" I asked.

"Oh! Yeah, just a second." I heard her riffling through papers and talking to someone. A deep voice replied—not Cruz, who I'd expected to be there.

"Where's Cruz?" I asked.

"He's dealing with something. Lennon's a fortress of impenetrable silence, so I didn't get enough out of him to satisfy my curiosity—"

"His first name's Lennon? How did I *not* know that?"

"Ah, because he doesn't like it," Millie said.

"Fuck that," I muttered, annoyed she knew more about my best friend on the team after two days than I'd learned in all the years I'd been playing and training with him.

"Luka," Millie said. She sighed. "We need to talk."

I stopped pacing and waited. Twice in ten minutes, I'd felt like my world was ending.

"Luka, it's not his money. It's *mine*."

I leaned against the wall, wondering if I'd entered the Twilight Zone or something. I swallowed. "That's…great."

"Actually, it sucks," Millie said glumly. "What do I know about running an empire?"

"More than me."

She snorted. "I seriously doubt that. I've seen you talk to your agent and PR person, remember? You're on top of your assets and time. Me? I know how to write code to search for oil."

"You do so much more than that, Millie. You were in charge of a team—"

"That I had to leave because of bed rest," she replied.

"Which you were doing to keep our baby safe," I countered.

"I don't know that I want her to be an heiress, Luka. That kind of money…it's evil."

Staring up at the ceiling, I tried to tease apart her words and her fears. "I don't think the money's evil," I said into the long silence. "I think your father did evil things with it." Like hide the fact that it was actually hers. Like force her toward a man who wanted the money, but not her.

"Well, I don't like what he did to me, but also to the companies he's bought and broken apart."

"No, I don't like that either."

"I'm scared I'll have to fight him for it. In court."

That was a given. "I'll be with you every step of the way."

She seemed to absorb that. "Thank you." Her voice broke. "You make this bearable—knowing we're a team. But Luka?"

"Yeah?"

She paused, and I heard her shaky exhale. "I'm still afraid."

I squeezed my hand into a fist, not unlike the one clamping my heart in my chest. "And I wish I was there to hold you."

"You can't be here, not when you're needed in Detroit. Sorry. I should have asked you sooner. How's Alyssa?"

Her voice was stronger. Millie liked to be the caregiver instead of the recipient. That was something she and I would have to deal with. I couldn't offer her much, but I was damn well going to take the best care of her I could.

I blew out a long breath. "She called me son."

Millie sniffled. "I'm glad you had her in your life."

Luka

Alyssa passed away soon after I returned to her hospital room. While it was peaceful—a soft sigh before the blaring of machines—Mikey shocked me. We cried and held Alyssa's hands after the hospital staff disconnected her from the monitors.

He was her son by birth and blood—I was the boy she'd taken in and who'd never felt good enough to fully accept her love.

"I'm gonna have her cremated," he said, staring at me with bleary eyes. "She wanted that."

"Okay."

"And she didn't want a funeral, but we're gonna have a party at her place this summer, after the season. I gotta get back— Coach is breathing down my neck."

I nodded. "That's because they need your pitching arm."

His smile was short and sweet—cocky as hell. I'd missed it.

"You know it. But now I gotta go out and throw those pitches, knowing my mom's never going to see another one of my games."

With that, he broke down in my arms. I held him up, and I held him tightly. Just as he'd held me during those years when my parents proved again and again and again that I didn't matter.

Once the storm passed, I gave him the moment to gather himself.

"I…"

"Don't you dare apologize," I said.

"I wasn't going to." He swiped at his wet cheeks, his grin

rueful. "I was going to say that you're going to make a great dad, Luka. A fucking *great* one. I'm kind of jealous of your kid because she's going to have such a good man in her corner."

I choked up as I grabbed the back of his head and slammed his nose into my pec. He grumbled for a moment before sighing, letting his body go loose.

"I miss her," I whispered. "Already."

"Forever, man. There'll be a hole where she was." He groaned.

"I heard that's the unexpressed love trying to get out."

He tugged himself out of my embrace and narrowed his eyes. "That's strangely poetic. Beautiful, man. Perfect. Yeah." He nodded. "Yeah. It's just all the love I still have for her." He clapped my shoulder. "You, too, right? You're gonna mourn her, too?"

"Every day."

He smiled and squeezed my shoulder. After a slow, deep breath, he tipped his head toward the door. "Guess we better get this over with. I need to be at the game tomorrow, and you need to get home to your girls."

"What's this about a woman and a baby?"

Every muscle in my body clenched as my mother waltzed into Alyssa's hospital room, as pretty as you please. As if she had a right to my grief, my decisions…my life.

After I recovered from the initial shock, talking to my mother in the hospital cafeteria wasn't the hellish experience I'd expected. In fact, I felt numb. Losing Alyssa and worrying over Millie had left me with none of my usual emotional energy to fret about my mom's approval.

"Why didn't you tell us about your girlfriend?" My mother's lips compressed as if she were disappointed.

"I didn't think you'd care."

She reared back. "Of course I care that I'm a grandmother."

I stared down into the sludge in my Styrofoam coffee cup. "You never cared about me."

She clasped my hand. "Of course we did! We paid for all that hockey equipment and camps and—"

I extricated my hand from hers. "No, you didn't. Alyssa raised most of those funds." I met her eyes. "Why are you really here?"

"To see you—"

"And how did you know I was in Detroit?"

Her gaze slipped to the side, her cheeks reddening a bit.

"Yeah, that's what I thought. Someone tipped you off. And now that I have money, you what? Want some of it?"

"We raised you—" Her voice was feeble.

"No, the woman I just cried over raised me. You birthed me, and I'm thankful, but we're not a family. Alyssa, Bob, and Mike were my family."

Mom straightened her back and lifted her chin. "I can't help that your father never wanted to marry me. Make us a family."

I dug deep, seeking patience when I really didn't have fucks left to give. "Neither you nor my father cared much for each other, me, the sanctity of marriage, or anything related to stability."

"We were free spirits."

"You both had lots of affairs and forgot about your kid at home while you were out partying."

"I deserved to live my life—"

I shook my head. We'd never agree on what her choices had done to me, so there was no point. I'd tried—again. Now I was done.

"Tell me about the woman who had your baby. Millicent?" Mom scrunched her nose like Millie's old-fashioned name was something unpleasant.

I sucked in a breath as my mother's reason for being here— how she knew where to find me—crystallized in my mind. "Who exactly told you I'd be here?"

She attempted nonchalance by picking at her thumbnail and refusing to meet my eyes. "What does that matter?"

"Who?" I kept my tone firm, my gaze unwavering.

"Trenton something." She waved a hand. "He seems to think you're shacking up with his fiancée." Mom leaned forward, her eyes gleaming. "Are you? Did you *steal* his bride?"

The numbness that had settled around me with Alyssa's passing crumbled. My mother didn't care about me; she wanted the story because she might make a few bucks selling it. Then she could get back to her life and the endless string of meaningless affairs that kept her from connecting with another person.

This woman had birthed me, but she'd also really fucked me up. For nearly twenty-five years, I'd thought her behavior was normal. Or that there was something wrong with me for wanting more—for wanting the closeness Alyssa and Bob had, the attention they'd showered on Mike and any other kid in the neighborhood who seemed to need it.

I'd told myself it didn't matter, that I was happy skimming through life like my mother. Because it's what I'd learned from her.

But then I'd met Millie. I'd looked into her beautiful eyes and seen a different future—one like Alyssa had with Bob, one I'd craved from the moment I'd seen them together.

I was building that now with Millie.

Or I would as soon as I returned to her, which needed to be soon, especially now that I knew that piece of shit Trent was keeping tabs. I rose from the plastic chair.

"Bye, Mom. Don't look me up again."

She gasped, outraged. "That's no way to treat your own mother!"

"Ah, but you've told me often enough that you didn't want to be one. Seems I got the message."

Once I'd escaped my mother, I called and spoke to Cruz and Coach about the latest turn of events with Trent and my mother, and they both promised again that Millie wouldn't be alone.

There was something so *slimy* about that man. Well, both Trent and Millie's father. I couldn't fathom what crazy plan they had concocted to keep all that money between them, but I knew I wouldn't like it.

I spent the rest of the afternoon trying to tie up as many loose ends for Mike as possible and ended up racing to the airport, nearly missing my evening flight. I barely hauled my ass through security and made it to the gate before the last boarding call.

I settled into my business-class seat and tucked in my ear pods, planning to listen to another book on parenting, until I realized who'd appeared in the chair next to mine.

Speak of the devil himself.

Deciding it was better to ignore him than act on my impulse, I shut my eyes and turned up the volume to my audiobook.

I made it through takeoff and up to cruising altitude with his elbow bumping into my side. When he tapped my forearm, I continued to ignore him, but I turned off my audiobook as discreetly as possible. I didn't want Trent to catch me unaware.

"I'm talking to you," he finally yelled.

I cracked an eyelid, making sure the surrounding passengers were looking, then closed my eyes again.

"Don't you dare pretend to ignore me," he ranted.

"Sir, is there a problem?" The flight attendant was a young woman.

I frowned, not wanting her to get involved. My guess was Trent took what he wanted—without thinking through the consequences.

"This *cretin* is ignoring me," Trent complained.

"He was sleeping," the passenger across the aisle spoke up. An older man, probably in his fifties. He frowned in judgment at Trent.

"He's not sleeping," Trent snapped. "He's ignoring me."

"Which is his right," the flight attendant said. "Why don't you move up to seat—"

"I'm not moving," Trent yelled. "I bought a seat specifically on this flight to explain to him that he's not stealing my bride or my baby."

The *fuck* was this douche running his mouth about?

Of course Bree was mine…wasn't she?

No, no, she was. They both were. *Trent is lying.* He'd hurt

Millie, manipulated her. And, yes, Millie had been scared, terri-fied, but there was *no way* she'd use me as a shield.

"Did she tell you we'd been together that same day? No, huh? We were working on our relationship. Getting back together. You ruined that and are trying to steal my kid, but I won't let you."

The mere idea of Trent touching Millie sickened me. His willingness to use her made me want to hurl. But the idea that Millie would have lied, even if it was to protect herself and the baby, infuriated me. How dare he throw her under the bus for his own purposes *again*?

Needing to stay on task—and the task was making sure I looked as innocent here as possible—I cleared my throat. "I'm pretty tired. I was up all night, dealing with a dear friend's passing."

Sympathy gathered on the flight attendant's face, followed by determination. I noted that another flight attendant—a large man—had stepped into the aisle behind her. She looked at Trent. "I'm going to have to ask you to move, Mr. Cox."

"No."

"That's no longer your choice," she said. She bent down to look into his eyes. "If you don't follow me, sir, I'll have to alert the captain—"

Trent stood so quickly his shoulder slammed into the poor woman's cheek. She reeled back into her colleague, her hand to her face. The man across the aisle gasped and flung the contents of his glass into Trent's face. Trent sputtered, cursing, and lunged toward the man. But before Trent could reach him, the two flight attendants had Trent on the ground, hands zip-tied behind his back. About thirty phones were now pointed toward Trent, who was howling and kicking.

"Get off me! Get off!"

He spewed more garbage about me being nothing more than a meathead jock—a fool who didn't understand the world, which apparently he thought revolved around *him*.

"Do you need some ice?" I asked the flight attendant.

She shook her head, her lips compressed. "No."

"I'd be happy to find you something cold," I told her.

She gave me an amused look. "Thanks. I know where they are. As soon as we get this guy subdued, I'll consider it."

She glanced at her colleague, who was dragging Trent by the legs toward the back of the plane. Trent kept twisting and screaming, especially when his head hit the metal chair legs or ran into passengers' feet. Someone booed, and soon the entire two hundred people on board were chorusing the word together, drowning out Trent's tirade.

The flight attendant returned her attention to me. "He'll be restrained in the back. Law enforcement will meet us at the gate when we land. I'm sure they'll want to talk to you."

I nodded. "Not that I'll be much help, but yeah. I'm happy to comply."

She nodded before trotting up to the front where she must have conferred with the pilots. A moment later, the speakers crackled. "Sorry about the disturbance, folks. Our people seem to have it under control, so we'll continue on to our scheduled destination."

The traveler across the aisle leaned over. He had finished wiping his hands on the small napkin that had arrived with his plastic cup.

"That guy was Trenton Cox—Chasten Jones' right-hand man." He grimaced. "What a douche."

I nodded. "You know him?"

"I've hated him since he bought into the company I built from nothing and ripped it apart without a single thought for my employees. Throwing that Coke in his face was the best interaction we've ever had. You know why he wanted to talk to you?"

"I have an idea."

"Well, I hope you bested him at his game. Both he and Jones deserve to come down a few pegs."

"I'll keep that in mind."

He smiled and picked up his book.

By the time I finished talking to the police when we landed—they asked both me and my new across-the-aisle buddy, George, for our statements—it was late. I was so exhausted I wobbled on my feet. Good thing I was calling a rideshare back to my place.

Cruz met me at my door, took one look at me, and patted my shoulder. Considering he looked just as bad, I offered him a gentle cuff back.

Then, I locked my door behind him and started taking off my clothes. I crawled into bed and wrapped myself around Millie, inhaling her sweet scent, thankful to be home.

"Luka! You're back," she said sometime later when she sat up. She hugged me, and I clutched her close. "What time is it?"

"Two thirty."

I groaned. "Mind if I sleep a little longer?"

"Go for it. I'm going to change and feed Bree."

I slipped back into sleep, but I felt Millie leave the bed. When she returned, she ran her fingertips lightly over my cheeks, nose, chin, and lips. She kissed me softly before snuggling into my chest.

"I can't believe how much I missed you," she murmured. "I'm not sure I can live without you."

"*Why* is there an article about you being accosted on the flight?" Millie set her iPad on the bed, still reading, and ran her hands up my arms, over my chest, and down toward my very evident erection. "By Trent? Oh, my—did he hurt you?"

I snorted as I collapsed back onto the mattress. "Please. As if that runt toothpick could. No. He poked me, got mad when I ignored him, started yelling, elbowed a flight attendant…" I told her the rest of the tale, following her to the nursery when Bree woke and needed to be changed—which I did, happily—and then fed, which I watched Millie do, happily.

"Wow," she whispered again and again. "Wow…" She reached over and cupped my cheek, searching my face. "Oh, Luka. He doesn't matter. You lost your *mother*." She squeezed my hands, her eyes filled with compassion. "I know how much it hurts," she whispered. "Do…do you want to talk?"

I took a deep breath and met her gaze. "I'm not sure the wedding's a good idea."

CHAPTER 16
Millie

Luka paced around me, clearly wound up to the point that he might snap. I sat on the edge of the bed because trembling prevented me from standing. Luka's sheets were linen, which was made from the flax fiber. Flax, like cotton, was a polymer made mostly of cellulose, but also with hemicelluloses, lignin, pectin, and possibly wax or salts.

I traced the weave with my finger. "You don't want to marry me? I'm sorry, Luka. I just thought—"

He slid to his knees in front of me, his eyes tortured, his beautiful chest on display. "I want that. Desperately. But you asked when you were afraid of your father's reach. Now that we're solving that issue, and we know the money is yours, you don't need my name, my protection, the Wildcatters resources. I don't want you to marry me out of obligation." He swallowed, his Adam's apple bobbing. Sweat pearled at his hairline.

He was falling apart. And there was only one explanation for the thing he knew.

"You heard," I said. My tone was flat. "Was it Gunnar or Cruz or Paloma who had you on the phone?"

"It was Cruz, but that's not what this is about."

I looked down at him for a long moment, studying his face. Luka's bones were elegant and harsh. The sharpness of his cheekbones led to such kissable lips. His nose, with its bump and slight twist from being broken in middle school, added to his mystique.

He'd read more books about babies than I had. His audiobook library was now full of books on maintaining a stable relationship with a partner, too. Luka considered himself less because he struggled to read on paper or a computer screen, but he absorbed so much knowledge through audio that I was in awe.

Still, sometimes, he was an epic idiot. Like now, when he was trying to be chivalrous.

"I didn't ask you to marry me out of obligation. That hasn't changed. But I'm not sure your assessment of the future is accurate either." I took a deep breath. "My father has sex tapes. Of me."

Luka stood so quickly, I fell off the bed.

"The fuck did you say?" he growled.

I didn't want to say it again. "Years ago, my father hired a PI to follow me. That investigator took video of me each time I went out. I'm not sure why, exactly…"

"But that PI followed you when you hooked up and *videoed* it?" He pulled me to my feet. "Do you think he's still following you?"

"Maybe. He may have video of us together. But I want you to know I was careful."

Luka clenched his fists and forced words past his stiff lips. "Trent said you were with him that same day, before you were with me. That Bree's *his* daughter."

My mouth opened, shut, opened again. I had to look like a dying fish, especially as the blood drained from my face. "No, Luka. The only time I've been in the same room as Trent since I walked out was at the airport."

There was a painfully tense silence.

"I never questioned you. About Bree," Luka finally said.

I tipped my head so I could see him better through my thick glasses. I'd taken to wearing them again, and Luka didn't seem to mind. In fact, he'd whispered in my ear, all those months ago, that he was wild for them on me.

"No, you didn't." My voice broke. "But you are *now*."

Luka rubbed the back of his neck. "No, that's not what I intend. I… *Fuck*, Millie. I hate all of this, what it's doing to you…to us. Gunnar thinks getting the paternity test is a good idea. So does Cruz. And, much as I hate to admit it, Trent got to me. It's not that I believe a word he said," he rushed to add. "But who knows what they're capable of…" He trailed off.

"I see." I wanted to be rational, to understand the smart move. But right now, this all just made everything hurt. I moved toward the door. "Give me a minute…"

"Where are you going?" he asked.

"I just need a break, Luka." Tears clogged my voice. I spun on my heel and walked into the nursery. The door shut with a soft click, but it might as well have been a slam. I didn't know how to move forward with the horrors of my past always nipping at my heels. I didn't know how to protect myself, my heart, when so much was happening so quickly.

Taking care of an infant took considerable time. It didn't, however, stop my mind from spinning.

My father was a manipulator. He'd had me followed and

videoed, without my consent. That was disgusting—still another betrayal of the trust he'd shattered years before by keeping me from my dying mother.

I've should expected these power plays and lies, attempts to undermine me and my relationship with Luka because that gave my father the stronger position. One he'd use to get what he wanted.

Luka spent time with Bree the next day, but gave me the space I'd asked for, though I wasn't entirely glad I had asked for it. But I let things lie. I was determined to have myself together, to find a rational headspace, before I dragged Luka into my drama again.

That afternoon, Cruz, Maxim, and Ida Jane came by.

"Mind if we go to the rink?" Luka asked.

I shook my head, not bothering to sit up from where I lay on the couch. I was tired and heartsick. "Enjoy."

"Yeah." He hesitated, then leaned down and kissed my temple. I wanted to snuggle in closer, wrap my arms around him, and hold on forever. Instead I tensed, waiting for the moment to end.

His lips brushed across my ear as he whispered, "I love you, Millie. You and Bree."

I gave him a tiny smile, then sighed with relief when he grabbed his hockey sticks from the front closet and tromped out after Maxim and Cruz.

Ida Jane plopped into the oversized chair, her chin resting on the arm as she stared at me.

"So…"

"Trent told Luka I was also with him the night Luka and I hooked up. That Bree's really his."

Ida Jane's eyebrows rose. "That was the day I got off work early so you could help me pick an outfit and we were together every minute until you dragged me to the party?"

"That's the one."

Bree cried, and I began to sit up.

"I'll get her," Ida Jane said as she hopped out of the chair. I heard her cooing at the baby and the rustle of the diaper change before Ida Jane brought my fussy daughter to me. She resumed her position in the chair as I settled Bree to nurse.

"She's no more than a pawn in this sick game of money and power," I said.

"So are you," Ida Jane said.

"I'm not innocent. Not anymore."

Ida Jane scoffed. "Why? Because over four years of your life you had ten lovers? Or because you didn't like your dad's choice for you and broke it off? Because you took control of your body and refused to let a man plan your future—trap you into a life you didn't want?"

"Yes."

We fell silent, and I flipped Bree to my other breast.

"Have you considered this from Luka's perspective?" Ida Jane asked.

Bree and I flinched. "What?"

"Well, I mean, he lost his mom—I know she wasn't his real mom, but the woman was a mom to him—then had to cut his real mom out of his life because she's looking for dirt on you and him to sell back to Trent—"

"What?" I breathed.

"He didn't tell you?"

I shook my head. Ida Jane took a deep breath. Then, good friend that she was, she grabbed me a bottle of water and chips and dished the details.

Bree stopped nursing, a drop of milk on her tiny rosebud lips as her face slackened into sleep. I cuddled her to my shoulder and patted her back, enjoying her weight and warmth against my skin.

"I'm so tangled up, Idge." Tears formed in my eyes. "I thought falling in love was supposed to be glorious."

She belly laughed until tears ran down her cheeks. "Cover that sweet pea's ears for me, Mil-bil." Once I did, she leaned forward, unconcerned about the mascara streaks down her cheeks. "Falling in love fucking sucked. Being in love, now *that's* rather glorious."

"No. The being in love is supposed to be work—"

Ida Jane waggled her finger at me. "Who's in love and who's struggling with the relationship?"

Snapping my jaw shut, I returned to rubbing my palm up and down the baby's back. I found it soothing. I hoped she did, too.

"*Falling* in love is one of the scariest things I've ever done. And that includes facing slimeball Dillon when he wanted to hurt me." She shook her head, a contemplative expression on her face. "Look. Relinquishing control to another person—someone who can hurt you? Believe me, I get the work of that. But it's also so…lovely." She smiled and her eyes turned soft. "Maxim sweats for me."

I blinked. "O-kay."

She giggled. "That, too. But in the house, I mean. He likes it so cold that I shiver. But he sets the AC to a higher temperature so I won't turn blue, and he sweats. I keep apple butter on hand because he loves it so much. He surprised me last week with the new line of Hanky Pankies—thanks for telling him I like that brand, by the way."

"Sure." I frowned. "But what does this have to do with being in love?"

Ida Jane sighed. "Everyone talks about the flush and heart palpitations of falling in love, but I think *being* in love is better. He knows my quirks. He accepts them. Embraces them. When he does that, he makes me feel even more cherished. And that makes me want to show him how much he means to me. We get in a serotonin loop. See?"

I nodded slowly. "Yeah. Ceding the control was hard though, wasn't it?"

"Nearly broke us," she said cheerfully. "Same with Cormac and Keelie and Silas and Paloma."

"Really?" Now that was a fascinating tidbit.

"And Naese? He's clearly in love with someone but fighting it. Or maybe she's fighting him. I haven't figured that part out yet."

I pursed my lips. "Cruz seems to fit your description, too."

"Mmm, good point. We'll keep an eye on him." She speared me with her gaze. "Think about what falling *is*, Mil-bil. It's letting go, taking a leap of faith. Believe Stolly will catch you, no matter how messy things are or what challenges await."

My chest clenched painfully. "No one has. Ever."

She rose and sat next to me on the couch. I rested my head on her shoulder as a few tears fell. I was so tired. And emotional. And leaky.

"Post-partum life is gross." I sighed.

"And yet Luka's still here with you. For you." She kissed the crown of my head. "So am I. So are Maxim and the rest of the guys. You won't splat if you leap, Millie. I can promise you that."

The next morning, as promised, Jonathan Dresden, the lawyer Gunnar had suggested we meet, showed up at our door. I was a mess—unshowered, disheveled, and so very tired. Tears kept streaming down my face due to lack of sleep—thanks to a newborn and my attempt to prepare myself well for this meeting—and stress.

I sat on the couch, Bree in a sling against my chest, and gave my attention to the impeccably dressed attorney.

Luka shuffled around the kitchen to get Jonathan and himself a cup of coffee. My mouth watered at the thought of the clarity-inducing hit, but I sipped on my jumbo bucket of water instead.

"How old is your baby?" Jonathan asked.

"Four days," Luka said.

"And we need a paternity test," I added. It was the right call. I knew that. Luka went rigid. "To make sure Luka and Bree are both protected."

Jonathan smiled. His eyes were sharp, focused, but kinder than the devil who'd shown up with papers in my hospital room. "That's smart. I can arrange that today."

"Thank you. I really should have insisted on it sooner." I looked over at Luka, trying to let him know I meant that. He stared back, his expression easing as tension slid out of him.

Bree fussed, and I patted her bottom.

"I remember when my kids were that age," Jonathan offered.

"You both look fantastic, considering."

I giggled. "Um…sure."

"Soon this will all be a vague memory, and you'll be packing them off to grad school." Jonathan shook his head. "I won't tell you to enjoy this. But try."

"Thanks," I said. I was surprised to find I liked this guy. I'd initially pinned Gunnar Evaldson as cut from the same asshole cloth as my father—but Jonathan seemed decent right off the bat.

"I'm assuming she'll need to eat soon, so let's get down to business." He pulled out a thick sheaf of papers identical to the stack I'd set on the table in the murky hours of the night. "Your father is suing for custody of your child, through the paperwork he'd already started on the conservatorship." Jonathan met my gaze. "He'll never win either of those cases, by the way."

My worry deflated, and my leaky eyes turned to actual tears. I covered my face with my free hand as I tried to steady my emotions. Luka rose quickly, grabbed a couple of paper towels, and offered them to me. I shoved them against my face and continued to breathe. This was a business meeting. Now wasn't the time to lose it.

Seemingly unperturbed by convention, Luka picked me up and put me in his lap, still holding the baby. I rested my head against his shoulder.

"That's a tremendous relief," I said.

Jonathan nodded, his face stern. "You can sue your father in civil court for infringing on your right to privacy with those videos of you that he's threatened to expose."

Luka stiffened again. "You mean the sex tapes?"

"The very ones," Jonathan said. He wrinkled his nose, breaking his professional demeanor. "Taking your mother's money is the better option, though."

I sucked in a breath. "At the time of her death, it was two hundred million dollars. That's pocket change compared to my father's current wealth."

Jonathan smiled, and it was sharp, predatory. "This is where it gets fun."

The attorney outlined my options, which ranged from requesting the money my mother had left me to a full civil suit to shoot for all my father's wealth, which he'd built off the lies he'd told me—which had been documented by house staff and my friends, including Ida Jane—and the money that was rightfully mine.

Let me say this: Jonathan Dresden came prepared.

I looked up at Luka, seeking his counsel. And I did really want it. We were a team—a partnership. Resolve formed in my gut, like something sliding into place. Thanks to Luka, I felt grounded in a way I hadn't realized I'd been missing.

"What do you think Millie has the best chance of winning?" Luka asked. He stroked my back, and as much as I wanted to relax against him, I just couldn't. I had to be ready for whatever came next.

"Clearly she has a right to the money her mother left her," Johnathan said. "And we have a strong case to take it all, if that's what you want to do."

"Why?" I asked.

Jonathan smiled. "There's a reason Gunnar sent you to me. I

was your mother's counsel."

I sucked in a breath. "You drew up her will."

"I did."

"So you know my father's a liar."

"I do."

I nodded. That would help this process. Some of my irritation toward Gunnar melted away. "First, I need that paternity test so I can have you draw up my will," I said.

Luka shifted, probably unsettled by my continued mention of confirming Bree's father. I ignored him and focused on Jonathan and what needed to happen. I'd done some reading of my own while Luka was in Detroit, and I needed to be methodical—and smart—about inheriting vast sums of money. "That takes three to five days, right?"

"I'll expedite for three at most," Jonathan said.

"Once we have that in place, we can file a motion to take back what my mother left me…" I sucked in a breath. "…and the rest of Chasten's money. If he'd shown even an ounce of caring for me back then, I wouldn't want him to suffer now."

Johnathan just nodded. "I'll contact the paternity-testing laboratory as soon as I leave and make sure they stop by to get the necessary DNA today."

I rose on shaking legs and offered Jonathan my hand. "Pleasure to meet you, and I look forward to working with you. If you don't mind, I'll have Luka show you out so I can get Bree changed and fed."

I made it to the nursery and laid Bree in her crib before I completely fell apart.

A couple of minutes later, Luka came in and once again pulled me into his lap. This time, I couldn't resist his scent or his comfort. The path forward had begun to take shape, but I was going to hate it every painful step of the way.

Luka

Millie was hurting, and I didn't know how to fix it. Emotions were horrible—so deep and thick, impossible to wade through. I gritted my teeth as I picked her up, adjusting her position in my lap.

Cowardly though it was not to meet her eyes as I bared my soul, she needed to hear the words, and I wanted to hold her close. Bree's soft breaths from the crib eased some of the tension from my muscles.

"I've never doubted that Bree was mine," I began.

Millie stiffened but remained quiet.

"I didn't. I need you to know that."

"Okay."

"No, this is important, Millie. I never once doubted your word about Bree. As for us...well, I hated feeling led on and ghosted. I hated that you didn't think enough of me to believe I could be the father our child deserves and that I want to be."

"Luka, I don't know how to be in a relationship," she said. "My parents didn't love each other."

"Neither did mine. And they didn't show me affection." I kissed the top of her head, reveling in my ability to do so.

"Exactly. And when I searched for love—"

"Your father made it sordid. Something to use against you."

She nodded, clearly too overcome to speak.

"Well, we know what not to do with *our* daughter."

She tipped her head back, so I dropped my chin to meet her gaze. "Ours, Millie. I know we still have details to hammer out—like your job, my job, where we'll live…"

She offered a faint smile. "Small details."

"They are and they aren't. They're small because they don't matter as much as loving you and Bree, being there for you and Bree." I looked over at the crib. "She means *everything*. Even if somehow she wasn't mine, I'd still love her as my own."

I'd realized that. I loved Bree. It was that simple. She was mine because I wanted her to be.

Millie's eyes widened and tears spilled down her cheeks. These were different, though. I could see that instantly, and I heaved a relieved breath. She wasn't sad and anxious. She was happy.

I'd made Millie happy.

"And I get it if you don't want to marry me right now. There's so much going on, and if you just want to see how things go—"

She shifted so she could kiss me. Her lips were soft and firm. She slipped her tongue into my mouth, and I groaned. I wanted to gather her closer, kiss her harder, show her just how much she meant to me. But Millie needed this moment just as it was, and so did I. She needed to be in charge of her life, to choose me out of love because she wanted that on top of everything else she faced—not out of fear of her father or a court-ordered conservatorship or because she didn't feel she had a choice.

I'd always give her a choice. And I'd love her, even if she didn't choose me.

I tried to pour all that into the kiss that tangled and twisted our mouths. When we finally pulled apart, she met my gaze for a long, painful heartbeat.

"Okay," she said.

"Okay."

"I'm tired," she said. "I think I'm going to nap while Bree's asleep."

I nodded, unsure how far to push.

"Don't you have practice?" she asked.

"Informal. I don't have to—"

"Go. Please. It will be good for you. And there's something I need to do." Millie rose, paused to look down at Bree in her crib, and walked out of the room.

Millie had been right. Getting a stick in my hands, flying across the ice, and slamming pucks into the net helped me clear my head. I had no idea how executives sat through meetings. That shit was brutal. Hockey made sense. Love, relationships…not so much.

Two and a half hours later, drenched in sweat and grinning like a loon as Maxim cursed me after a fucking *fantastic* deke, I leaned over, hands on knees, and let myself glide across the ice.

"You good now?" Cruz asked as he skated up beside me.

"Yes. But no."

Cruz made a humming noise. "What did you do?"

I rose to my full height and glared. "Why do you think I did something?"

Maxim slapped his giant paw on my shoulder. "Because

we're men and we fear our feelings and do dumb shit to make them go away."

Cruz skidded to a stop at the rink's exit and pointed at Maxim. "That." He led us off the ice.

I sighed, demoralized, as I admitted that I had, in fact, been stupid. Or at least not approached Millie's feelings with the care I should have. I told them about Trent's comments on the plane and her guarded, hurt reaction to my suggestion of the paternity test.

Cruz gave his head one shake, then let it drop. "That's partially my fault. I should have considered how she'd take that— especially knowing what a snake her father is. And Gunnar's asshole comments."

"There's so much on her plate right now. She just had a baby, for God's sake. She shouldn't have to litigate her entire life on top of that. Yet that's exactly where we are, and I can't make any of it go away."

Maxim nodded, meeting my gaze when I finally lifted it.

But it was Coach Whittaker who answered. "Sounds like what I did when I freaked out about how much I loved Trix and Paloma, even though I knew I wasn't good enough for them."

I glanced over my shoulder, too tired and heartsore to be angry my coach was eavesdropping. "But you're happy now?"

He smiled. "Yeah. Even when they make me crazy, which is often." He pressed his lips together. "Those two are good at it."

"Because they know you so well. And it's probably part of their love language," Cruz offered.

Millie

My hands shook as I picked up the small box I'd had delivered while Luka was at his practice. My heart pounded, but my grip was sure. I met him in the living room when he returned.

He was freshly showered, but his face was pinched. He searched my eyes, seeking answers I hoped I could give him.

"Would you sit down?" I asked.

He moved toward that giant armchair and sat. I walked toward him, my legs wobbly, and dropped to my knees between his spread ones. I set the box on his thigh.

"What's—"

"Your engagement ring," I said.

"You bought *me* an engagement ring? That's *a thing*?"

I nodded. "Oh yeah." I shrugged. "The jewelers off Montrose had many choices."

We both smiled. Montrose was at the epicenter of the vibrant gay scene in the city. Houston was a lot more cosmopolitan than outsiders gave it credit for; probably because the city also embraced its roughneck roots.

Maybe that's why I loved Houston so much—it was messy, effervescent, chaotic, and so *alive*. "I think I'm going to want to continue working," I told him. "But I'm going to want to be around for Bree, too, so I don't know what that future will hold. But it'll be here. Here in Houston."

"You're sure? I mean, I know the city holds bad memories—"

"I'm sure." I heaved a breath. "I've always loved the city. I love Ida Jane and the CATS. It's my father I feared. But with you, I'm not scared of him anymore."

Luka smiled, his fingertips grazing my cheek. "I'm glad to hear that, sweetheart, but you understand I may get traded."

"I understand that. But you won't be traded to Sri Lanka." I opened the box. "I want us to be a family, hopefully here, but wherever we need to go. I want Bree to know how loved she is, every day. And I want you to know how loved you are by me. Every day."

I scooted closer to better show him the thick platinum band, inset with a tiny channel of rubies. "Since we're both June birthdays, I went with our birthstone, but if you hate it—"

He lunged forward, his hand cupping the back of my head, and kissed me. The ring went flying, but I wasn't worried. We'd find it soon enough.

After an intense make-out session that ended with my toes in pins and needles and the rest of my body primed for more than we could do safely, Luka crawled around on the floor until he found his ring.

"Put it on?" he asked.

I slid it past his knuckle. "I wasn't sure if you'd want a wedding band, too—"

"Yes. Both. *All* of it." He grinned with such joy, my breath caught. "I'm fucking engaged!" he crowed.

Bree shifted and then cried. We looked at each other and laughed.

"I'll change her and then we can talk plans while you nurse her, okay?"

I nodded.

"Good." He paused, suddenly seeming shy. "I have ideas about the wedding."

"I want to hear them," I said.

"And I want to go back to Colombo, but not to live."

I smiled. "No, not to live. But we'll visit. It's a magical place."

"I want to get married soon."

"Then we will." I kissed him, and he kissed me, until our daughter squawked again.

Keelie and Ida Jane insisted on watching our eight-day-old daughter for Luka and me while we went to a meeting our lawyer, Jonathan Dresden, had set up with my father. I was grateful, but leaving Bree with my besties almost made me more nervous than facing the man who'd lied to me for years. Though bringing Bree along would have definitely been worse.

I pulled the lapels of my suit jacket over my breasts as we waited at the conference table, hoping I didn't have another milk accident like the one yesterday. Luka must have been thinking the same thing because he leaned in and whispered, "I'd pay ten grand to see you hit him in the eye."

I laughed but also gagged a little. I didn't want my father in contact with any part of me, even my breast milk.

A minute later Chasten Jones strode into the room like he owned it—with Trent and the smarmy lawyer from the hospital in tow. I reached for Luka's hand, and he held on, letting me know he was there. I glanced over at him, accepting his slight nod. He'd let me handle this—we'd already talked about that—but he offered the vote of confidence I needed. He believed in me.

"Mr. Jones," I said, my voice whip sharp. "Mr. Cox. And...
attorney."

"Millicent," my father said, evidently accepting my use of
his surname as his due, as opposed to the distance I was putting
between us. "Andre Castinelli is my legal counsel."

"Right. Well, this shouldn't take too long. Jonathan, if you'd like
to explain," I said, looking his way as the others took their seats.

"My pleasure, Millie." Jonathan passed Andre a brief, and
the other lawyer picked it up lazily. "My client is suing you for
the entirety of the funds designated for her in the will of her
mother, Allison Seymore Jones. She's also suing for damages
created by the lies told to her regarding her mother's illness,
the subsequent forced removal from her home, and the emotional cruelty created by the attempts to coerce her into a
conservatorship."

"That's ridiculous—"

"Actually," Andre said, setting down the document. "It's legal.
And smart." He scowled at Chasten. "Based on your deceased
wife's will, Ms. Millicent Jones was the sole beneficiary. That's not
the will you shared with my firm."

"Because, because she *changed* it."

"No, she didn't," Jonathan said. "And I'm sure of that
because I was her legal counsel at the time, which is why I'm
representing Millie now." He leaned forward. "You committed
fraud, lied to your only child, and used her money to try to
coerce her into a life she never wanted. In exchange for the
money and properties and businesses you bought using her
funds, we won't press criminal charges."

Trent sat back in his chair, mouth gaping. Clearly he'd believed Chasten was the wealthy one—the holder of the cards—not me. I tried to squelch the satisfaction rolling through me as he turned paler and began to sweat.

Okay, I didn't try very hard—*at all*, really. Trent deserved to sweat and worry after telling me he'd keep me locked in the house, where a woman belonged, while he went out and lived his life. *Misogynist scum.*

Luka settled our clasped hands on his thigh. I rubbed my thumb along his muscle enjoying the flex under my caress.

"That's preposterous," my father—no, *Chasten* exclaimed. His face was a mottled, deep red.

Luka shifted his hand, and his engagement ring rubbed against my finger, causing me to smile.

"You think this is funny?" Chasten snarled.

I wondered if he might have a heart attack or a stroke. That would be…sad. Yes, I'd feel bad if my father, my only blood relative besides Bree, was gone. But I wouldn't miss him. I couldn't. He'd never really been a part of my life.

I cleared my throat. "No, what you did to me—what you tried to do—isn't funny at all. But I do guess I'll get the last laugh, because despite your awfulness, I found Luka, and I have a beautiful daughter. A family. Something you've never achieved."

Andre Castinelli smirked at me, and Luka squeezed my hand a little harder. I knew he was struggling to let me handle this my way. No doubt he wanted to shove his fist through Chasten's teeth.

"What are you going to do with my holdings—should you manage to weasel them away from me?" he asked.

I shrugged. "Nothing."

Both he and Trent seemed to relax at that, and I let them. I wouldn't do anything with those companies. People counted on them for their livelihood, and I wouldn't disrupt their lives. I would fire Chasten and Trent, of course, and if they hadn't had egos the size of Texas, they would have figured that out already.

Sometimes others' entitlement really paid off.

CHAPTER 17
Luka

The next morning, after the team's morning skate, I sat down in the chair in Coach's office—his fancy management office located in the Wildcatters' executive suite. This space was even nicer than the office at the arena. The chair supported me with sumptuous cushions made of some fine, soft material. Coach's desk was an eclectic mix of wood and glass and metal—a sculpture in its own right. Thick carpet muffled his footsteps as he rounded the desk to sit in the chair behind it.

I couldn't help feeling as if I was the peasant, and Silas Whittaker was the judge, jury, and probable executioner of my future. I reminded myself that Millie and Bree were at my condo. They were my *home*, not a city or even the walls that housed us. Wherever the three of us were *together*, I could flourish.

"This is really a formality, but I prefer to meet with my players face to face."

I clenched my hands where they lay on my thighs.

"Gunnar will be here shortly, as he has a few things he wanted to say to you, too."

I dipped my head, unwilling to open my mouth. I might as well have swallowed nails. Leaving Cruz, my unexpected best friend and, yeah, my brother—I loved that scary-ass son of a gun—not to mention Cormac, who'd overcome so much to earn that sheen of perfection. Then there were Naese and Maxim. The guys had been more of a family to me than my parents ever were. How was I going to do it?

"I don't think we have to wait for him on all of this, though," Coach continued. "I sent the details to your agent before you came in. We wanted to get ahead of your contract negotiations during the next off-season, Luka. We don't want to wait. We consider you one of the Wildcatters most valuable core members, and we're offering you a five-year extension with a nice pay bump. I hope you'll consider what we're doing here and how we want you to fit into that plan, because I'm almost positive Colorado's going to beat our offer." Coach's nostrils flared and his lips pinched. Everyone knew Coach was the most competitive of us all. He hated losing anything, ever, including a bidding war.

I swallowed as his words sank in. "You want to keep me?"

Coach smiled and tilted his head. "You thought otherwise?"

"Well, yeah, I wasn't sure you'd see me as a good fit after all the drama."

"Do you know what I've witnessed this past season?" Coach asked. His gaze remained direct, his hands folded on top of his desk. His nails were short and neat, his hands now smoother than any player's. But if you looked closely, he still had the nicks and scars of a former player. That was another reason I respected Coach so much. He'd sweat and bled and stressed over the game just like the rest of us.

I shook my head, a knot of barbed wire bobbing in my throat.

"I've watched you go from unfocused and sometimes lazy— using your talent and athleticism to skate by—to a man who's dedicated and focused. One who prioritizes his family and has the other younger players turn to him when they have questions about growth."

I swallowed as I stared at my hands. "I want to stay in Houston," I began.

"And we want you to," Gunnar said from the door. "You show excellent potential to be one of our next-gen franchise players."

Weight sloughed from my shoulders like dirt from the bottom of a shoe. I grinned. "That means a lot. Everything, actually." From the moment I'd heard about the Houston expansion team, I'd known it was going to be life changing. Being here, learning from Silas, Cormac, Maxim, Cruz—all the guys—had taught me what it meant to be a man as much as how to be a better hockey professional.

"Plus, everyone sings Millie's praises," Gunnar added. "Adam said she's a good influence on Naomi—has helped her settle down. And obviously Ida Jane loves your partner."

"Paloma has also enjoyed spending time with her. She said Millie's head is on straight," Coach said.

I looked over at Gunnar. "What happens to the franchise if you don't go through with Chasten's deal?" Because that wouldn't be happening.

His eyes gleamed. "Nothing."

I raised an eyebrow. "Nothing?"

"I don't need Chasten Jones' money. We have a healthy fan base and sell out most games. You guys are popular with the locals, so we have robust jersey and merchandizing sales. I was more interested in Chasten's community connections, wanting to make inroads into some programs we haven't yet been able to ramp up."

"Like a summer-long hockey camp for local kids," Coach offered.

"Or at-risk teen mentorships," Gunnar added.

"Those programs sound fabulous," I told them.

"They do, but they'll wait until we find the right person," Gunnar said. "Chasten Jones is not that person. He wanted to force his daughter into a conservatorship so he could maintain control of money that wasn't his." Gunnar's lip curled. "Or even worse, take a baby from loving parents as a power play—a *bargaining* chip."

I leaned forward, hands clasped between my knees, unsurprised that Gunnar knew as much about my situation as I did. "All three of us did the buccal swab, and we already have the results."

"Did the answer change anything for you? I mean, how you feel about the baby?" Coach clarified.

I huffed out a laugh. "I didn't even want to bother with the test because Bree's been mine from the get-go. But indisputably, now everyone can know it's me. I'm her dad. Though, I have to say once again, Millie's word was enough for me."

The two most powerful men I knew nodded their understanding, approval shining from their eyes.

I'd found it. My place. My home.

I'd needed Millie and Bree to settle me, to help me prioritize what was important—my family, my team, then my job. For the first time since my parents had skipped my pee-wee championship, I felt peace.

Whole.

I needed to tell Millie. But first…

"If Millie pries that money away from her father, which she will, would you be interested in working with her?"

Gunnar and Coach exchanged a look.

"She'd need to bring us a proposal," Gunnar said.

"One that funnels some of Ida Jane's clients into the program?" I asked.

Gunnar chuckled and clapped me on the shoulder. "You should be the one negotiating your contract. You do a better job than your agent."

With a wave, he left, and I returned my attention to Coach.

He'd leaned back in his chair. "You really pulled your head out of your ass, Stolly. You've come a long way this year. Why don't you go share the news with your woman so I don't regret saying that—or offering you such a juicy contract?"

I left the office with a near-skip and a mile-wide grin. I called my agent and left a message to let him know I was accepting Houston's offer. He called back immediately, again and again, but I let those go to voicemail, knowing he'd rail against me not including him in my decision-making. He'd huff and puff about the money I'd left on the table when I accepted the Wildcatters offer and not Colorado's. But I'd call him back in a couple of days—once the ink was dry on my contract—and remind him that he'd just earned a fat paycheck. His job was to look out for my best interests, and those were in Houston, with the Wildcatters.

My smile remained in place as I opened the door to my

condo. Millie's voice drifted down the short hall, nearly drowned out by Bree's ragged cries.

I kicked off my shoes and padded toward the chaos. My chaos, my *family*. Love swelled in my chest, choking me.

Millie stood in the middle of the room, swaying slightly as she bounced Bree. "Is it always going to be this way, little Bree? Every time, you fight sleep like a demon. Why, baby? You're so tired. Mommy's tired. What if you gave in, and—oh, Luka!" Her eyes widened as she took in my expression.

My cheeks ached, so I must've still been grinning like a damn fool. I wrapped my girls in my arms. Bree quieted, as she always did once she'd worn through the last bit of her energy. Her eyes drooped, and her little pink lips parted on a soft sigh. So sweet and precious. She was a beautiful baby with a feisty streak, and I loved her fiercely. I kissed her silky head.

"I have so much to tell you about my meeting, but first and foremost, I want to say this: I love you, and I'd never hold your choices—your attempts to find a connection with another person—against you, Millie. Hell, I did that for years before I found you."

I bent down to kiss her lips, and I took my time. Slow and soft, lingering so I would have this moment pressed always in my mind. I pulled out the ring I'd found for her—the one that matched mine. Her band was thinner, and I'd added opals to the channel that led to her large, pink ruby. "The opals signify our meeting last October. I wasn't ready for you, but I was so ready for being here. Will you wear it?" I asked, holding it poised over her trembling ring finger.

"Y-yes. Of course!"

I slipped it on her and smiled as I twined our fingers together. This was what I'd wanted with Millie from the start, the togetherness I'd been unable to put into words.

"Wow," Millie murmured. She rested against my chest, her gaze still on our rings, baby Bree cuddled in our arms. She'd slumped more, a sure sign she was asleep.

"Why the change of heart?" Millie asked.

"I didn't have one. I just got…clarity." I nodded. "Yeah, clarity."

"I'm glad to hear that."

"Let me put her down. You can shower or—"

"Celebrate with my sexy hockey star," Millie murmured.

"I like the sound of that." I plucked Bree from Millie's arms. Something about holding my daughter calmed me—gave me perspective, a centering. I'd thought for so long that a family would be a weight for me to overcome, but now I realized they were the very reason that kept me going. I'd been such a fool. So young and naïve. Millie had opened my eyes. Bree had opened my future.

Millie slipped from the room and I held my daughter for another moment before I laid her in her crib. After ensuring her monitor was on and she was warm enough, I exited her room, shutting the door with the softest of thumps.

And I went in search of Millie.

I found Millie asleep in the middle of our bed. I smiled, more than happy to snuggle in close and hold her until our baby needed us again.

I woke to Millie's fingertips drifting over my cheeks. "Can we wait six weeks or so to get married? So I'm all healed down there? I want a proper wedding night with you." She slid closer and wrapped her arms around my shoulders, resting her head against my chest. "And I want to feel beautiful in my dress, not self-conscious about the baby weight in my tummy."

"You're gorgeous, Mil—"

"To you, maybe," she cut in. "But I want to feel gorgeous for you. And for me." She looked up at me. "But most of all, I want you to know in that thick head of yours that I love you. That I'm marrying you because of that love. That there is no one else for me, ever, because I couldn't possibly love another person like I love you."

With each of her words, heat sizzled through my veins. I stared into her eyes, needing her to understand what I was offering—me, *all* of me—to her, the unloved child, the broken, traumatized teen, the bitter, untrusting woman, the caring partner, and the well-loved mother and soon-to-be wife.

Millie

Clutching his cheeks, I looked into his eyes. "I love you, Luka Aaron Stol. I love you. You. Only you."

"And Bree."

I smiled. "And our baby. But not like I love you with all this passion and fire and lust."

His lips kicked up. "I am irresistible."

"To me."

He dropped his hands to my hips and squeezed gently. "I

think I really needed to hear you say that." His voice was soft. His expression was open and filled with contentment but also a tension that vibrated through him. It was fear, I realized.

"I'm not your parents, Luka. I'll *always* find you worthy, and I won't be angry about your dyslexia or consider your need to move while you learn too difficult. I won't ever, ever denigrate your intelligence or your work ethic or you." I leaned in and kissed him, just a brush of my lips across his before I pulled back. "You're not perfect, which *is* perfect because neither am I. And it's our imperfections that fit together so very well. I'm sorry it took me so long to fight for you—for us. But I'm in this with you. We're a team."

He managed a nod, his eyes shining.

"Tell me about your meeting," I said.

"Later."

I tugged his shirt up so I could run my hands over his chest and abdomen. "Now."

He groaned against my lips. "Five years with an extension clause for another three. Part of the reason is you, your influence on the CATS."

I leaned back and blinked up at him. "What?"

"Coach loves your presence in our community and your impact on *me*. You're a wonderful person, Millie."

"I…"

"You've made me a better man, which led to me being a better teammate." He nuzzled my neck, and my hips tilted into his warm, hard body.

This man made me lose my senses in the best possible way. I

knew he respected me and loved me and wanted me—just as I respected, loved, and desired him. "And the rest?"

He explained his salary and the housing allowance, which was a substantial upgrade. "We can buy a house."

We could have bought a house with my money—well, the soon-to-be my money that neither of us really wanted. But I knew Luka needed to feel like he'd taken care of us. He did take care of us, showing me that a genuine man wasn't one who belittled others to make himself feel bigger. Luka focused on my wellbeing, showing love and respect. He built me up to be the best version of myself and encouraged me to do the same for him.

This time, he leaned in and kissed me—with tongue and that nibbling followed by soothing licks that made me so damn hot I thought I'd combust.

After a moment he met my gaze. "I love you Millicent Anne Jones, soon to be the much better name of Millicent Anne Stol."

I grinned widely. "We'll all match. You, me, and Bree."

He kissed my nose. "Forever."

I hugged him tighter. "I wish I could get naked and love you up the way you deserve."

"You are loving me the way I deserve—like I love you, with my whole heart."

I shifted again. "Dammit, Luka. Stop being so sweet. I'm…" My cheeks flamed. "I *need* you," I whispered.

"Good."

"Good?"

He tightened his embrace. "Good. Now you know how I've felt since I sat across from you at that restaurant last year.

Yearning like that fucks with your head."

"But not your performance." I giggled.

"Oh, that, too. Thankfully, I have stamina." He rocked me gently. "And patience."

I sighed into his neck. "You start training next week."

"I do."

"So we won't see you as often."

"You won't."

"I'll miss you."

"Not as much as I'll miss you." He was silent for a moment. "Tell Bree not to do anything new and cute while I'm at work, okay? I want to be present for all her firsts."

I smiled as I snuggled closer. How could I not adore this man? "I'll do my best."

He laid his hand over my stomach, his breath tickling my neck, and I knew, without a doubt, I was home.

In the city I couldn't wait to leave, instead I'd found my future. My family.

My purpose.

EPILOGUE

TEN WEEKS LATER

Luka

"Pouting isn't becoming of a bride," Naese said, though without his usual snicker. He'd become increasingly morose since that day he'd come over and told me a woman from his past hated him.

I glared. "Fuck off."

"No can do, Stolly. I'm part of your wedding party." He found his grin for a moment as he shifted closer, hand raised. "Let's make sure you're pretty for your pictures."

"Touch him, and I rip off your thumb," Cruz growled as he rose from his spot near the door.

Naese backed away. "That was viciously specific."

"It's his wedding day," Cruz said as he strolled over.

I was getting married exactly one year after I'd sat down at that tiny table and stared into the thick-lensed glasses of my future bride.

I was a lucky bastard.

Cruz's size and quietness really shouldn't have gone together, but now I knew his secret: he took ballet. I'd gone with him a few times, so had Cormac and Maxim. That shit was *hard*.

We'd wanted our new goalie to make it part of his daily routine, but hadn't thought it fair to ask of him if we weren't willing to try ourselves. At least, that's what Cormac and Maxim had said when they shoved me into the class with Cruz and watched through the window.

Once they realized I was getting a damn good workout and was more flexible than they were, they came in and jumped all over the springboard floor. Hockey players would always be competitive, and we loved nothing more than getting the edge over our opponents.

"This is a nice place," Maxim said, looking around. "I mean, I guess I knew Houston had good wedding venues, but I like this one."

We were at the Bell Tower on 34th, the premier wedding spot in the city—my stipulation for waiting two months. Because we were getting married on a Wednesday night, we hadn't had a problem with securing any of the vendors, even with such short notice.

Coach had given us Thursday off, and next week we'd start our preseason with an away game against Colorado.

"He touched my hair, didn't he?" I asked. Grumbling, I stalked to the mirror on the opposite wall. *Good*. Naese hadn't messed anything up. I'd spent way too long fixing it so it looked like I hadn't done anything at all—just the way Millie liked it. I straightened my pale pink tie and turned to find all the guys staring at me.

"What?" I asked.

"Proud of you, man," Cormac said, slapping my back hard enough to make me hide a wince. "You stepped up for Millie and Bree."

"And the team," Maxim said.

"And taking her piece-of-shit father down about seventeen pegs had to feel fantastic," Cruz said.

"Not as good as I'd hoped. Knowing Bree's mine and Millie will be today, though, that makes me happy."

The guys grunted. "Fucker rolled quickly when he realized his freedom was at stake," Maxim growled.

"Didn't hurt that Trent turned on him as soon as he realized he was facing some pretty spectacular criminal charges," I said. "Millie and I bought those flight attendants season tickets for life."

"Shit, yeah," Naese said. "I wanted in on that action. Those two were stone cold and unwavering. Still wish Trent would end up in jail, though."

"I do, too, for Millie's sake. But knowing her father's being indicted on a bunch of charges for bribing that judge and lying on his taxes helps."

The guys all nodded in agreement.

"I like happy endings," Naese said, though his expression fell as he turned away.

"Not happy so much as justified," Cruz said.

Bree squawked through the baby monitor clipped to my belt.

"I'll get her," Maxim said.

He'd fallen in love with our daughter, and he rarely wanted to let her out of his sight. Ida Jane had confessed he wasn't too sure about kids of his own, but I knew my sweet baby girl would change his mind.

Maxim came back into the room holding Bree, who now sported a full inch of rich honey-colored hair on her tiny head. She wore a pink crocheted circlet of roses and a pale pink dress a shade lighter than the bridesmaid's dresses and our ties. Her dress was made of silk so it wouldn't irritate her skin, and she wore satin slippers in the shape of ice skates.

I'd insisted we get two dresses, which Millie found silly based on the cost, but I figured we had a better chance of getting nice photos that way. One thing about my daughter—she shat at the worst times. Every. Time.

"She looks adorable," Cormac whispered.

My chest puffed out. I had chosen the dress, after all. "She does."

"Aw. She does. I wanna hold her," Naese said, holding out his arms.

"Try to take her from me and I'll rip you in half," Maxim snarled before he tickled Bree's tummy, making her giggle and kick her legs.

Already she'd outgrown her newborn clothes. Time was flying by.

I clapped Naese on the back. "Time for some pictures, and then I get married."

He nodded, his mouth pressing flat.

"And then we work out a way for you to get your woman."

He snorted. "That ship has sailed."

~

Millie walking down the aisle toward me took my breath away. Not going to lie—tears burned. Cruz pulled out a handkerchief and unabashedly wiped his eyes, and even Maxim looked a little misty.

Who the hell would have thought I'd talk about my emotions with Maxim Dolov, but I did, and often. He still held Bree, who seemed fascinated by the lights and the new teething toy Maxim had pulled out of his suit coat a moment earlier.

My smile turned into a full-blown grin. I was getting married, and Maxim was in love with my daughter.

Life couldn't get any better.

Then it did.

When I slipped Millie's wedding band onto her finger and said my vows, I knew I'd found my forever. My family. She smiled up at me, her eyes so full of love that I just knew, no matter what else life threw at us, we'd make it.

She repeated the vows, slipping the matching platinum ring she'd insisted on buying onto my finger. It settled next to my engagement ring. The two hooked together, fusing us into one. I liked the metaphor, but I enjoyed kissing Millie, now Mrs. Stol, much, much more.

And I loved watching her laugh and smile with our guests. I loved sitting quietly with her in a room off to the side when she pulled down her halter top and nursed our daughter. Millie had the best tits—plump and pretty—almost as perfect as that juicy ass I couldn't wait to get my hands on later tonight.

We'd waited a few additional weeks to make sure Millie and I could have the wedding night we wanted. It had been torture, but it also made tonight special.

I kissed her, tasting the cake and champagne she'd just imbibed.

"I've been thinking about your ass," I said.

She grinned as she kissed me again. "That's because it's the one—well, one of a few parts of me you haven't seen recently."

"True, but also because I love it. I love you."

"Take me home?"

"I'll take you anywhere, Millie."

She grinned. "Back to Colombo?"

"I love that place. And we own a condo there."

Millie had taken an extended leave of absence, not sure she'd be ready to go back to work next month, and not sure what to do with her new wealth. While she wanted to work eventually, she wasn't sure she wanted to stay in petrochemicals, and she wasn't sure how she wanted to frame her days.

So far, we hadn't hired a nanny, but I figured that would come—probably after we bought a house in the neighborhood where Maxim, Cormac, and Naese lived.

Now that I thought about it, it was weird that Naese had bought a big, family house in the neighborhood with the rest of the team. I'd bet just about anything it had something to do with his mystery woman. He and I were definitely having a talk. Soon.

But anyway, as long as Millie was happy with her choices, I was, too.

"Let me just make sure Maxim has everything he needs for Bree," I said. I kissed Millie again before I broke away.

When I found them, Bree was snuggled against the D-man's shoulder, a tiny droplet of drool on her lip. I kissed her head.

"You good with my kid, Maxim?"

He scowled. "You know I am. We went over everything yesterday and the day before. And the day before. We set my air conditioner at sixty-eight, and I may die of heat stroke, but your baby will sleep...like a baby."

"In her pack and play. Not with you."

"I know, Stolly. And what I haven't learned, Ida Jane knows thanks to having such an enormous family." He leaned in closer. "Enjoy your wedding night. We'll see you at brunch tomorrow."

He and Ida Jane had set up a morning brunch that all the Wildcatters would attend. It was also a wedding and baby shower combined, so I expected we were going to need a trailer to haul our gifts out of the place.

I ran my hand down Bree's tiny back once more and then bee-lined to my wife.

Millie

My pulse pounded with nerves as I stepped out of the bathroom. I'd run a brush through my hair and put on Luka's jersey. The wool caressed my bare skin underneath, and my nipples peaked.

I tugged at the hem, which hit mid-thigh, as I entered our bedroom. Luka—that mass of muscle and hotness—lounged against the pillows and headboard.

"You, Millicent Anne *Stol*, are a vision."

I smiled. "You're just saying that to get in my pants, husband of mine."

"Nope." He popped the P in the word as he rose. His fingertips trailed up the outer edge of my thighs and over my hips before sliding forward to meet at my belly button. I quivered as he sent his hands back down, over my sex and between the soft petals of my center. "I already did that." He winked.

"You did," I breathed. "And we have the most precious little girl because of it."

"Not just a baby girl, but a family."

I looped my arms around his neck and kissed his chin.

"My family," he murmured. The seduction was soft, sweet, and thorough.

"Also, you're not wearing any pants," he whispered against my cheek before he nipped my earlobe. "You're so sexy. So beautiful. So wet," he groaned the last word.

I loved that I made him feel that way. Who would have thought the player of hockey players would want me?

He slipped two fingers into my channel while his other arm banded the back of my thighs, bringing me flush against his muscular torso. He spread his legs wider to give himself room to manipulate his hand between my legs. "Just keeps getting better and better," he murmured.

His kiss was deep, darkly seductive, and a little wild. Just like Luka. He was everything I never let myself dream of and more—so much more than most people gave him credit for.

He flicked my clit, and I leaned forward, pressing my mouth to his shoulder as I cried out. Ecstasy washed over me in a thick rush of tingles from my core out to my fingertips, toes, and the top of my head. He continued to nuzzle into my neck, his fingers massaging to bring me down slowly. I fell, boneless, to the mattress and stared up at him as he came to rest next to me.

I cupped his cheek. "You, Luka Stol, are the best man I know. Will ever know." I used one of my jiu jitsu moves and reversed our positions so that I was over him.

His grin widened. "You gonna fuck me, Mrs. Stol?" he rasped.

"I am. But I'm also going to love you. Now, tomorrow, always."

His abdomen contracted as he rose, his big hand sliding to my nape, and kissed me. I tasted all Luka—that rich, distinct flavor I'd been addicted to from our first night. I shifted my knees, reached down to grasp his erection, and slid him home. He continued to kiss me as he pressed my pelvis to his, rooting deep, joining us from hips to lips. I reveled in his warmth, his hardness, his gentle power.

Then he pulled back, making space, dragging that luscious cock from my channel and creating friction that sparked my latent lust. He thrust in and I gripped his shoulders, my short nails digging into his skin. Out, in, thrust after thrust, Luka fucked me.

"So…good…" I moaned.

"You're beautiful. You're *so* beautiful."

He snapped his hips faster, rooting deeper, owning my body with a rhythm that was pure Luka. I clung to him as passion flooded my veins. We tumbled off the knife's edge as the tension slid into bliss. I collapsed onto his chest, and he wrapped his arms around me, encasing me in him.

"I love you, my hockey man," I said.

"And I adore you, Millie."

I smiled against his shoulder, content, relaxed, in love.

There was nowhere I'd rather be. Nothing I'd rather be doing than Luka Stol. He'd shown me it was okay to let go—that he'd catch me when he could and love me through the pain when he couldn't.

With Luka, I was safe, whole. Happy.

Millie

The pulsing beat of Genuwine's "Pony" blared through the stadium's speaker system as Millie, Ida Jane, Keelie, Naomi, and the rest of the CATS made their way out toward the ice. Naomi was in the front, and she stopped so suddenly, the rest of the women bonked into her.

"The hell?" asked Hana, Naese's former college sweetheart.

After a few nudges and a firm shove, Naomi moved and the rest of the women stepped onto the rink floor.

A collective gasp sighed around us. The guys were on skates, without their pads or gloves or helmets. They wore, well, way less than I was used to seeing them wear on the ice.

"Holy shit balls," Ida Jane whispered. "Maxim's doing…"

Keelie fanned her face. Her eyes went glassy. "They… I never knew Cormac could move like *that*!"

The song ended, and the guys regrouped in the middle of the ice. Cormac and Cruz each said a few words before Naese cupped his hands and yelled, "Again!" up at the sound personnel.

He turned back to the guys huddled at the far end of the ice. "This has to be perfect."

"This has to be a surprise," Naomi muttered. "We shouldn't be here. They're obviously working so hard to make it—*shit*! They noticed us!" She turned around, eyes wild. "Lie," she hissed. "*We saw nothing!*"

www.ingramcontent.com/pod-product-compliance
Lightning Source LLC
Chambersburg PA
CBHW070726280626
47159CB00023B/2811